"Mac! What—"

"No, no, honey," Mac said quickly, placing a finger on her lips. "Let's not talk about it. I've told the sheriff what happened . . . that we had an argument and that you couldn't possibly have anything to do with that bank robbery."

"But, Mac—"

"Now that he realizes you're my wife, he'll have to let you go."

"But, Mac!"

He grabbed her arms and hauled her against him, shocking her silent. His first contact with her momentarily stunned them both. She was firm yet soft, and felt so good against him. Better than his wildest dreams, and he'd had plenty of those in the last few years.

He gazed meaningfully into her wide eyes, hoping she wouldn't notice *his* reaction to her nearness. His voice low and vibrant with emotion, he said, "It scares the hell out of me to think of you in danger during that bank robbery." And it was the truth; it *did* scare him. "So what do you say, darling? Shall we kiss and make up?"

"K-kiss?" she stammered.

Mac told himself he had no choice as he kissed her. Her lips were warm and soft against his, and she tasted sweeter than he'd ever dreamed. Coaxing, moving his mouth experimentally against her lips, he kissed Savannah until she gave up and kissed him back, pulling him closer and wrapping her arms around his neck.

"Ahem," said the sheriff . . .

Hero
for
Hire

Sheridon Smythe

JOVE BOOKS, NEW YORK

HERO FOR HIRE

A Jove Book / published by arrangement with
the author

PRINTING HISTORY
Jove edition / May 2001

The Penguin Putnam Inc. World Wide Web site address is
http://www.penguinputnam.com

ISBN: 0-515-13055-9

A JOVE BOOK ®
Jove Books are published by The Berkley Publishing Group,
a division of Penguin Putnam Inc.,
375 Hudson Street, New York, New York 10014.
JOVE and the "J" design
are trademarks belonging to Penguin Putnam Inc.

PRINTED IN THE UNITED STATES OF AMERICA

10 9 8 7 6 5 4 3 2 1

For my mother, Helen Francis Johnson. Although you live a hundred miles away, you are always in my thoughts and in my heart. I miss you constantly. Sometimes I don't realize just how much until I see you, hear your sweet voice, and feel the warmth of your loving hug. Thanks for being so proud of me, and for giving me your unconditional love.

Sherrie Eddington

I would like to dedicate this book to several people: My friend, who is always there to share my secrets and has my back in any situation. My lover, whose passion and caring when we are together, keep me warm through cold lonely nights when we are apart. My financial advisor, who even though he is not always right, advises all the same. My protector and my provider, who checks out the things that go bump in the night because my imagination won't let me.

So this book is for my friend, my lover, my financial advisor, my protector and my provider. I hope I didn't miss anybody, because I'm trying to include all the people that my husband is to me.

For William Woodrow Eller. I love you most.

Donna Smith Eller

Thanks also to the Dunklin County Library for their invaluable time and patience in helping with our research.

Chapter One

Angel Creek Bank was an easy target, especially to someone familiar with the layout.

Pulling the dusty bandanna over his mouth and nose, Mackenzy Cord pushed through the glass doors of the bank and strode with easy assurance across the shiny, massive floor to the counter. The sharp clicking of his boots announced his approach, but there was no help for it.

"Raise your hands, nice and slow, and you won't get hurt."

The low, menacing voice he used startled the bank teller. The teller lifted his hands high, backing away from the cash he'd been counting. For a long moment they studied each other across the window ledge.

One corner of the teller's handlebar mustache began to twitch.

Laughing, Mac yanked the concealing bandanna from his mouth and chin. "How in the hell do you always know it's me?"

It was a game they'd played a hundred times over the years. Telly Kramer had worked alongside Mac's father at Angel Creek Bank for twenty years before his death. As a young boy, Mac had often accompanied his father to work, sweeping the massive floors to earn a few pennies for candy, and generally making a nuisance of himself until his father sent him home.

Telly tried to look affronted as he adjusted his black bow tie. "I *didn't* know. One of these days my ticker's going to give out, and you're going to feel bad for scaring an old man to death."

"Hogwash." Mac laid his money purse on the counter and shoved it forward. "I'd like that added to my savings account, please."

Hefting it in his hand, Telly let out a low whistle. "Feels like you've got a good haul this time, Mac."

Mac shrugged. "I did all right." Bounty hunting was hard, lonely work, but with the money he made, his savings account had grown steadily over the past few years. Still, it wasn't fast enough to suit Mac.

He had plans—big plans—that involved a certain banker's daughter with honey-gold hair and violet blue eyes.

"Who'd you catch this time? Anyone I know?"

"You remember the train robbery a few months back?"

"You mean, the Cowgil brothers? The ones who shot poor old Cooter because he wouldn't leave the engine room?" When Mac nodded, Telly looked impressed. "No wonder you got a good haul. I heard the railroad was offering a two-hundred-dollar reward for that pair of dogs."

"Yes." Mac's jaw hardened. When he'd caught up with them, both brothers had proudly confessed to the murder, although there had only been one fatal shot fired. After a week of listening to their bickering about who had killed the poor engineer, Mac had been more than glad to hand them over to the sheriff.

"How much have I got?" Mac asked abruptly.

Telly reached beneath the counter and withdrew a leather-bound ledger. He consulted the book, figuring in the two-hundred-dollar deposit. "Look's like eight thousand, two hundred and twenty dollars."

A few more jobs, Mac swiftly calculated, and he could give up bounty hunting. He planned to sell his modest childhood home, buy a bigger house, and take over Sheriff Cannon's job when he retired. The mayor had already assured him of the position, and if he was careful, the rest of his savings would supplement his sheriff's salary for a good many years.

The only thing left was to convince Savannah Carrington to become his wife.

Mac refused to dwell too much on the fact that to date Savannah didn't have the slightest notion of his plans. When he *did* think about it, he got a cold knot of fear in his gut.

So he tried not to think about it. Whatever it took, Mac was determined to win Savannah's heart and make her his wife. From the moment she had shyly offered to share her candy stick with him at the age of ten, he'd known Savannah was the only woman for him.

"Oh, I nearly forgot," Telly said, glancing from side to side before leaning foward. "Mr. Carrington said to let him know the moment you get back into town. He's got a serious matter to discuss with you . . . about Savannah."

Mac stiffened. "Is she all right?"

"Yes, yes." Telly fiddled with the ends of his mustache as he added mysteriously, "Well, I *suppose* she is. Mr. Carrington will fill you in. He's in his office now."

Glancing at his dusty clothes, Mac hesitated. "I need a bath."

"Hm. I agree, but I think in this instance Mr. Carrington will hardly notice."

The gravity of his statement sent Mac spinning on his heels. Striding across the gleaming floor, he paused in front of the door to George Carrington's office and knocked. His mouth had gone desert dry as his imagination took flight. Something had happened to Savannah, his true love, his future wife—

"Come in!"

At Carrington's impatient call, Mac opened the door and stepped into the office. His boots sank into plush carpet, but Mac hardly noticed.

George Carrington, a short man who had lost sight of his waist years ago, sat behind a massive oak desk with his chin propped upon steepled fingers. His eyes, which Mac knew were as blue as Savannah's, were closed tight.

In the four months since Mac had last seen him, the banker had aged. Dark circles beneath his eyes added a gaunt look to his usually florid face, and there were lines there Mac swore hadn't been there four months ago.

Mac's apprehension deepened. "Mr. Carrington?"

The banker's eyes shot open; Mac noted they were bloodshot and puffy. For a moment, Carrington stared at Mac as if he didn't trust his vision.

"Mac? Thank God you're back! And not a moment too soon, either. Come in, come in! Have yourself a seat."

As Mac took the leather chair in front of the desk, Carrington moved to a sideboard against the wall and poured amber liquid into a glass. He paused and lifted a brow in Mac's direction. When Mac shook his head, the banker tipped the glass against his mouth and drained the whisky in a single swallow.

Now Mac knew the reason for the bloodshot eyes. Yes, something was very, very wrong, for he'd never known Carrington to be a drinking man.

To hell with subtlety: he had to know. "Is it Savannah?" he demanded, jamming his hat onto his knee. Every muscle in his body felt tight and anxious.

Carrington filled his glass again and resumed his seat at the desk. "Yes, it's about Savannah. You see, the wedding was to take place next Saturday."

Around the sudden, painful lump in his throat, Mac sucked in a slow breath. "Savannah's?"

"Yes." The banker nearly spilled his drink as he aimed for his mouth.

He's drunk, Mac decided dazedly, wondering if hearts really could break. "I think you've had a little too much to drink, Carrington." With every fiber of his being, he prayed that he was right, that Carrington's announcement was the ranting of a drunken lunatic.

"Damn right I've had too much," Carrington snapped. "You'd drink, too, if your only daughter was off gallivanting with God-knows-what type of riffraff!"

"Savannah's gone?" More confused than ever, Mac struggled to make sense of his words.

"Gone! Ran off. Left me a note saying she'd never come back to Angel Creek." Carrington bit back a muffled curse and drained the glass again. He wiped an unsteady hand across his mouth. "It's my fault. I should have listened to her, instead of ignoring her concerns and pushing her to marry Jon Paul DeMent."

Mac's heart gave a hopeful leap. "She doesn't want to get married?"

Morosely Carrington stared into his empty glass. "No, she doesn't. Told me so, but I wouldn't listen." Tears glistened in the older man's eyes as he continued. "I was afraid for her, Mac. When I die, she's going to inherit a lot of money. I want her married to someone I can trust before that happens."

Keeping his voice steady with an effort, Mac said, "And you think you can trust DeMent?" Mac had only met him a few times, but he wasn't impressed by the man's air of superiority toward others—including himself. He couldn't imagine kindhearted Savannah attracted to a man like De-Ment.

"DeMent's the son of my friend and colleague. I've known him since he was a little boy."

Just like you've known me, Mac thought. Although he liked Carrington well enough—the banker had always been kind to him and his father—Mac knew the man was a bit of a snob; he would never consider Mac for a son-in-law. Mac hoped that changing jobs would go a long way in changing the banker's way of thinking.

Carrington's slurred yet urgent voice snagged Mac's attention.

"Mac, I want you to find her and bring her back. I know your reputation as a bounty hunter and I know you can do it."

"And if she doesn't want to come back?" Mac asked softly. At twenty-two, Savannah was old enough to make her own decisions, and the thought of forcing her to do anything against her will left a nasty taste in his mouth. In fact, he didn't blame Savannah for leaving.

The hands that Carrington clasped together trembled visibly. "If you bring her to me safe and sound—*by any means*—I'll pay you five thousand dollars."

Despite himself, Mac nearly choked at the amount. "That's a hell of a lot of money."

"To get the opportunity to right the wrong I've done Savannah, I'd do anything—I'd pay a hundred times that much!"

It hit Mac then, a brilliant idea, a plan that might get Carrington *and* himself exactly what they wanted. All he would need was Carrington's agreement and Savannah's cooperation. The first he felt confident he could get; the other he could work on during the long trip back to Angel Creek once he found Savannah.

He leaned forward, mentally bracing himself for Carrington's reaction. "If I can convince Savannah to come home . . . and if she'll have me, will you give us your blessing?"

Carrington's well-padded jaw dropped to his chest. Finally he worked it closed. "*You* want to marry Savannah?" He flushed as he realized how Mac might interpret his disbelief. "I didn't mean—what I mean is, are you certain?"

Mac had never been good at sharing himself with others. Even Telly, whom he considered his closest friend, didn't know about his yearnings for Savannah Carrington. So it was with great reluctance that Mac confessed, "Yes, I'm certain. I've been saving money, planning to court Savannah and convince her to become my wife." He could do nothing about the flush that crept into his neck and face, but to compensate he thrust out a proud chin. "I've wanted to marry Savannah from the moment I first laid eyes on her."

"Well." Carrington was still in shock. "No wonder Savannah balked at marrying Jon Paul! She never mentioned a word to—"

"That's because she doesn't know," Mac inserted in a low, embarrassed voice.

"Doesn't . . ." The banker frowned and cleared his throat. "Has she given you *any* indication of her affections?"

"We've been friends for many years." Mac's flush deepened at Carrington's logical question. What had sounded good in his mind sounded feeble and ridiculous spoken aloud. Mac could just imagine what Carrington must be thinking. To cover the awkward moment, he said gruffly, "The way I see it, you have nothing to lose. If I succeed, then you not only get your daughter back, you won't have to worry about what happens to her after you die."

"Mac, you're a good man, and I had the highest respect for your father, but bounty hunting is rough, dangerous work—"

"I plan to take over Sheriff Cannon's job next spring, and I've got eight thousand dollars in the bank. I can buy a decent house with that kind of money, with plenty left to see to Savannah's needs." Mac looked Carrington dead in the eye in a challenge the other man could hardly mistake. "Does that address *all* of your concerns, sir?"

Mac would have been a lot happier if Carrington's hesitation hadn't lasted a full moment and if the banker hadn't sounded so damned unhappy when he did get around to answering.

"Like you said, I've guess I've got nothing to lose by agreeing."

"Then it's a deal?" Mac held his breath. Even without Carrington's blessing, he planned to pursue Savannah, but his blessing would be a bonus.

"That depends on Savannah, doesn't it? I won't make the same mistake by trying to push her into another marriage."

"I'm glad you see that it *was* a mistake," Mac said, stung by Carrington's not-so-subtle doubt that Savannah would not want to marry him.

"How do I know *you're* not after Savannah for her inheritance?"

"You don't. But you have the word of Mackenzy Cord, and if you took the time to ask around, you'd find out my word is as good as my aim." Standing abruptly, Mac held out his hand. He wanted the deal sealed. Carrington reluctantly shook hands. "Now, let's get down to business so we can both accomplish our goals. I'll need any information you have about where Savannah might have been headed."

Chapter Two

She'd done it! Savannah could hardly contain her exhilaration as she waited in line at the bank in Jamestown, New York. She'd traveled clear from Angel Creek, South Carolina, to the bustling excitement of Jamestown without a hitch.

"It's a mite different from your small hometown, wouldn't you say, Miss Carrington?"

With a gracious smile, Savannah turned to the dark-haired man behind her. Ned Barlow and his sweet-natured sister, Raquel, had been a godsend during the long, tedious train ride. They had even insisted on seeing her safely to the bank while she deposited the money she'd hidden in the hem of her traveling dress.

"Why, yes, it is," she agreed, her gaze wandering among the crowd of people inside the bank. "Daddy would be pea-green with envy to see this many people clamoring to put their money in the bank."

Standing beside her brother, Raquel laughed at her remark. "Are you going to take my advice and send a telegraph to let him know where you are and that you're safe?"

"I don't know. . . ." Frowning at the reminder, Savannah stepped forward as the woman in front of her completed her transaction. She handed the teller the carefully stacked money, watching as he counted it.

"I think it would be a good idea," Ned said. "In fact, I think I'll insist upon it. He'll need to know where to send the ransom money."

Savannah started to laugh at his outrageous jest, but the sudden pressure against her spine strangled the words in her throat. There was no mistaking the click as Ned Barlow cocked the hammer on the gun.

"Would you be kind enough, Miss Carrington, to move aside so that I might make a withdrawal before we leave? Starting with your money, of course."

"Miss Carrington checked in three days ago," the Imperial Hotel clerk informed Mac when he arrived in Jamestown a week after his discussion with George Carrington. "But I'm afraid you won't find her in her room."

Mac was tired, dirty, and in no mood to play guessing games with a bored hotel clerk. "Do you have a notion of where I might find her?"

"You mean you haven't heard?"

With exaggerated patience, Mac said, "I've just arrived in town."

The clerk's eyes began to gleam, giving Mac his first inkling that all was not as it should be with his lady love.

"Then you *don't* know."

Snapping his teeth together, Mac growled, "Just what is it that I'm supposed to know?"

"About Miss Carrington, sir. She's in jail."

Despite his fatigue, Mac threw back his head and laughed uproariously. When he finally managed to control his mirth to some extent, he gasped out, "I think you must be talking about another woman."

"Hair the color of ripened wheat? Sort of tall—for a woman, that is—and cornflower blue eyes? Dressed real fancy, with a right nice smile . . ."

Before the clerk could finish his startlingly familiar description, Mac was on his way to the hotel entrance. He hailed a passing carriage, barked out his destination, and urged the driver to hurry.

Mac hung on for dear life as the driver sent the horses into a fast clip, skillfully navigating the crowded street. What was Savannah doing in *jail*? Try as he would, he couldn't imagine the refined, gentle Savannah behind bars. In fact, the hazy image he *did* conjure made him shudder.

Fifteen minutes later the carriage pulled alongside the boardwalk in front of the Jamestown Jail. Mac paid the driver and jumped down, anxious to get to Savannah. George Carrington would suffer a *stroke* when he heard about this. Hell, *he* felt close to panic as well!

The sheriff, a burly, bearded man with tobacco-stained teeth and a stubborn glint in his eyes, stopped Mac at the door. Beyond the sheriff's shoulder, Mac could see several deputies milling about, but no sign of Savannah.

"I'm here to see Savannah Carrington," Mac announced, meeting and holding the sheriff's suspicious gaze.

"Miss Carrington ain't seein' nobody until she tells us where Barlow's hiding out," the sheriff said, firmly blocking the doorway.

This was insane, Mac decided, growing angrier by the minute. "What exactly are you holding her for?"

The sheriff switched a wad of tobacco to the other side of his jaw, planting his fists on his hips. "Bank robbery."

For the second time that day, Mac laughed. He couldn't help it. First the hotel clerk had informed him Savannah was in jail, and now the sheriff was telling him Savannah was involved in a bank robbery.

There was obviously some mistake. A *big* mistake.

"I don't see the humor in breaking the law, mister," the sheriff snapped. "So, unless you're some kin to the *lady* in there, get yourself lost."

"Well, Sheriff . . . ?"

"Porter."

"Sheriff Porter. I *am* kin." Mac stood eye to eye with the sheriff as the blatant lie rolled from his tongue. "I'm Mac Carrington, her husband." Well, he *wanted* to be, so that should count for something, although it stung his pride to use the Carrington name instead of his own.

Sheriff Porter's eyes narrowed with suspicion. His gaze crawled along Mac's lean form down to his dusty boots. "She didn't mention no husband."

Mac quickly formulated his plan. In his line of work, it paid to lie—and be good at it. Otherwise, he'd never get close to the wily outlaws he hunted. "We've had an altercation, so I'm not surprised she didn't mention me." He lifted a brow for emphasis as he added, "If you know what I mean."

"Ran off, did she?"

"Yes, right after the argument." Mac gave his head a rueful shake, lowering his voice. "You see, we've only been married a few days, and Savannah . . . well, she's already talking about babies and—"

"Tell you what," Sheriff Porter said, looking uncomfortable with the subject. "I'll give you five minutes with Miss—*Mrs*. Carrington. If she *doesn't* know you, I'll throw your mangy hide in there with her." He gave Mac a hard, meaningful look and lifted a bushy eyebrow. "*If* you know what I mean."

The sheriff wasn't as dull-witted as he appeared, Mac realized. "You've got a deal, Sheriff."

Porter waved him inside. With an inward sigh of relief, Mac followed him through a cluttered office into a dim hallway. The success of his plans counted on Savannah being glad to see him. She always *appeared* happy to see him when he returned from his bounty-hunting trips. He reckoned there was no time like the present to find out if she was sincere. Of course, there was always the chance she'd realize right away that he'd followed her to Jamestown, and figure out who'd sent him.

"Mrs. Carrington? You've got a visitor."

Jarred back to the present by the protesting sound of metal as the sheriff opened the cell door, Mac quickly stepped through, his gaze on the statuesque blond woman perched on the hard cot.

She was every bit as beautiful as he remembered, from her upswept blond hair to her narrow feet encased in sturdy brown traveling shoes. Her gaze remained focused on the gloved hands folded demurely in her lap, and as Mac scanned her pale features, he was relieved to note she looked understandably upset but unharmed.

Unaware of Mac's presence, she said, "I've already told you, Sheriff Porter. I have no idea where Ned Barlow was headed when he left the bank with *my* money."

Although there was strength—and a hint of lingering anger—in her voice, Mac saw her bottom lip quiver before she caught it with her teeth. The betraying movement caused a peculiar ache to bloom in his heart. Lovely, brave Savannah. She was frightened but determined not to show it.

Reaching into his coat pocket, he withdrew a candy stick and removed the protective paper. Slowly he approached Savannah, aware that Sheriff Porter watched them covertly. One wrong word, one wrong move, and Mac knew they'd both be in a pickle barrel without an opening.

"Darling . . . can we put this silly argument behind us and get on with our lives?" Mac pleaded softly, holding out his sweet offering.

Savannah's gaze focused on the candy stick, then flew upward; her stunning blue eyes widened in recognition. "Mac! What—"

"No, no, honey," Mac said quickly, placing a finger on her lips. "Let's not talk about it. I've told the sheriff what happened . . . that we had an argument and that you couldn't possibly have anything to do with that bank robbery.

"But, Mac—"

"Now that he realizes you're my wife, he'll have to let you go."

"But, Mac—"

Mac grabbed her arms and hauled her against him, shocking her silent. His first body-to-body contact with Savannah momentarily stunned *him* as well. She was firm yet soft, and felt oh-so-good against him. Better than his wildest dreams, and he'd plenty of those in the last few years.

He gazed meaningfully into her wide eyes, hoping she wouldn't notice his even more shocking reaction to her nearness. His voice low and vibrant with emotion, he said, "It scares the hell out of me to think of you in danger, as you must have been during that bank robbery." It was the truth; it *did* scare the hell out of him to think of Savannah in the midst of violence. "So what do you say, darling? Shall we kiss and make up?"

If her eyes had been wide before, they nearly swallowed her face now. "K-kiss?" she stammered.

Smiling at her dumbfounded expression, Mac nodded.

"And I've changed my mind. I want to have *lots* of babies with you." It was so easy, Mac thought, because everything he said was the God's honest truth.

"Mac!" Savannah squeaked, her cheeks flaming with gorgeous color. "Have you lost your—"

Mac told himself that he had no choice as he kissed her. He would have preferred a more private, romantic setting for the glorious, memorable occasion of their first kiss, but there was no hope for it. At least, he mused with an inward smile, it would be a tall tale to pass on to their children.

Her lips were warm and soft against his, and she tasted sweeter than he'd ever dreamed. Coaxing, moving his mouth experimentally against her lips, he kissed Savannah until she gave up with a little sigh and began to kiss him back. Her arms came up and around his neck, pulling him closer.

Her response gave Mac a burst of hope. Savannah was kissing him as though she meant it—as if she *wanted* to.

"Ahem." When clearing his throat didn't work, Sheriff Porter gave his keys a noisy jangle.

Reluctantly Mac pulled free of Savannah's moist, kissable mouth and placed his lips near her ear. "Are you with me now?" he whispered. He felt her slight nod against his chin. "Good. Because if we're going to get out of here, we need to be convincing."

Slipping his arm around her waist, Mac turned toward the sheriff. "Sheriff, as you can see, my wife is clearly not a bank robber." Mac smiled as if the mere idea were ludicrous. "We'd like to get on with our honeymoon, if that's all right with you."

Sheriff Porter hesitated, glancing at Savannah's flushed face and glazed eyes. "I've got about a dozen witnesses that heard Barlow call her by name. He called her 'Sweet Savannah.' "

Mac didn't have to invent the jealous scowl at Porter's remark. He'd like to know the answer to *that* riddle himself. In the meantime, he'd have to improvise. "Anyone who knows Savannah knows that she never meets a stranger." Slanting her an admonishing glance, he said, "I've told you about talking to strangers, haven't I, darling? Now look what's happened. You've got Sheriff Porter here thinking you're a bank robber!"

There was an answering spark in Savannah's eyes as she gazed back at him. "But it all worked out for the best, didn't it, *darling*? After all, we *kissed* and made up, and we're going to have lots of *babies*." The spark became a definite flame. "I'm sure *Daddy* can't wait to bounce grandchildren on his knee."

So, she'd gotten over the shock of seeing him and figured out why he was in Jamestown, Mac mused. Well, what had he expected? She'd traveled all the way from Angel Creek to escape her overbearing father and an impending marriage she didn't want. It wasn't likely she'd agree to go home without a fight.

Mac wasn't too concerned about the time-consuming task of convincing her—if it meant he'd get to spend more time in her company. Linking her hand with his, he smiled into her glittering eyes. "Come along, darling. We've got some making up to do."

Her fingers tightened meaningfully. "Yes, we *do* need to talk."

"You plan to stay in town long . . . *Mrs.* Carrington?" Sheriff Porter asked.

Sensing the sheriff harbored a few lingering doubts, Mac answered quickly, "Yes. We plan to stay a few days and see the sights."

"Good. If I have any further questions, I'll know where to find you."

Another delay . . . and more time to spend with Savannah. Mac could hardly believe his good luck. With dreamy visions of candlelight dinners, moonlit walks, and tender kisses, he offered his arm and led Savannah out of her temporary prison.

Chapter Three

"I'm going after Ned Barlow, and I'm going to get my money back. If you won't go with me, then I'll hire someone else."

Over my dead body, Mac thought, but was wise enough not to voice his thought aloud.

They were seated in the sitting room adjoining her bedroom at the Imperial Hotel after a hasty meal in the restaurant downstairs. In all the years he'd known Savannah, it was the first time he'd seen her angry. Yet there was no mistake—she was furious. Her eyes had deepened from violet to nearly black.

"That—that smooth-talking *thief* has a thousand dollars of my money, Mac, and he's not going to get away with it. He—he also took something else of mine that was very dear to me, a locket that once belonged to my mother. I thought I lost it on the train, but now I realize that he must have stolen it right from under my nose!"

Mac tried not to speculate on just what Barlow had been doing when he managed to steal the necklace. "You heard the sheriff," he argued gently. "He practically ordered you not to leave town."

The truth was, he suspected he'd feel the same way in her place. But then, he was a man—a bounty hunter. Savannah was the pampered daughter of a wealthy banker. She was soft, tenderhearted; he was hard and had faced death many times in his twenty-five years.

After they returned to the hotel, Savannah had changed into a dove-gray dress trimmed in black. The style outlined her trim waist and generous bosom, sweeping in gracious folds to her feet. Savannah wasn't a conventionally small woman, but to Mac she was the most fetching sight he'd seen in a long time. Even more so with her stunning eyes now darkened with emotion. He wondered if her eyes would darken that way when she was aroused. . . .

"He has no valid excuse to hold me here in Jamestown, and you know it."

"Maybe. Maybe not." Mac rose from his chair and strode to the cold fireplace. He propped a booted foot upon the hearth. A previous occupant of the room—perhaps a child—had traced a smiling face in the cold ashes. "Savannah, this isn't just about the money, is it? Sheriff Porter said Barlow knew you." He glanced at her and with growing interest watched a flush creep into her cheeks. Jealousy quickly followed. "Savannah?" he prompted. "Don't you think it's about time you told me what happened?"

Her direct gaze clashed with his. "Why? So that you can report back to Daddy? So that you can tell him what a gullible fool his daughter is? Tell me, Mac, how much did my father pay you to bring me back?"

Mac winced and considered evading the question, but figured she'd find out soon enough. "He offered me five thousand dollars." *But I didn't take it.* If he told her that, then he would have to explain why, and he wasn't—*she* wasn't ready to know. *He* was ready all right. More than ready.

"Dead or alive?"

"Don't be ridiculous. Your father loves you." *And so do I.* Mac shifted his weight and placed his elbow on the mantel. "Tell me what happened. We've been friends"—Mac nearly choked on the platonic word—"for a long time, Savannah. That hasn't changed, has it?" To his relief, the fierce light in her eyes softened at his coaxing tone.

"Yes, we have." She glanced at her folded hands, her cheeks still flushed. "There isn't much to tell. I met Ned Barlow and his sister on the train, and we became friends." She frowned in remembrance. "Mr. Barlow seemed like a nice man. Witty, funny, and charming. A gentleman, or so I believed. We ate our meals together—with his sister, of course." Savannah's lips twisted in a self-derisive smile. "It wasn't long before I found myself telling them about Daddy and why I left Angel Creek."

"So he knew your father was a banker." Mac was beginning to see the ugly picture take shape. No wonder Savannah was furious with Barlow!

Savannah nodded. "I never had the slightest notion Barlow was anything but a gentleman, and his sister Raquel anything less than a lady."

"An honest mistake, by the sound of it," Mac offered softly.

"A mistake you would never make, Mac."

Mac flushed at her compliment. Before he could deny it, she held up a detaining hand.

"Believing they were my friends made the conclusion all the more humiliating. Continuing his pretense as a gentleman, Mr. Barlow insisted on accompanying me to the bank to deposit my money. The moment I handed it to the teller, he robbed the bank and tried to force me to leave with them. He was planning to hold me for ransom."

A shiver crept along Mac's spine as he imagined Savannah in the hands of Barlow had he succeeded. Obviously, though, his plans had gone astray. "How did you get away?"

For the first time since finding her in the jail cell, Mac saw a genuine smile. She lifted a hand to the hat perched on her thick, upswept hair.

"I—I was wearing a hat decorated with a big purple feather. It must have startled the horses. I managed to run back into the bank, and once I was inside, the teller locked the bank doors."

Mac grinned. "That's the most amazing hat story I've ever heard."

"It's not funny, Mac. I've never felt so foolish in my life!"

"About the hat?"

"No! About believing . . . You know what I mean!"

"Doesn't it make you yearn for the quiet, safe atmosphere of Angel Creek?" Mac asked hopefully.

"No, it doesn't." The stubborn glint returned. "I'm not going back, so don't waste your breath."

"Have you forgotten? Barlow took your money. How do you plan to live?"

"Have *you* forgotten?" she retorted with a lift of her finely arched brow and a steely glint in her eye. "I plan to get my money back from Barlow."

"I can't let you do that, Savannah. Besides, that's Sheriff Porter's job."

For a long moment Mac held her challenging gaze. She finally looked away, but he didn't think she'd given up.

"You're right. How foolish of me to think I could go after Ned Barlow."

Sauntering to her, Mac tilted her chin until she looked at him again. "Do you know where he's gone?" *God, a man could lose himself in her eyes,* he thought. They were like a huge, glistening, violet lake . . . inviting, irresistible.

"I told Sheriff Porter—" she began.

"*I'm* asking now." Mac rubbed his hand along her jaw, remembering her soft lips and equally soft body. He wondered if she thought about the kiss as he did. As he waited for her answer, her tongue came out to moisten her lips. Mac sucked in a sharp gasp, hoping she hadn't noticed his reaction. He didn't want to move too fast and scare her away.

But moving slowly was damned near killing him.

"He—he mentioned something about a sister in West Virginia and a ranch called Sunset about thirty miles south of Cornwall."

"And you think he was telling the truth?" He moved his hand along her jaw and into her hair, marveling at its soft, luxurious texture. It wasn't difficult at all to imagine it unbound and flowing around her shoulders.

Or spread across his bare chest.

"Why would he lie? He planned to take me with him and hold me for ransom."

"You've got an excellent point," Mac agreed huskily. Wisely he left her and moved to the window. Judging by the shadows filling the room, it wouldn't be long before full darkness was upon them.

The hotel overlooked Main Street, a muddy, rutted road filled with carriages and wagons. Through the thin glass panes of the window Mac could hear shouts and cursing as the drivers fought for space. Venders made last-minute attempts to sell their wares before nightfall, and couples strolled along the boardwalks in front of the numerous shops.

Across the street a solitary figure leaned against a lamppost. His long black coat flapped against his legs, and the black hat he wore shaded his expression. A thick silver band circling his hat glinted in the rays of the dying sun.

He appeared to be watching the hotel.

Mac stiffened, wishing he could see the man's face. Someone sent by Sheriff Porter to watch them? Although Mac did not feel threatened by the man, he supposed he *should* find out his business. In Mac's line of work it was impossible not to make enemies, mean ones who had no compunction about getting revenge.

And now he had Savannah's safety to consider.

"Mac . . . if you don't mind, I think I'll retire early. I'm a little short on sleep."

"Good idea. Tomorrow, we'll make good our promise to the sheriff and take in a few sights." He managed a casual shrug and glanced at Savannah over his shoulder to gauge her reaction to his offhand invitation. "Might as well. Looks like we're stuck here for a few days."

For a split second he saw a flash of something that might have been regret in her eyes before she blinked and glanced away.

"Yes . . . it does look that way. Mac, I can't go back to Angel Creek."

"Why don't you think about it?" Mac suggested. "Maybe in a few days you'll feel differently." *Especially if he had anything to do with it.*

Dry-mouthed, Savannah watched him stride to the door. Broad-shouldered, lean-hipped, and long-legged. She noticed every detail, right down to the interesting motion of his tight buttocks outlined by his trousers.

Mac was a man of action, and it showed.

In her mind she saw again the vibrant green of his eyes, framed by thick black lashes. His hair, more auburn than brown, brushed the collar of his shirt in a careless way that made her fingers itch to smooth it, then muss it again. A day's growth of beard lent him an air of danger, yet the stubborn cut of his jaw and easy way he walked spoke of confidence and an inbred sophistication he seemed unaware of.

He was definitely a man any woman would look at twice, yet Savannah was seeing *this* man for the first time.

The moment the door shut behind Mac, Savannah brought her hand to her mouth and traced her lips. Mac had kissed her. Not just a friendly, polite greeting sort of kiss, but a man to woman kind of kiss. A passionate kiss, pressing his body length against hers in an intimate *un*-Mac way that jolted her heart into a flat-out gallop.

In the past few months Jon Paul had kissed her many times.

She'd never reacted like this; hot, flushed skin, weak knees, and a curious tumbling sensation low in her belly. Gingerly she brushed her hands over her breasts. She sucked in a startled breath. Through the fabric of her dress, her nipples were hard and tingly to the touch.

So *this* was passion, that forbidden word spoken in hushed whispers during her earlier years, but more openly as she grew older without finding a suitable husband.

Mac . . . Her dear friend. He'd kissed her to convince the sheriff he was her husband, and in the process he'd opened Savannah's eyes to a few facts she hadn't considered before.

Now Mac wasn't just a friend; he was a *man,* an attractive man who made her feel very much a woman. Savannah frowned, still finding it difficult to believe she could know someone so long and not realize how attractive he was. And there was no doubt she was attracted to Mac! Using her hand as a fan, she attempted to cool her hot face.

Lord! Mac would probably *die* of embarrassment if he

had any inkling of her naughty thoughts! He thought of her as he might think of a kid sister! If he knew, he'd probably run right back to—

Savannah held her breath at the thought.

If Mac knew, he'd be beyond embarrassment. He'd fear breaking her heart. She knew he loved her in a sisterly way. They'd been friends forever, it seemed.

Would his fear of hurting her prompt him to give up the chance to make five thousand dollars? Savannah rose and paced the floor, her mind tumbling as fast as the waves in her stomach. No, she couldn't do that to Mac, as harmless at it sounded. She valued his friendship too much.

Pausing at the window, Savannah surveyed the street below. She had only one recourse left, but she wasn't looking forward to it.

She'd have to search for Ned Barlow on her own.

Chapter Four

The gentle click of a door closing woke Mac. It was a distant sound, but he heard it loud and clear. Mac never slept soundly. In his line of work, sleeping soundly could be deadly. Besides, Savannah's easy acceptance hadn't fooled him.

Rising from the bed, Mac reached for his gun and tucked it into his pants. He didn't have to pause to put on his boots; he never removed them unless he was at home.

Footsteps—a woman's, he determined—moved down the hall past his door. Mac waited until they faded away before he eased through the door and followed.

Downstairs and to the left, the hotel restaurant lay in darkness. On the right, the clerk behind the desk snored softly, his chin propped in his hand and his elbow balanced on the counter. Mac paused briefly until Savannah disappeared through the hotel entrance.

Questions crowded his mind as he passed the sleeping clerk. Where could Savannah be going at this late hour? Could she be meeting someone? Could that someone be *Barlow?* Was it possible he didn't know her as well as he thought? Both possibilities sliced through him like a knife and awakened his earlier jealousy. He pushed quietly through the door and moved to the shadows, trying to determine which direction she had taken. Didn't she know it wasn't safe for a lone woman to walk the streets at night?

"Oh, you frightened me!"

It was Savannah's voice. Then Mac heard another voice, one he didn't recognize. His hand went unerringly to his gun as he pressed closer to the wall.

"My apologies, Mrs. Carrington."

"You—you know me?"

Exactly Mac's thought. His fingers tightened on the butt of his gun. He started to step out of the shadows, but the stranger's next words gave him pause.

"Where is your . . . husband, Mrs. Carrington?"

So, Mac mused. Not a threat, but a nuisance. One of Porter's men, sent to make sure Savannah didn't do a disappearing act, and to perhaps nosey around. Very quietly, Mac edged back to the entrance and pushed open the door. He let it slam.

"Savannah, I've been looking—" Mac broke off, nearly barreling into Savannah. He looked surprised, then suspicious as he glared at the deputy. "Who the hell are you?"

The deputy peered at Mac in the dim light. "Who are *you?*"

"He's—"

"I'm Savannah's husband," Mac inserted hurriedly, stepping to Savannah's side. He slipped an arm around her waist and pulled her against him, curling his fingers into her waist in warning. "She—we—I'm afraid you've caught us in the middle of a squabble."

Despite his warning, Savannah attempted to pull away. "He's—"

Mac shushed her with a finger to her mouth, gazing into her eyes with all the loving he could muster—which was plenty. "Darling, why must you always run when we fight? It's not safe for you on the streets."

"Ma'am, is this your husband?" the deputy demanded, clearly suspicious of her reluctance.

"Of course I'm her husband!" Mac growled. "The question is, who the hell are *you?* And how do you know my wife?"

"Mac—"

Swallowing an exasperated sigh, Mac covered Savannah's open mouth with his own, thrusting his tongue inside in the hopes of shocking her speechless.

She begin to struggle. Aware of their skeptical audience, Mac tangled his fingers in her hair to hold her mouth to his, wound his arm tightly around her waist, and pulled her against him. He deepened the kiss, groaning inwardly as his manhood leaped in response to her soft, womanly curves.

Mac was fast discovering that it was impossible to be this close to Savannah and not respond.

Assuring himself it was necessary, he slowly ground his hips against her, capturing her startled gasp in his mouth. She gave a little shudder and began kissing him back with a fervor that made his blood heat.

Prudently he released her. If the deputy wasn't convinced now, he'd never be, Mac thought with a rueful, inward chuckle.

More than a little shaken himself, Mac's lips lingered against her sweet-smelling hair before he turned to confront their audience.

The deputy was gone.

"I guess we convinced him," Mac said, his voice noticeably husky.

"Yes . . . I'm sure we did." Savannah's voice matched his own. She cleared her throat and tried to move away.

Mac held her tight, surveying with interest her blushing face revealed beneath the gas lamp. To be honest, he wished the deputy had lingered awhile longer so that he could do some more *convincing*. "Where were you going, Savannah?"

She wouldn't look at him as she mumbled, "Just for a stroll. I—I couldn't sleep."

"Is the money that important to you?"

Her eyes flashed fire. She made no attempt to deny his accusation. "It's not *just* the money, Mac, and if you knew me at all, you would know that."

"Pride, then." Mac's smile held a rueful understanding, yet he wasn't entirely convinced of her motives. "But to go after Barlow alone? Haven't you considered the danger? He intended to hold you for ransom. Are you planning to give him the opportunity he missed the first time?"

"I don't *plan* to give him the chance!" Savannah said.

Before Mac could anticipate her move, she twisted from his grasp and produced a small derringer. She aimed it at his midsection.

"You see, Mac, I may be a lady, but I'm not stupid. I had a plan."

Mac let out an admiring whistle, then promptly plucked the derringer from her hand. "I'm hoping you were just demonstrating your skills, and that you weren't intending to use that on *me*."

"Don't be ridiculous. I was showing you that I can take care of myself." When Mac handed the gun back to her, she slipped it into a hidden pocket of her dress and dusted her hands. "Since you're a bounty hunter, it might interest you to know the bank is offering a hefty reward for the capture of Ned Barlow and the retrieval of their money."

It was on the tip of Mac's tongue to deny interest in the reward, but he caught himself in time. He wasn't ready to divulge that his *main* interest was her. Because she expected it, he asked, "How much?"

"Five hundred dollars. Of course, it isn't five thousand . . ."

"Tell you what," Mac said, settling her gloved hand on his arm and leading her back into the hotel. Her eyes narrowed, but she didn't resist. "I'll make you a deal."

They passed the slumbering clerk and climbed the wide stairs, arm in arm. She paused on the top step and eyed him with suspicion. "What kind of deal?"

"Let's talk about it in your room," Mac suggested. Probably wasn't the best idea, but neither was *his* room, and the only public place was closed. He might have worried about her reputation . . . except they were *supposed* to be man and wife. The clerk did, however, give him a hard look when he asked for a separate room earlier that evening. Mac had rolled his eyes and mumbled, "Women, I'll never understand them."

Watching the enticing sway of her hips as she moved ahead of him to unlock her door, Mac sighed. Twice he'd held Savannah close and kissed her, yet he still didn't know if her response was natural or part of an act they were forced to play.

If it was an act, she was mighty good at it!

He closed the door and locked it. When he turned around, he froze. Savannah had not continued to the safety of the sitting room as he'd expected. She'd taken a seat on the bed and was now patting the space beside it—a very *close* space. He stared into her innocent blue eyes and silently quoted every Bible verse he could remember.

"Come sit with me and tell me about your deal. I'm all ears."

The ears he could handle. It was her soft curves, thrusting breasts, and moist lips that tempted him, Mac thought with a hard swallow. God, he'd loved her, dreamed about her, and wanted her for so long . . . Now she was sitting on the bed, her cheeks flushed, her eyes wide and expectant.

Trusting him.

Mac tore his hand from the doorknob and slowly approached the bed. He sat, not where she indicated, but several inches beyond that. Beyond temptation.

It didn't help. He could smell her sweet fragrance—was it jasmine?—and see the visible rise and fall of her breasts through her blouse. Her lips looked swollen from his kiss, and a sexy wisp of golden hair had fallen loose and now lay curled fetchingly on her shoulder.

With great effort, Mac kept his hands to himself and tried to resume the role he'd always played around Savannah; that of a good, trusted *friend*. Men flocked to Savannah, either for her money or her stunning looks, and he never wanted her to think that he was one of them.

"Mac?" Savannah prompted softly. "Was your *deal* just a trick to get me into the hotel?"

How about into bed? Mac shook the naughty thought from his head and blinked. He was going to have to make this conversation very short indeed. If he didn't he was deathly afraid he would do something he'd regret.

"Ah, no, it wasn't a trick."

"You look strange. Are you sick? Your face is flushed. . . ."

He'd bet it was! Thank God his trousers were roomy in the crotch, or she'd be even more alarmed. "I'm fine. I was just thinking. What if I agreed to help you find Ned Barlow?"

"What's the catch?"

Mac wondered what her response would be if he said, "You have to agree to fall in love with me." His hopeful thought prompted an old familiar surge of anxiety. What if she *never* loved him? What if no matter what he said or did in the next few weeks to convince her, she could think of him as nothing more than a friend? How would he live without her?

"Mac . . . are you *certain* you're all right? I've never seen you look this way."

No, she hadn't. He'd been very careful to keep his true feelings from her. Until he could offer Savannah the life she was accustomed to living, he hadn't wanted her to know.

"I'll help you look for Ned Barlow . . . if you'll agree to come back to Angel Creek with me."

"Mac, I can't—"

"Your father wants to apologize for attempting to force you to marry DeMent," Mac inserted.

Savannah's eyes rounded. "He said that? I can't imagine Daddy backing down. He's the stubbornest man I know!" Suddenly her shoulders slumped. "I don't know why I'm blaming Daddy. It's not really his fault."

"What do you mean?" She looked so dejected Mac had to grip his own hands to keep from comforting her. Nothing wrong with comforting . . . if he could actually stick to comforting.

"It's the money. No matter who I fall in love with, I'll never really know if he loves me for *me* or because I stand to inherit Daddy's money. It's one of the reasons why I decided to come to Jamestown. Nobody knows me here."

"They do now," Mac said dryly. "By the way, how *were* you planning to live?"

Her chin came up at the question. She looked proud and beautiful, and the sight of her spirited reaction made Mac more determined than ever to make her his wife.

"I'm going to open a hat shop . . . and design my own hats."

Not *was,* Mac noted, but *am.* "You could do that in Angel Creek," he pointed out. He wouldn't mind having a working woman for his wife, as long as it made her happy. He gave a startled jerk as she reached for his hand. A tremor of desire shot along his arm, but he didn't pull away. He *couldn't.*

"Mac, you're missing my point. Everyone in Angel Creek knows me as George Carrington's daughter. That will never change."

It will when you marry me. Because he was helpless to resist, Mac began to rub his thumb back and forth along her soft palm. "Won't you consider returning long enough to make amends with your father?"

Her darkened, luminous eyes studied him for a long moment. Finally she said, "And if I agree, you'll help me get my money and my locket back from Ned Barlow?"

"A week. If we don't find him within that time limit, we head for home." She hesitated, pulling her hand from his and rubbing at the same spot *he'd* been rubbing . . . as if it tingled? Well, hell, a guy could hope!

"All right, you've got yourself a deal."

Mac moved from the bed and put a couple of safe yards between them. "One more thing, though. You're to remain here while I go after Barlow."

"Like hell I will!"

To Mac's surprise, Savannah rose from the bed and approached him, finger pointed at his chest, eyes flashing with ire. She stopped short of poking him.

"I'm fed up with being treated like a princess, Mackenzy Cord. It's about time you found out that I'm *not* breakable! So if you think I'm going to just sit here meekly while you're out searching for *my* money, think again."

Choking back a smile, Mac said, "Whoa, Sav, I didn't mean—"

"Oh, I know what you meant!" Savannah continued to rage, her voice rising. "You've always thought of me as a pampered butterfly with no backbone and no brain. You're just like all the rest of the men in Angel Creek!"

Mac took offense at that. "Wait a damned minute! I never said you didn't have a backbone. Obviously you've got *plenty* of backbone or you wouldn't be here. I just don't want you anywhere *near* Barlow. He's dangerous."

"You're not leaving me behind!"

"Yes, I am!" Mac shouted right back.

Someone pounded on the door, interrupting their heated exchange. Without thinking, Mac jerked it open.

It was the clerk, looking sleepy-eyed and irritated. "Is there a problem? I heard you shouting downstairs." The clerk looked past Mac to Savannah. "Should I call the sheriff, ma'am?"

To Mac's chagrin, Savannah seemed to be considering the clerk's offer. She wouldn't . . . would she? Narrowing his gaze at her, he said softly, "We're having a discussion, aren't we, darling?" When she continued to hesitate, Mac took a step in her direction, fully intending to take her into his arms again. If that's what it took to gain her cooperation, then he was more than willing to comply. Again and again and again. With pleasure.

"Yes, yes," Savannah said hastily, apparently recognizing his intent. "My . . . husband and I were just having a silly little argument. But we've come to a compromise, haven't we . . . *darling?*"

This time *her* meaning was very clear. While Mac had to admire her clever maneuver, he was not happy with the outcome. She had no idea how dangerous bounty hunting could be. If something happened to her while she was in his care, George Carrington would have a bounty on *his* head.

And Mac would never forgive himself.

He could always slip away in the night. He nearly smiled at his ingenious solution. If he left her behind, Savannah would be fit to be tied on his return, but at least she wouldn't be in danger.

"As a matter of fact," Savannah added in a sugar-sweet voice that immediately alerted him and made him wonder if he'd spoken his thoughts out loud, "he was just about to get his things from his room."

She sashayed to him in a way that made his mouth water, gazing at him in a loving way that almost convinced Mac she was sincere. The little minx.

"No sense wasting our money, is there, darling? After all, we're a married couple. It's silly to keep separate rooms after we've reconciled our differences."

Mac decided that instead of kissing her this time, he might have to choke her.

Chapter Five

"Are you out of your ever-lovin' mind?" Mac demanded the moment the clerk disappeared after volunteering to retrieve Mac's belongings. "We can't stay in the same room together!"

Savannah folded her arms across her breasts, her chin tilted at a stubborn angle that was beginning to look very familiar to Mac.

"Why not? Everyone thinks we're married."

"Because—because we're *not* married," Mac argued, remembering to lower his voice. His face began to heat. "You're an unmarried lady, and unmarried ladies do not stay alone in hotel rooms with men."

"You're not just any man, Mac," Savannah chided. "You're my friend. We've known each other for ages. I trust you."

"I'm not made of stone."

At his low-voiced confession, Savannah's jaw dropped. She stared at him for a full moment before she began to laugh.

Mac didn't find a single thing about the conversation humorous.

"Mac! You are priceless. For a moment there I almost believed you. But you forget—I know you, and if you think I'm going to fall for your pathetic attempt to frighten me, think again. I'm not letting you out of my sight so that you can sneak off without me!"

Frustration was a mild word to express how Mac felt. His very first attempt to let Savannah know how he truly felt about her, and she laughed in his face! Somehow he had to convince her that sharing a room was a terrible idea. Since she didn't believe the truth, lying seemed the only solution. "If I promise not to leave without you, will you give up on this insane idea?"

Those luscious lips firmed with resolution. "No, I won't. I trust you to be a gentleman, but I don't trust you to keep your word. You'd justify it by saying it was for my own good."

They fell silent as the clerk returned with Mac's bags. When he'd gone, Mac locked the door and began unfastening his shirt. "Fine," he said, shrugging out of his shirt and moving his hands to the tie of his trousers.

"Mac . . . what are you *doing?*"

He nearly smiled at her squeaky voice. "I'm getting undressed for bed."

"But—but—you can't undress *here!*"

Mac paused with his hands on the waist of his trousers. He lifted a brow. "I can't? Why can't I? You said yourself that you trusted me. Besides, I'm tired, so I'm going to bed. Since I do not sleep in my clothes, it stands to reason that I would have to remove them." He slept fully clothed when he was away from home, but she couldn't know that.

Savannah's hand went to her throat. Her eyes appeared huge in her suddenly pale face. "You should undress in the sitting room . . . where you're going to *sleep,*" she emphasized.

"I don't see what difference it makes where I undress," Mac tossed out casually. But after a second glance at her pale face, he took pity on her. He left his trousers riding loose on his hips. While he was angry enough about her tricking him to shock her, he didn't want her fainting on him. Chances were Savannah had never seen a naked man before, and he wasn't just naked; he was partially aroused. "Remember, this was *your* smart idea. We've been *friends* forever, right?"

"Yes, we have, but—"

"And since this *wasn't* my idea, I shouldn't have to suffer, should I?"

"Well, no, but—"

"I'm not shocking your tender sensibilities, am I? Strong backboned woman that you are," Mac added in a drawling voice.

"You're making fun of me."

Mac bit back a wicked smile at her injured tone and tried to sound innocent. "I'm certainly not! By the way, would you mind helping me off with my boots?"

"Who—how do you remove them when you're alone?"

"I don't."

"Oh."

"So, will you give me a hand?" He strode to the bed and sat down, beckoning her with curled fingers. Hesitantly she approached him. "Now, turn around and lift your skirts."

"I beg your . . . pardon?" she stammered hoarsely.

Wondering just how far she'd carry the challenge, Mac stifled a laugh—and the urge to pull her onto his lap and kiss her senseless. He placed his hands on her hips and turned her around. "Now lift your skirts. Trust me, this won't hurt a bit."

Savannah gathered her skirts, but shot him a warning

glare over her shoulder. "If you're teasing me, Mac, I'm going to sock you in the eye."

Mac blinked innocently at her. He lifted his leg and slid it slowly between hers—was that a gasp he heard? "Now, grab my boot and pull."

Grunting, Savannah pulled and yanked on the errant boot while Mac took shameless pleasure in watching her wiggling bottom. There was no question about him dropping his drawers now! She'd faint for certain.

Finally she managed to remove his boot. Her face was flushed, and several tendrils of hair had worked loose from the pins. Before she could catch her breath, Mac offered the other boot, again taking his time sliding his leg between hers. He could feel the warmth of her thighs against his leg and groaned.

Savannah immediately froze. Her breathless, "Am I hurting you?" twisted his insides.

"Ah, no. Not at all." To Mac's disappointment, the second boot was easier to remove than the first. When she faced him again, he couldn't resist drawing out the torture. And it was pure torture! "Don't you have trouble undoing all those buttons yourself?" He reached behind her and ran his hand along the long row of tiny buttons on her blouse.

Her eyes flared wide. She arched her back and moved slightly to the side, dislodging his hand. "I—I can manage."

Mac arched a brow. "Why manage when I'm here? Besides, I owe you one." Just as he'd hoped, Savannah couldn't resist the challenge. She whirled around and presented her back to him.

The delightful curve of her spine gave Mac pause. Maybe he'd been a little hasty in teasing her.

• • •

With her back turned, Savannah couldn't see Mac, but the image of his bare chest remained emblazoned in her mind.

She'd never seen a man so perfectly formed, so ruggedly handsome. Ripples upon ripples of muscles rolled along his stomach, followed by a dark line of hair that disappeared into his trousers. She'd even managed to count the scars—three in all—that in no way detracted from the beauty of his skin. It was golden from the sun, smooth and hard-looking, and Savannah wished she was brave enough to reach out and touch it. Or even more scandalous, trace that mysterious line of hair right into his—

Mac's fingers brushed her back as he reached for the first button in a long line of many. Her naughty thoughts turned in a different, equally naughty direction. What would it be like if they *were* more than friends? How would it feel to have Mac stroking her with those rough-padded fingers all over?

Savannah held herself very still, her hand against her pounding heart. When Mac had slid his leg between hers, she'd gotten this strange feeling again, the same one she'd gotten when he kissed her both times. As if . . . as if she had a hundred butterflies fluttering around in her stomach.

She *knew* that Mac was taunting her, that she'd made him angry by tricking him into sharing her room. But what if he truly turned on that wicked charm she'd glimpsed earlier? Could she resist? Would she want to? Savannah gave her head a slight shake.

"Something wrong?"

Shivering as Mac's warm breath stirred the curls at her neck, Savannah shook her head again. "No. What could be wrong?" *I'm just tingling all over, and I want you to kiss me like you did before—without an audience so I'll know it's real.*

But she couldn't say that to Mac. He'd be embarrassed

at her brazen display, and right now she didn't want to give him a reason to leave before he helped her find Barlow. After they got her money back, *then* she might find it useful to scare Mac by letting him know how he affected her. She felt a stab of shame at the thought of deceiving him.

Then she recalled *his* reasons for fetching her home; five thousand dollars. As if *she* were bounty to be hunted, instead of a flesh-and-blood person with feelings. If Mac could be so callous, then why couldn't she?

Money. Savannah's lips twisted in bitter remembrance. She was beginning to hate wealth and the hurt it could cause. She had believed that Jon Paul DeMent truly loved her, until she'd overheard his boast that he would be richer than ever when he married her. Her daddy hadn't believed her when she told him what Jon Paul had said. He'd accused her of making excuses not to marry, and had insisted she go ahead with the wedding.

Mac's fingers worked their way down her buttons, seeming to take a long time in their task. Savannah shifted restlessly. Just the thought of Mac doing something as intimate as unfastening her blouse caused a strange ache in her breasts. She glanced down, gasping at the sight of her puckered nipples through the fabric.

"You're tense," Mac whispered, his seductive voice sending a delicious shiver dancing along her spine.

Tense? Oh, he had no idea how tense she was! Prudently Savannah clasped her arms over her telltale breasts to hide her aroused state. "Just tired, is all."

"Me, too. I'm almost finished."

And a good thing, too, because the curious ache had spread to her belly and was slowly seeping into her thighs. It was making her knees wobbly.

"All done."

For a shocking moment his big, warm hands slid into

her open blouse and massaged her tense shoulders. He gave her back a friendly clap and stepped away.

"I think I'll turn in now," he announced as if nothing momentous had happened between them. Savannah couldn't help feeling disappointed. "Oh, when you order your bath in the morning, don't throw it out. I'll just use your water."

Savannah, still prudently turned away from him, listened to his soft footsteps as he made his way to the sitting room. Her mouth was dry and her mind numb with the image of Mac, naked and dripping wet, emerging from his bath.

"Good night, Savannah, and sleep tight."

It took a moment to form the words, and when she did they were betrayingly husky. "Good night, Mac." Maybe he wouldn't notice, or would put it down to weariness.

When the sitting room door clicked shut, her knees gave way. She moved backward until she felt the bed against her legs. Lord have mercy! she thought. Could this be love? Could she be in love with . . . *Mac?* Not that he wasn't gentle and kind, and handsome. Oh, yes, he was definitely handsome!

But . . . *Mac?* Mac was her friend. They'd known each other since childhood, when Mac's father came to work for *her* father many years ago. And other than his admittedly admirable qualities, was he really any different from other men who couldn't be trusted? She'd heard her father brag on Mac on more than one occasion about how ambitious and hardworking he was.

Did she dare hope Mac could see her as someone other than a friend . . . or the rich daughter of a rich banker?

Chapter Six

"Mac . . . do you truly think it's necessary to kiss me each time we pass someone?" Savannah asked, sounding flustered.

They were strolling along Main Street enjoying the warm September day, doing a wonderful job of pretending to be in love. Only Mac wasn't pretending. He considered her question and decided to be honest. "I don't want people to think I'm insane."

"Beg your pardon?"

"For *not* kissing such a lovely wife at every opportunity."

Savannah squeezed his arm and laughed. "If I didn't know better, I'd think you had taken lessons on flattery from Ned Barlow!"

She could not have known, Mac told himself, how much her careless remark wounded him. "He said things like that to you?" he demanded, forgetting to hide his jealousy.

"Not exactly . . . and *he* never kissed me."

Was that a *wistful* note in her voice? Mac wondered, struggling against an overwhelming urge to yank her against him and wipe Barlow from her memory once and for all. But there was no one watching at the moment to justify his actions . . . dammit.

"By the way, Mac, you *did* know that we're being followed?"

Mac gave a start, resisting the urge to look behind him. Of course he had known, but how had *Savannah* known? She wasn't trained, as he was, in the art of following and being followed. "Probably one of the sheriff's deputies," he lied, instinctively pulling her closer. He'd planned to confront the man, but in the past two days Savannah had insisted on dogging his every footstep. She hadn't been exaggerating when she said she didn't trust him.

"He's not a deputy, at least not one that I recognize. Aren't you going to find out what he wants?" Savannah persisted.

"No."

"Why not? I'd be curious to know—"

"Which is why *I'm* the bounty hunter," Mac said, then immediately regretted his words when she stiffened. "I'm sorry. I didn't mean that the way it sounded."

She sniffed. "No, I'm sure you didn't." She didn't sound at all sure. "Imagine, little ole me, a bounty hunter! Why, I'm much too busy deciding what to wear to go chasing after mean ole outlaws!"

"Stop it," Mac growled. "I said I was sorry."

"Of course, I could *pay* someone to do the job for me, I suppose, since I'm rich."

"Savannah . . ."

"You know, Mac, that's not a bad idea. I could go into the bounty-hunting business, hire a few men, and just sit back in my office and pull in the money. Maybe you'd like to work for me?"

Mac saw an opportunity to shut her up. Striding in their

direction was Sheriff Porter. Hoping Savannah had yet to spot him, Mac pulled her against the wall of the feed store and gazed into her startled eyes. "God, Savannah, I want you so badly it hurts!" he announced passionately.

"W-what?" she squeaked, glancing behind them. The boardwalk was deserted—if one could discount the constant shadow that quickly slipped into an alley.

Before she could search the other direction, Mac turned her face back to his. "I want you. I want to take you back to the hotel and make mad, passionate love to you." He lowered his voice to a husky whisper, nuzzling her ear. "Do you want me as much?" He slipped his hands over her bottom and pressed her hard against him, proving to her just how sincere he was.

He felt her shudder. She curled her arms around his neck and pressed closer, sounding confused and breathless. "Mac—"

"Looks like you two lovebirds need to mosey on back to the hotel," Sheriff Porter said, startling a shriek from Savannah.

She stepped slowly away from Mac, her face blazing. Before he realized her intent, she hauled off and slapped him hard enough to make his ears ring.

When she had stomped out of earshot, Mac rubbed his stinging jaw. He stared after her. "Can't seem to satisfy that woman," he muttered with a rueful laugh.

The burly sheriff stared after Savannah through narrowed, assessing eyes. He shuffled his boots on the boardwalk. "Looks like you got a real hellcat on your hands," he agreed. "What'd you do this time?"

"I called her a daddy's girl," Mac lied smoothly. "She's been after me to take her home."

"Don't reckon there's any need in you two hanging

around, although I still think she knows more than she's lettin' on about Barlow."

Mac ignored the sheriff's comment and forced himself to look like a besotted fool. Wasn't as difficult as he thought, since he *was* besotted with Savannah. "Mighty obliged, Sheriff. I wasn't looking forward to spending another night on the sofa."

"Maybe you should have kept your room," the sheriff said pointedly. "And I guess you got a perfectly reasonable explanation for registering as Mackenzy *Cord.*"

The sheriff was smart, but he'd alerted Mac with his earlier comments, and Mac was ready. "As a matter of fact, I do. It's called pride. I was hoping that by registering under a different name, people wouldn't know my own wife kicked me out of her room."

Sheriff Porter fell silent, and Mac took it as a good sign. "Well, you two see if you can't leave *quietly,* you hear?"

Swallowing another bit of his pride, Mac simply nodded. When the sheriff left, Mac made his way back to the hotel. Right now would be the perfect opportunity to slip away from Savannah and go after Barlow, but for some baffling reason, Mac found he couldn't do it.

So his father was right; a good woman *could* soften a man.

Mac wasn't certain he liked the change.

"Come on, Savannah. Open the door and let me in. I need to talk to you. I said I was sorry."

Through the door, Mac heard her muffled, furious, "You *said* you were sorry right before you made a fool out of me! You'll have to come up with a better excuse this time."

Mac contemplated the door. For a reckless moment, he considered breaking it down. Finally he sighed and resorted to pleading again. "Please open the door. I've talked to Sheriff Porter, and he said—"

The door opened abruptly, nearly spilling him into the room. Savannah stood ramrod straight in the doorway, eyes narrowed and glittering.

"If you're lying to me, I'm going to rip your heart out. And another thing; if you plan on kissing me again, you'd better make *damned* certain I know why you're doing it!"

"I'm not lying." Mac stepped into the room and shut the door, but wisely kept his distance. It wasn't easy, because her anger made her more beautiful than ever.

"Mac . . . I don't remember you tormenting me this way in the past."

"And *I* don't remember your tantrums," Mac said. It was true, not that he was complaining. Since he'd found her in the jail cell, he'd discovered many surprising facets of Savannah's personality he hadn't been aware of—most of which he admired. And he had to admit he'd deliberately provoked most of her tantrums.

"Why is it that when a woman voices her opinion, she's throwing a tantrum?" Savannah folded her arms. "Yet when a *man* voices his opinion, it's quite a different matter. *He's* showing intelligence."

Belatedly Mac realized he'd stepped into yet another pile of horse manure. The space between them seemed to be populated with the stinky mounds lately. He was mighty relieved when her voice softened, hinting that her anger was cooling.

"Mac, what's changed between us? Do you think— could it be all this kissing we've been forced to do that's causing the problems?"

"Problems?" Mac growled. He didn't like the direction of *this* conversation any more than he'd liked the other.

"What's wrong with kissing?" *And please don't make me stop!*

"But we're *friends,* and since all this kissing began, you've been acting strange, and I've, well, I haven't been myself, either."

Hard to deny, Mac mused, speculating on the reason for her blush. She was right on both counts, but he didn't think it was a good idea to explain *his* reason for the change. If her agonized expression was any indication, he wasn't ready to hear her explanation, either. He suspected it might hurt too much.

He needed more time. Maybe the best thing to do would be to ease back into their earlier relationship for a while, at least until she could relax.

Friends again.

Mac wasn't fond of the idea, and expressed his dislike with a muttered oath. To her credit, Savannah-with-the-Backbone did nothing more than lift a questioning eyebrow at his language. It was just the boon Mac needed to muster a convincing grin. So his smile felt a little stiff, and his heart felt heavy. He hadn't given up, and that's what counted, right? A week looking for Barlow, and another week to get home. Two whole weeks to woo, court—or seduce her if he had to. Sometimes, he was fast discovering, a man had to be ruthless in his quest for love.

Thrusting out his hand, he said, "Friends again?"

Her smile was a little uncertain, and there was a lingering confusion in her eyes Mac would have given his eye-teeth to decipher. But her grip was strong and sure as she softly repeated, "Friends again."

Whew! Savannah thought to herself as Mac disappeared into the sitting room to pack his things. She was very glad they'd gotten that uncomfortable matter settled. One more kiss and she suspected she would have blurted out the appalling truth! Or worse—she might have humiliated herself and ruined their friendship by throwing herself into his arms and begging him to make love to her.

How did Mac manage it? How could he kiss her as if he meant it with his whole heart, yet continue to think of her as just a friend? Savannah folded her nightgown and placed it in the trunk on the bed. There had been a few times when she'd felt a part of him—a very *hard* part—against her that had seemed a little more than friendly, but she couldn't be certain. She wasn't as naive as most unmarried woman about the act of love, but she wasn't physically experienced, either.

Savannah began to fold the dozen or so dresses she'd brought with her and place them in the second trunk. Perhaps that particular part of a man's anatomy became rigid with any type of friction, in which case she wasn't necessarily the cause.

This theory disappointed her, which in turn made her giggle at her brazen thoughts. If Mac knew . . .

Mac would run. And right now she needed him. In fact, she rather enjoyed their spirited exchanges these past few days. With a sigh, Savannah closed the second trunk and opened the third. She began haphazardly pitching items into the bottomless pit: hairbrushes, combs, pins, chemises, drawers, and countless pairs of stockings. Instinctively she sensed that with the end of their pretend marriage, there would be little sparring between them. A pity, because she'd lied when she indicated to Mac that she was disturbed by the wicked side of his personality. She was disturbed, all right, but in an unmentionable, naughty way.

But she'd lied out of necessity to preserve their friendship and to rescue herself from probable humiliation. She slammed the lid shut and snapped the buckles closed. If only she'd noticed how she felt about Mac years ago, before she became so distrustful of men, and before they'd had years and years as *friends*.

She'd nearly blown it with that last kiss. Unaware of Sheriff Porter's approach, she'd allowed herself to believe for a sizzling moment that Mac meant the bold things he whispered in her ear. How close she'd come to telling him she felt the same way!

The rat had known all along that the sheriff was approaching. Now that Savannah was over her anger, she smiled at the memory, then winced when she recalled the wallop she'd given him. She supposed she should apologize to Mac.

But on the other hand, it *had* been a dirty trick. She didn't recall seeing this mischievous side of Mac, so her instinctive reaction had been—understandably—outrage. Now, thinking back, she realized he'd been teasing her. *He* didn't know her pretense of kissing him had stopped being a pretense on her part after their first scalding kiss.

A kiss, no less, that had left her aching and trembling from head to toe and thinking thoughts about Mac that made her blush through and through!

What a mess. Savannah felt tears sting her eyes at the irony of her situation. Out of all the men who had vied for her hand over the years, she wanted the one man she could never have.

Mackenzy Cord.

Chapter Seven

Maybe, just *maybe,* he needed to rethink his desire to wed Savannah—or any woman—Mac thought, surveying the mountain of trunks and hatboxes crowding the train station platform. They all belonged to Savannah, and he'd had to hire two carriages to bring them to the station.

"Er, Savannah?"

Dressed in a fetching rose-colored traveling suit trimmed in gray and wearing a perky gray hat that highlighted her mass of golden curls, Savannah whirled around to face him. She nearly poked him in the eye with the sharp tip of her frilly parasol, and didn't seem to notice.

"Yes, Mac?"

"I've got a question."

"*Yes,* Mac?"

With a bewildered sweep of his hand, he indicated the mountain of luggage. "How did you manage to *sneak* away from Angel Creek?"

She smiled at his dumbfounded expression. "It was easy. I bribed the housekeeper, the cook, and the gardener. I then sent the luggage ahead in a separate carriage to the train station and told Daddy I was going shopping." She frowned, tapping the tip of her parasol against her chin. "I also had to bribe Milton, which *wasn't* so easy."

"Milton?"

"Our driver. He's been with Daddy for ages."

Mac shook his head, deciding he'd never understand the rich. "Obviously not so long that he couldn't be bribed," Mac said dryly. "You'd better keep an eye on your trunks while I get the tickets." He started to turn away, then hesitated, eyeing the flouncy folds of her dress. "If anyone bothers you—"

"I'll handle it, Mac." Patting her dress, she indicated the small derringer hidden God-knew-where, then pointed the sharp edge of the parasol at him. "Don't worry, I can take care of myself."

Reluctantly Mac went to buy their tickets.

When he returned scarcely fifteen minutes later, Savannah wasn't alone. Two young boys tugged a trunk back and forth between them. Mac could hear them arguing as he approached.

"The lady asked me first!" the smaller of the two growled, yanking at the trunk.

The taller one stabbed his chest with his free hand and snarled back, "She didn't! She said we could both help." He gave a mighty yank and tumbled backward, knocking his hat to the ground.

Mac helped him to his feet and handed him his hat. He fished a few coins out of his pocket and gave them to the smaller boy, who looked to be twelve or thirteen and in need of nourishment.

"Thanks for your help."

"But, I didn't—"

"We can handle it from here," Mac added. "Now run along."

The kid's mouth worked for a moment. Finally he threw

the coins on the ground and spat, "I don't take charity, mister!" Holding his thin shoulders stiffly, he turned and walked away.

Savannah started to go after him, but Mac restrained her with a gentle hand on her arm. "Leave him. He'll come back for the money after we're gone."

Her gaze held a hint of censor. "Why didn't you let him help?"

Mac glanced at the boy standing next to the trunks. His gaze strayed to the silver band around his hat. "Because it's *this* one who interests me," he said.

"But, why—" Savannah's eyes widened in recognition. "You mean, *he's* the one who's been following us?" she whispered. When Mac nodded, she stepped closer. "But, Mac, he's just a child!"

"If he's old enough to follow us, then he's old enough to tell me why."

Without giving Savannah time to protest, Mac approached the unsuspecting boy and took his arm, pulling him out of earshot—just in case the conversation turned ugly. "I'll give you three minutes to tell me why you've been following me before I turn you over to the sheriff," Mac ordered. The young boy's eyes flared in surprise, confirming Mac's suspicion that the boy wasn't aware he'd been seen.

But his surprise didn't last long. He jerked free of Mac's hold and brushed at his sleeve. "I don't think you'll be turning me over to the sheriff, Mr. *Cord*."

"And why wouldn't I?" Mac asked softly. He didn't like the smug gleam in the boy's eyes.

"Because I know who you are and I know that you're not *her* husband"—he jerked his head at Savannah, who watched them as if she were attempting to read their lips—"or anyone's husband."

"Is that a fact."

Boldly the boy grabbed the lapels of his long coat and looked Mac in the eye as he said, "That's a fact."

The train whistle blew, reminding Mac he didn't have time to waste. "What do you want?"

"I want be a bounty hunter."

Mac yawned. "Have you got a name?"

"Yes, sir. It's Roy, sir."

"No last name?" Roy flushed at that, but Mac hadn't forgotten the boy's threat, and he never did like to be threatened. "People with no last name usually have something to hide."

"So do people with a *fake* last name," Roy said. When Mac started to walk away, he added quickly, "Okay, okay. The last name's Hunter. Roy Hunter."

Mac sighed and reached for the handle of the trunk closest to him. Obviously God had been short on imagination by the time He got to this kid. "Okay, Roy *Hunter*. Give me a hand with this trunk." When Savannah's pile of luggage was safely loaded, he urged her to go ahead so that she could find a window seat. Mac handed Roy a few coins.

With a scowl Roy handed them right back. "I told you! I don't want money—I want to learn how to be a bounty hunter!"

"First of all," Mac told him, folding his arms and leaning his back against the train. The vibration rumbled through him, reminding him the train would be leaving soon. "I don't need an apprentice. What are you, fourteen? Fifteen? Where are your folks?"

"None of your business!"

"That's the second thing. I don't trust people who don't trust me. Your last name's not Hunter, is it?" When Roy remained stubbornly silent, Mac shook his head. "In fact, I doubt your *first* name is Roy."

"It is!"

"Thirdly, I don't like to be threatened by a snot-nosed little kid with more balls than sense."

The train began to move. Mac flung himself away and hopped aboard, looking down into Roy's frustrated, angry face as he raced alongside the train to keep up with him. "Go find yourself a real job, kid. There are a lot of better-paying, easier jobs than bounty hunting."

"Go to hell, Cord!" Roy shouted after him, lifting his fist and shaking it at Mac. "You just hide and watch! I'll be a bounty hunter some day, and I'll be better than *you* ever were!"

Mac chuckled at the kid's enthusiasm and went to join Savannah. Too bad he planned to change his profession; training a brassy kid like Roy might be interesting.

When he spotted Savannah, he realized that she'd been watching the scene from her window. She was still watching Roy as he ran alongside the train, red-faced and shouting obscenities.

"What did he want?" she asked when he settled onto the padded leather seat beside her.

"Apparently he has aspirations to become a bounty hunter." Carefully Mac placed his arm along the seat just inches from her neck. He relaxed his thigh so it touched hers. When she didn't seem to notice, he relaxed further.

"He's persistent."

"Yes, he is." Mac leaned a little closer and inhaled the flowery fragrance of her hair, dreaming of a time when he could remove the multitude of pins and let it fall free around her bare shoulders. . . .

"Mac."

"Hm?"

Finally she turned from the window to look at him, catching his nose in her hair. He jerked back and cleared his throat.

"Did you forget? We're not in Jamestown any longer. We don't have to pretend to be husband and wife now."

Hell. Not only had he forgotten, he wished *she'd* forget! Running a restless hand through his hair, Mac shrugged. "You're right, I did forget. Habit, I guess." Habit he *wished*. They'd only been on the train a few moments, and he was already missing the touches, the kisses, and the heated looks they'd made a habit of exchanging.

"Why won't you help him?"

Mac blinked. "Help who?" His mind lingered on the memory of those heated looks. There had been a couple of times when he could have *sworn* she wasn't act—"

"Mac!"

"Sorry, honey. I mean, Savannah." He grinned sheepishly. "See? I told you it was a habit."

Her lips twitched in response. "I was referring to the boy."

"Roy Hunter, who wants to learn to be a bounty *hunter*." *Just like I want to learn to be a good husband*, Mac thought.

"What's wrong with wanting to be a bounty hunter?"

Again Mac had trouble focusing on her question, because he was too intent on watching her beautiful mouth move. She had ripe, curvy lips . . . just made for kissing. He liked kissing her. *Loved* kissing her.

"Mac!"

"Hm?"

"Do I have something on my mouth? You keep staring at it. If something's there, then *please* tell me. I insist." She began to wipe frantically at her mouth with her gloved fingers, deepening the cherry-red glow.

If something had been there—a bit of jelly left from their breakfast, a crumb of toast—Mac would much prefer removing it himself. With tiny, lingering little nibbles of his lips. "No, no. Your mouth's fine." More than fine. Beautiful. Luscious. Kissable.

She shot him a quelling, suspicious look and continued wiping. "You're lying, otherwise you wouldn't still be staring at my mouth."

That's what you *think, my dear.*

Someone tapped him on the shoulder. Mac turned to find a bearded, stern-faced man bending close to his ear.

"Mr. Cord, I wondered if you would mind coming with me."

"What's this about?"

Looking harassed, the conductor shot Savannah a meaningful glance and said, "I'd rather show you, if you don't mind, sir."

Savannah grabbed Mac's arm as he started to rise. "I want to come with you!" she whispered.

"Stay here."

He should have known that she wouldn't listen, Mac mused, hearing the rustling of her skirts behind him as he followed the conductor along the narrow aisle.

Several coaches later, the conductor stood aside and indicated for Mac to go first. When Savannah followed fast on Mac's heels, the conductor looked startled, but wisely didn't comment.

"Do you mind telling me what this is all about?" Mac asked again, glancing casually around. They were in the baggage car. Other than a mountain of luggage stacked haphazardly from floor to ceiling, the car looked empty.

A muffled sound snagged his attention. Mac peered into a shadowed corner of the compartment. It didn't take him long—Savannah neither, judging by her gasp—to recognize Roy struggling to speak around the gag in his mouth.

"Found this stowaway in the mail coach. He says he knows you," the conductor informed them in an aggrieved tone.

"And if I don't?" Mac asked softly. He didn't know whether to be exasperated or impressed by the boy's persistence.

"Then I'll do what I always do with stowaways. I'll throw his carcass from the train."

"You most certainly will *not!*" Savannah cried, waving an admonishing finger beneath the conductor's nose. "How dare you even *think* such a thing? He could be killed!"

The conductor remained firm. "If he don't pay, then he don't ride. Same as everyone else."

Savannah's gaze narrowed on Mac. "Mac, you will give the conductor money for Roy's ticket."

Not *will you?* But *you will,* Mac noted. He suspected that if she had any money of her own, she would have gladly presented it by now. Still . . . he didn't much care for her commanding tone. He settled his hands on his hips. "I might, if you say please nicely—"

"Please," she spat ungraciously before he could finish.

Mac continued as if she hadn't spoken, aware of the conductor watching them with growing amusement. "And I believe I'll take a back rub to go with the please—at your convenience, of course."

"A—" Savannah choked on the words and began again. "A *back rub?*"

From the corner of his eye Mac saw that the conductor was now grinning. "Yes, a back rub. I think I might have pulled something while loading your trunks onto the train." He rolled his shoulders and grimaced. "Yes, I'm sure of it."

"Mackenzy Cord," Savannah began in a low, furious voice. "You'll buy Roy a ticket, or I'll—I'll give you more than a *back* rub!"

The conductor burst out laughing. Mac chuckled and gave his eyebrows a suggestive wiggle.

Savannah, belatedly realizing what she'd said and how it was taken by the conductor, flushed a deep red. Mac had to admire her spirit, though. While most women might have fled the room in haste, Savannah tossed her head and pushed by them to reach the struggling boy. On bended knee she untied Roy's hands and removed his gag.

Still chuckling, the conductor told Roy, "You're lucky, boy, that Mrs. Cord decided to stick up for you."

Simultaneously Mac and Savannah began, "Oh, but we're not—"

They stopped, staring at each other in consternation. Mac was remembering his scandalous request in front of the conductor, and her equally scandalous response. He suspected that she was as well.

"Not newlyweds?" the conductor guessed inaccurately when they remained silent. He beamed at them. "Well, I never would have guessed you'd been married long the way you two carry on. It does my heart good to see a couple still so much in love. Me and my missus are the same way."

Roy snickered and opened his mouth to speak. Mac saw Savannah step casually near him and bring the heel of her shoe down on the boy's foot. Roy let out a howl and began hopping around the compartment.

Savannah grabbed his skinny arm and dragged him, half-hopping, half-walking, to the door. "Roy, I think you should stick close to us until we get to Virginia so that you don't get into any more trouble." She flashed Mac a brilliant smile over her shoulder. "Don't you agree . . . darling?"

Mac didn't have to feign a happy smile. He had only to think of all the delicious possibilities that could arise—and would if he had anything to do with it—in posing as her husband between now and Virginia. "I certainly do agree, *darling*."

He especially liked the *Mrs. Cord* part.

Chapter Eight

Two days later, after countless stops, little sleep, and bad food, Mac, Savannah, and Roy arrived in the rugged little town of Cornwall, West Virginia. Mac wasn't in the best of moods, considering he'd spent the better part of the journey fighting Roy for a seat next to Savannah.

And just to spite him, Savannah had chosen the brat over *him*. As a result, Mac had lost countless opportunities to kiss her or touch her as a husband was expected to kiss and touch. How much easier it would have been if Savannah hadn't followed him when the conductor came to fetch him, Mac mused with a frown. Roy *Hunter* might be dusting his backside along the tracks somewhere while *he* got down to the serious business of wooing Savannah.

"I need three rooms," Mac growled to the desk clerk in Cornwall's only hotel.

"I'm sorry, sir. We only have two rooms available."

Mac cursed loudly and without remorse. He refused to share a room with Roy. "Fine. Do you have a place in the stables for the boy?"

"Mac!"

At the sound of Savannah's protest, Mac groaned inwardly. He would *not* share a room with that—he sucked in a sharp breath as an idea came to him. It would probably put him in hot water with Savannah, but the probability *did* have its advantages.

If Savannah didn't want Roy to sleep in the stables, then she shouldn't object to sharing a room with *him*. All he had to do was make up for his first mistake. Thinking quickly, Mac said, "All right. My wife has not been feeling well, but under the circumstances I'm sure she can make an exception and share her room with me." He leaned close before he added, aware that Savannah and Roy had also leaned close, "She's going to have a baby and doesn't like to be . . . disturbed, *if* you know what I mean."

The clerk's head bobbed knowingly. "My own missus was like that with our third baby," he confided. "Best not to aggravate the situation more than you have to, sir."

"I'll keep your advice in mind," Mac murmured. He could almost feel the heat of Savannah's glare burning through his back. Speaking of backs . . . He reckoned that back rub she owed him was out of the question tonight.

She wasted no time lighting into him when they reached their room. "First I'm Mrs. Carrington, then Mrs. Cord. Now I'm Mrs. Cord and going to have a *baby?* Is there anything you *haven't* lied about, Mac?"

Mac winced. It was an unfair question, but he had to admit he could understand why she'd asked it. Since he'd arrived in Jamestown, he'd had no choice but to tell lies on top of lies.

But there was one tiny little point she seemed to have forgotten.

"If I hadn't lied to Sheriff Porter, you'd still be sitting in jail in Jamestown." Now it was *her* turn to wince. "I also seem to recall that on the train it was by mutual agreement that we continue the pretense as husband and wife."

Savannah's eyes widened with incredulity. "And why is that? *I* seem to recall you placed me in a very embarrassing situation with your outrageous conversation, Mackenzy Cord. My reputation was at stake."

He knew when she started using his full name that he was in trouble. "Maybe so, but you have to admit that sharing a room makes sense. It's not only cheaper, but also it keeps your precious protégée out of the stables."

"He's not *my* protégée, he's yours."

Mac gave his head a vigorous shake. "I never agreed to train him, Sav, and you know it. He's just a kid, and bounty hunting is dangerous work. He'd wind up dead."

"*You* didn't," Savannah pointed out.

Her eyes began to sparkle with something other than anger. Mac braced himself as she sauntered close to him. She fiddled with the collar of his shirt, her voice turning soft and persuasive.

It was a new side of Savannah—a seductive side Mac wasn't sure how to handle.

"Mac, why don't you show him a few things?" she pleaded.

He'd like to show *her* a few things. Mac held his breath as she leaned closer. A peculiar weakness flooded his groin.

"If I were a man, I'd want to be a bounty hunter just like you," she continued, walking her fingers along his chest. "It sounds like an exciting adventure."

Mac caught her wrist and held her still. The only thing that stopped him from jerking her against him and kissing her as he ached to do was the suspicion that she had absolutely no idea what she did to him. "I can't do it, Savannah. The fact is, I'm taking over Sheriff Cannon's job next spring. I'm giving up bounty hunting."

Her eyebrows climbed at the news. "Oh. I didn't know. Roy's going to be disappointed."

"He'll get over it," Mac said huskily. He could feel her pulse beat where he held her wrist. What would she do if he brought it to his lips and traced a tender path along the soft, delicate skin? he wondered.

Savannah tugged her hand free. "I'm going to have a bath sent up, then get something to eat. I'm starving."

"Me, too. Want to save time and take a bath together?"

She threw back her head and laughed at his outrageous suggestion, revealing a tempting length of her smooth white throat. Mac chuckled only because he knew she expected it. She'd never guess how heartfelt his suggestion had been, or how he ached to slide his mouth along her exposed throat.

"Oh, Mac! You'd be in big trouble, my friend, if I ever started taking you seriously! I never knew you had such a wicked sense of humor, but I'm getting used to it."

Mac managed a smile. Inside his gut was churning with frustration. He was beginning to think he'd *never* get Savannah to take him seriously. "Yeah, well, there's a *lot* you don't know about me."

"I'm looking forward to finding out."

And he was looking forward to showing her.

"Mac . . . have you noticed anything different about our room?" Savannah questioned, all humor suddenly gone from her voice.

Alerted by her tone, Mac surveyed the small room, his gaze lingering on the bed. There was a wash table, a chest of drawers, a dresser, and a mirror. The furnishings weren't as lavish as the Jamestown Hotel, but fairly standard. He frowned. "No, I don't." When he turned back to Savannah, she was clutching her throat, her expression solemn.

"There's no sitting room. There's no *sofa*. Just one bed."

So, Mac mused, holding back a delighted smile, here was proof that God truly *was* a man.

Savannah couldn't stop staring at the bed. Her bathwater was rapidly cooling—which meant that Mac would have to take a cold bath—but she couldn't seem to take her eyes from the double bed in the middle of the room.

Of course Mac had been teasing when he suggested they *share* the bed, just as he'd been teasing when he suggested they bathe together.

But both suggestions had prompted naughty images that quickly joined the others that had yet to fade from her mind. If he'd only stop teasing her with his outrageous suggestions, she might be able to revert to her earlier way of thinking about Mac as a friend.

Savannah sighed and slapped at the water. She knew that hope was a crock of rancid butter! Once she became aware of Mac as a man, her mind—and her shameless body—refused to let it go. She ached to know him as a woman, to feel him touch her and kiss her, and not in a pretend way. The pretend way was arousing enough; Savannah could just begin to imagine how Mac could effect her if he truly wanted her.

The possibility that she might *never* know Mac the man made her heart ache fiercely. If she had an ounce of sense, she'd take advantage of every opportunity to get close to him . . . in the guise of pretend wife and in the guise of friendship. Savannah rose and grabbed a towel, drying herself as her mind continued to plot ways to get the most out of her time with Mac.

Believing she thought of him only as a friend, he would never suspect as long as she was careful. Of course, there were limits to how far she could go without arousing suspicion.

As she slipped a fresh chemise over her head, Savannah smiled. She'd just thought of the perfect start—a *perfectly* innocent suggestion and one he could hardly object to, since it was his idea in the first place.

Chapter Nine

The hard floor was torture, but knowing Savannah rolled restlessly on the bed above him was the *worst* kind of agony. Well, Mac thought, attempting to find humor in the impossible situation, at least it couldn't get any worse.

"Mac, are you awake?"

Or maybe it could, because the last thing he needed was her soft, sexy voice to go with the arousing image in his mind. Gruffly he said, "I am now." As if he had been thinking about sleep at all—ha! Instead he'd been staring at the darkened ceiling above his head for what felt like hours.

"I was just thinking," she whispered.

Uh-oh. The covers rustled, and the shadowy image of her face peered at him over the bed.

"About that back rub I owe you," she added.

"Forget it." Mac clenched his teeth, his hands, and his thighs to keep from leaping up and joining her on the soft mattress. The bedsprings squeaked. He jumped as her hand landed on his bare chest. Every nerve in his body froze.

"But I can't sleep, Mac, and from the sound of your voice, you can't sleep, either. Maybe a back rub will help."

It might help you, but it won't help me! Mac growled silently. If only her offer didn't sound so—so *friendly.* Out loud, he said, "Count sheep or something if you can't go to sleep. Tomorrow's going to be a long day."

To his relief, she moved her hand from his chest. He had just begun to relax when she popped into view again. If he knew it wouldn't be so painful, Mac could have turned onto his stomach to get away from the tempting sight. But something was in the way. Something that made turning over impossible.

He couldn't make out distinct features in the weak moonlight streaming through the window, but he knew that her hair was down; he'd watched her brush it until it shone. The nightgown she wore was thin cotton, with delicate lace at the collar and sleeves.

He knew these things because he'd seen her before the lamp went out—seen right through the material to the shadowy outline of her sex, and the faint outline of her nipples.

Which was exactly why he couldn't sleep now.

Grim-faced, he gazed at the sweet face hanging above him and waited. What now? he wondered. And how much more could he take and still remain a gentleman . . . a *friend,* as she so trustingly believed him to be?

"If you won't let me give *you* a back rub, will you give *me* one?"

Mac didn't bother to hide his exasperation. She had to be the single most persistent woman in the world.

In one smooth roll he came to his feet. In keeping with what he'd told her at the Jamestown Hotel, he had removed his boots and shirt, but he'd drawn the line at taking off his pants to enforce his lie. He would have had a difficult time explaining his state of arousal had he gone that far.

Savannah moved to the middle of the bed to make room, but Mac perched on the edge. "Turn onto your stomach," he ordered, making a valiant attempt to sound impersonal.

She quickly did as he asked. Mac took a deep, fortifying breath and leaned over her, kneading her shoulders. Before a full moment had passed, Savannah shrugged his hands away and proceeded to draw the edges of her gown away from her shoulders, baring the smooth skin of her back to his hungry gaze.

Her voice was muffled against the pillow as she explained, "I think this will work much better, don't you? I like to feel the rough pads of your fingers against my skin."

Mac swallowed hard. So, she'd noticed.

"Mac?" Her voice was muffled and husky with impending sleep. "You didn't fall asleep on me, did you?"

Hardly. In fact, the way his nerves were jumping beneath his skin, he couldn't imagine sleeping again—ever!

"Hm. It's nice of you to do this for me. You're the best friend a gal could have."

Gritting his teeth, Mac gingerly settled his hands onto her skin. It was silky to the touch and warm. He moved his fingers lightly, tracing the delicate bones of her shoulder blades, then back again to the feminine curve of her spine.

"Hm, that feels good, but could you do it a little harder, please?"

Hell. Mac smothered a growl in the nick of time. The woman would be the death of him yet! He felt as if he were going to explode. Desperately focusing his mind on anything but the sound of the soft, little mewling noises emerging from her throat, Mac dug his fingers into her muscles and began to knead with a vengeance.

"No, Mac. Here, let me show you."

Before he could protest, she rose and pushed him onto the bed. He fell forward into a new torture, for the pillow reeked of Savannah's scent.

Thank God the pillow muffled his gasp as she straddled his hips and began to work her expert little hands over his tense back. But when he felt the heat against his buttocks and realized exactly *where* it was coming from, he moaned loudly and distinctly.

"There, doesn't that feel good?" Savannah purred with smug satisfaction. Obviously she'd misinterpreted the sound. "You know, if it were anyone but you, doing this would be out of the question."

Oh, yeah. Most definitely. Mac bit his tongue—hard.

"Which is why I'm glad we're friends."

If he heard that term one more time from her mouth, he was going to smother her with the pillow, he decided. Her *friend* was poking a hole in the mattress.

"Mac? You awake?"

He didn't trust his voice, so he grunted.

"Good. Because I was thinking . . ."

Again? This time Mac's groan wasn't entirely due to his uncomfortable state.

"It's silly for you to sleep on the floor when there's plenty of room in the bed for both of us."

"Huh?"

Fingers tiptoed along his spine, leaving a rash of goose bumps in their wake. "Oh, I know what I said earlier, but I *am* a woman, and everyone knows that women are entitled to change their minds."

Her hands got busy again, working their magic and driving him insane. Mac's mouth formed a very definite "no," but the sound refused to follow.

"So if you go to sleep, that's all right with me. I'll just

snuggle up beside you. I've always wondered what it would be like to sleep with a man. It'll be fun."

Fun. Mac repeated the astounding word in his mind. Surely she couldn't be *that* naive? Granted, she'd never been married, but—

"Of course, that's if I *decide* to go to sleep," Savannah continued with a delighted little laugh that curled his toes. "I feel as if I could do this to you all night long. Would you like it harder? You feel pretty tense. Maybe you *did* pull something carrying my horrible old luggage."

Mac's mind was still frozen on her offer to do it harder. With a string of oaths thankfully muffled against the pillow, Mac twisted onto his back.

Savannah rode the waves without a single squeak of alarm, which further infuriated Mac. Any woman with any sense would have been leaping for the other side of the bed, but not Savannah. She clenched her sweet thighs and stayed put.

Now she was astride him, looking like a naughty angel in the moonlight, regarding him quizzically as if she didn't have the slightest notion of the savage desire boiling between her legs.

Frowning, she leaned forward to peer into his face. The move opened her legs wider until she was fully embracing his arousal. Her heat seeped through his trousers as if the rough clothes were nothing more than a slip of silk, creating an inferno between them. *How in the hell could she not notice it?*

This time Mac tasted blood when he bit down. He grabbed her hips and held her still. If she kept on moving, he knew he'd spend himself against her. Long months of abstaining had its drawbacks, he discovered. The irony was that he'd been saving himself for *her.*

Well, she was about to get him, but the biggest irony was she didn't even know it!

"Mac?"

"Be still," he ordered.

She froze at his harsh tone, much to Mac's relief. In a tiny little voice, she said, "I hurt you, didn't I? You look like you're in agony."

Yes, but it's the sweetest kind of agony! He felt blood surge into his face. He was going to have to explain the situation to Savannah, and he wasn't looking forward to it. One wrong word, and he could lose her forever. She might turn from him, either from embarrassment or fear. Or both.

"Savannah . . . there's something I have to tell you, and I don't want you to be embarrassed." He sucked in a sharp breath as she shifted against him. "No—be still!"

"I—I'm sorry." She immediately became still again.

"Don't be sorry. It's not your fault." Mac's rueful smile felt stiff on his face. "Your mother died when you were young, did she not?"

She nodded, watching him with wide, anxious eyes. Her hands rested lightly on his outstretched arms.

"Then it's possible that you don't know . . ." Mac hesitated, embarrassed beyond belief at his predicament. He wanted very badly to make love with Savannah, but he wanted her full cooperation and knowledge—and her declaration of love. "You might not know that a *man* doesn't have to be—have to be—in love with a woman to want to—to be intimate with her." There, he'd said it! Mac let out a harsh breath and waited for her reaction.

Savannah regarded him for a long, suspenseful moment. Finally she said slowly, "Mac, are you saying that even though we're friends, you still want to be intimate with me?"

"No!" Mac shook his head, confusing himself. "I mean,

yes! It's not always something a man can control," he added quickly. "What you were doing to me . . . what you're doing right now caused a reaction—"

"You mean this?"

To Mac's horror *and* pleasure, she wiggled her buttocks, causing a ripple of sensation along his thighs and an ominous surge in his arousal.

"But I thought—" This time it was Savannah's turn to blush. "I thought it was supposed to be like that. All the time. I've never actually *seen* a real one. Is it—is it always this big?"

Mac had to laugh. Savannah wasn't frightened, and she didn't seem all that embarrassed; she was *curious!* He would have been a lot better off if she'd been frightened, because she was still sitting on top of him, doing and saying things that made him want to forget about being a gentleman.

"Mac."

He stopped laughing at her serious tone.

"When you laughed, it felt good. Do you suppose . . . that a *woman* could have the same reaction? I mean, even if she were just *friends* with the man?" As she spoke, her voice grew husky. She leaned forward again, and this time she deliberately pressed hard against the outline of his throbbing length. "Because it does indeed feel good," she added in an awed whisper.

"Dear God!" Mac howled his agony, knowing his limit; he'd definitely reached it! "Savannah, I want you to move away from me very quickly and forget this ever happened," he rasped, breathing hard. She was moist—he could feel her dampness right through his trousers, feel her all around him, hot and pulsing. Maybe it wasn't too late—

"Is it . . . okay if I do this, Mac?" she asked breathlessly as if he'd never spoken, sliding back and forth. "Because it feels very good. Yes, I think I want . . . to . . . continue."

Mac let out a guttural moan of surrender and clutched her hips, directing her moves as she continued to rub against him. In the dim moonlight he watched as his sweet Savannah threw her head back in abandon, totally enthralled with the sensations they were creating. He freed her hips and closed his hands over her thrusting breasts. Her nipples were taut and hard. He rolled them between his thumb and forefinger urgently.

She let out a gasp that quickly became a moan of unfettered pleasure.

"Mac . . . something strange is happening to me!" She gasped, moving faster and faster.

Her innocent bewilderment fueled the flames of his raging passion. He wanted more than anything to slide inside her hot warmth and spill his seed, but he knew he'd never make it in time. Her name began as a strangled whisper and ended on a shout as he began to spasm against her. "Savannah!"

"Oh, Mac, Mac, this is—it's—ahhhh!" Mouth open in shock, she collapsed against his chest and moaned into his neck. Shudders continued to rack her body.

Mac didn't know who was breathing the hardest. Both stunned and appalled by what had just happened, he wrapped his arms around her and held her tight. He loved her more than ever, but he never intended for this to happen—at least not yet, and not in this way.

How would Savannah feel about him now?

Later, when he determined by her soft snores that she was asleep, he tried to move her, fully intending to return to his pallet on the floor and figure a way out of the mess he'd made.

He got his answer sooner than he expected.

"Don't go," she murmured, clinging to his chest. "We're still friends, Mac. We're still . . . friends."

Chapter Ten

Warm fingers of sunlight slanting across her face woke Savannah from a deep, restful sleep. Before she could open her eyes, her mind filled with lusty images of last night with Mac.

A blush warmed her body from head to toe.

She jerked fully awake and sat up. The space next to her was empty. Scrambling across the bed, she peered over the edge.

Mac lay sleeping on his pallet on the floor, sprawled on his back with one arm flung over his face as if to block out the encroaching sunlight. Savannah let out a sigh and propped her chin on her folded arm, content to watch him as he slumbered. Her interested gaze slid along his length, paused for a moment on the bulge in his trousers, then returned to his face. He frowned in his sleep.

Savannah frowned with him. Was he dreaming about last night? The first time he'd tried to slip away from her, she had tried to assure him she expected no commitment, that they were still friends. But sometime in the night he'd left her and returned to the floor.

How would Mac feel about her this morning? she wondered. Would he be embarrassed? Regretful? Horrified? Would he think that she had fallen in love with him, and worry about her feelings? Or would he be disgusted by her behavior and believe that she was a woman of loose morals?

She hadn't meant for things to go so far, hadn't meant to risk losing his friendship *or* his respect. But how was she to know that being intimate with Mac would be so wonderful? She'd only planned to touch him . . . maybe do a little more of that kissing she enjoyed. Instead she'd started a fire she couldn't put out. The results had been very memorable indeed, but what happened now? Did they go back to being friends—pretend it never happened? Was Mac dreading the confrontation or looking forward to it? He hadn't attempted to deny that he desired her. Did she dare hope his desire might eventually turn into something deeper?

Savannah sucked on her bottom lip. So many tough questions! Her instincts urged her to use her womanly wiles on Mac and see what developed, but her heart hesitated. Mac had been in her life for a very long time . . . as a true and trusted friend. Deceiving him—deliberately setting out to *seduce* him—seemed very, very wrong. Of course, she hadn't *meant* to seduce him last night, just get close to him.

Okay, so she had miscalculated—due to her naïveté concerning male body parts and a man's reaction to a woman's touch. She *hadn't* known men were so easily aroused. Yet when Mac had explained in his adorably hesitant way, she hadn't shrieked with maidenly outrage, or outwardly revealed her surprise.

Perhaps she should have, but Savannah could not regret what happened.

Unless, of course, Mac did.

• • •

It was the steady drip-drip of water on his forehead that pulled Mac from the depths of the best sleep he'd experienced in ages. As a result, he awakened heavy-eyed and disoriented. Not a feeling he liked.

"Rise and shine!" Savannah sang out.

Mac focused on the lovely vision bending over him. His eyes narrowed on the pitcher of water Savannah held in her hand. "I take it that it's *not* raining and the roof of this crumbling castle they call a hotel *hasn't* sprung a leak?"

Savannah laughed. "No, no, and this *crumbling castle* isn't so bad. I slept like a log." Fully dressed and looking sassy and happy, she added, "And now I'm starving. Hurry and get dressed so that we can have breakfast. Roy's working on his third stack of flapjacks."

That got him good and awake. He jackknifed to a sitting position. "At whose expense?" he demanded.

She flashed him a sunny smile. "Yours. You know that *I* have no money—thanks to Ned Barlow. Now, here's your wash water."

Without preamble she handed him the pitcher. Mac grabbed it before it soaked his lap. His gaze followed the sassy sway of her hips as she moved to the door. *The hell with breakfast,* Mac thought with a groan, *I'll just have a helping of last night with a side order of kisses.*

"I'll meet you downstairs when you're finished," she flung over her shoulder.

The moment the door clicked shut, Mac scrambled to his feet. Savannah had acted as if nothing had happened between them. He didn't know whether to be chagrined or glad.

He gave a start as the door opened again. When Savannah stuck her head through the crack, he hastily held the pitcher in front of him. Watching the enticing swing of her bottom had awakened the mad beast again.

"By the way, I had a wonderful time last night, so if you ever need another . . . *back* rub, just let me know."

Mac's jaw dropped at her brazen offer—and the sight of one gorgeous blue eye closing in a meaningful wink. The door slammed shut again, leaving him dazed. He pinched himself to make certain he wasn't dreaming. Had he imagined her emphasis on *back,* or was it only wishful thinking? Because the back rub was already a distant memory . . . while the *other* rubbing lingered sharply in his mind.

In a daze he took the pitcher to the washbasin and filled the bowl. He splashed his face repeatedly with the cold water, but it failed to clear his mind of Savannah's brazen offer and equally brazen wink. What had he unleashed with his inability to control himself around Savannah? By claiming he wasn't in love with her, yet able to get aroused, had he given her the wrong impression about lovemaking?

It was an alarming possibility. Savannah seemed mature and levelheaded, but last night proved she was innocent in the ways of men. He couldn't deny the proof of her innocence pleased him, yet it dismayed him to think he may have somehow twisted her perceptions about the relationship between a man and a woman.

Mac buttoned his shirt and combed his hair with his fingers, wondering how he could reverse the damage he might have inadvertently caused. Without a doubt he would have to talk to her, explain to her that what happened between them *shouldn't* have happened unless they were in love, or better yet, married.

But she'd made it clear just before drifting off to sleep that she still thought of him as a *friend.*

Hell, how he was coming to despise the word! Yet, what if they *weren't* friends? Wouldn't he be one step further from getting her to fall in love? His parents had been friends before they married, as his mother had been fond of telling him. They'd had a long, loving marriage based on trust, loyalty, and friendship. Mac wanted that for himself, with Savannah. Wanted it so badly he could taste it.

And by God, he was going to do everything in his power to see that it happened. From here on out he was going to treat Savannah like the lady she was. No more embarrassing, dangerous scenes—however wonderful—like last night. Even now he flushed with remembered humiliation. If it had been anyone but Savannah, they would have laughed at the way he spent himself against her like a young boy with his first woman.

Savannah deserved his respect. From now on, that's what she'd get.

With this firm resolution, Mac quit the room and made his way downstairs to join his lady love and the brat.

He paused at the entrance of the restaurant, quickly spotting Savannah and Roy at a table near the window overlooking Main Street—or what there was of it. Roy was busy stacking thick slices of bacon onto a biscuit.

"Leave anything for me?" Mac demanded in a grumbling voice as he took a seat next to Savannah. For once Roy wasn't plastered to her side. It was a small comfort.

Roy's mouth was stuffed, so with his free hand he indicated the platters of sausage, ham, and bacon. There was steaming biscuits, gravy, and scrambled eggs. A pitcher of milk sat near Roy's elbow; there was no sign of a glass.

There was one flapjack left on the plate. Lips twitching despite himself, Mac noticed a stream of dark molasses dripping from Roy's chin. It wasn't difficult to guess Roy's favorite.

Meeting Savannah's amused gaze, Mac couldn't hold back a smile. He glanced at the biscuit by her cup of tea. "I thought you were starving."

Roy finally emptied his mouth long enough to mumble in response to Mac's earlier question, "I ordered plenty."

"So I see," Mac drawled, dragging his gaze from Savannah's. "Expecting an army?"

"No, just you."

Mac scowled at the brat's sassy remark. "You might recall who's paying the bill."

Apparently Savannah decided it was time to intervene. "Are we taking a carriage out to the ranch or riding?"

"*We* aren't riding anywhere."

"I'm *not* staying here!" Savannah insisted.

"Neither am I," Roy added, grabbing another biscuit and a slice of fried ham.

"I'm going alone, and that's final." Mac was adamant. "If Barlow's there, he'll recognize you. He doesn't know *me*."

Roy hastily swallowed a mouthful of biscuit. "He doesn't know me, neither!"

"If you're going to be a bounty hunter, the first thing you need to learn is to obey orders," Mac told Roy in his sternest voice. "You'll stay here with Savannah."

But Roy heard only part of Mac's words. "You mean you'll agree to train me?" he cried, his face lighting up.

"That's wonderful, Mac!" Savannah clapped her hands, gracing Mac with a brilliant smile that never failed to make his heart skip a beat. Suddenly her smile faded. "What if you get into trouble? What if . . . what if you need our help?"

"Yeah, you might *need* us," Roy emphasized, puffing out his skinny chest like a rooster about to crow.

"I've been taking care of myself for a long time. I think I can manage." He hesitated before adding, "Besides, if I do catch Barlow, I'll have to force him to tell me where he's hiding the bank's money. It might get ugly."

He'd been worried about bruising Roy's pride; he'd forgotten entirely about Savannah's. She didn't hesitate to remind him.

"After last night, you still think of me as a spineless ninny?" she challenged softly. "Really, Mac. I'm hurt. I didn't run from *you,* did I?"

Roy, who was watching the exchange with unabashed curiosity, couldn't possibly have known the meaning behind Savannah's reference, but the knowledge did little to quell the rush of heat into Mac's face.

"Something happen that I should know about?" Roy demanded, glancing from Savannah's stubborn face to Mac's red one. He sounded injured that they might have excluded him from something.

"No," they snapped simultaneously.

Completely ignoring Roy now, Mac focused on Savannah. God, she was so beautiful and strong! It petrified him to think of her falling into Barlow's hands. "Barlow isn't your *friend,* Sav. Best you remember that." He would elaborate the moment they were alone, but for now he hoped she gleaned his meaning.

Judging by the flush that suddenly suffused her face, she did. But her chin remained high. "Can't we at least go halfway with you, make camp, and wait for your return?"

"And if Barlow was to find *you* before I found *him?*" Mac countered softly. "What then? This is a dangerous man. He not only robbed the bank of a lot of money, he intended to hold you for ransom. Have you forgotten?"

"Roy would be there, and I have my own protection. Have *you* forgotten?"

Mac requested a cup of coffee from a passing waitress, then stared pointedly at Roy. "Do you own a gun, brat? Do you know how to shoot?"

Roy looked offended. "Of course I own a gun."

When the boy's guilty gaze dropped to his plate, Mac prompted, "And you know how to use it?"

His silence was damning. "I was hoping you'd teach me," Roy finally mumbled.

Slanting an I-told-you-so look at Savannah, Mac leaned back as the waitress deposited his cup of coffee in front of him. "That settles it, then. You both stay here and wait for me."

"By the way," Roy asked belatedly, pausing to drink from the pitcher of milk. He wiped his dripping mouth with his coat sleeve. "Who *is* this Barlow guy, and why are we chasing him?"

Chapter Eleven

Getting information out of the people of Cornwall was like pulling an ornery tooth, Mac thought with a growl of disgust.

Everyone obviously knew Barlow's sister and the location of the ranch, but their vague responses left Mac with the strong suspicion they were protecting him—or *someone*. Possibly Barlow himself?

On his way to the livery stable located at the edge of town, he passed several unsavory-looking men whose faces looked familiar. He was certain that if he took the time to search through the pile of wanted posters in his satchel, he'd find a match or two right here in the uncooperative little town of Cornwall.

With a sigh of regret for the lost bounty, Mac entered the dim building where the barber grudgingly assured him he could get a horse.

A man emerged from the shadows as if he'd been waiting for Mac. He thrust his hand out before Mac's eyes could fully adjust to the dim light.

"Mason West, at your service."

Warily Mac shook the big, meaty hand. "Mackenzy

Cord. I need a horse for a few days." At his request, Mason nodded—too quickly for Mac's peace of mind.

"Got just the horse for you, Mr. Cord. He's a might frisky, but you look like a man who can handle it."

Mason stepped into the light then, and Mac got a good look at his face. He barely suppressed a shocked gasp; one side of Mason's face was hideously disfigured. Mac glanced away out of politeness, but the sight of his scars once again tickled Mac's memory.

"Happened when I was a boy," Mason volunteered with a careless wave of his hand. "Injuns burned our house plumb to the ground with my ma and pa in it." As he talked, he led the way through the stalls into the heart of the stable. "I tried to pull 'em out but I was a puny thing back then."

Swallowing a murmur of sympathy he suspected Mason didn't want, Mac eyed the man's broad shoulders and thick arms. It was hard to imagine the big man as a puny little boy.

"This here's Buckaroo." Mason paused at a stall and opened the door. He grabbed the horse by the mane and led him out. "He's strong, but like I said before, he's got a stubborn nature. Once you show him who's boss, he'll come around."

He was a beautiful horse, stocky and strong-looking, but a bit short for Mac's taste. Mac held out his hand to be sniffed, but the horse snorted and gave a disdainful toss of his head.

Mason laughed. "Told you he was a bit feisty."

"I don't mind feisty," Mac said, casting a narrow-eyed glance along the stalls to the other horses. "But I'd like to make my own choice, if you don't mind."

"Wouldn't mind at all," Mason said with a toothy smile. "If I had something else for you to choose *from*." He indicated the three horses on down the line from Buckaroo. "Billy there, she's going to drop a foal any day now, and the other two horses are spoken for."

Feeling unaccountably contrary, Mac moved to the stall housing a tall, beautiful bay gelding. He dismissed the third horse—a gentle-looking, smaller gray filly. "I don't mind paying extra for what I want."

"Well, I—"

"How about five dollars—plus the dollar a day?"

The amount seemed to temporarily rob Mason of his speech. He looked indecisive for a moment before finally nodding. "I reckon five dollars might persuade me to make an exception."

Mac had suspected that it might. He paid Mason, adding an extra dollar to the five he promised him. "I'll need a bedroll if you've got one handy, and enough supplies to last me a few days."

Now that Mason had made his decision, he was eager to be helpful. "I'll have everything you need, Mr. Cord. Cactus will be ready when you are."

"Good, I'll be back in an hour." Deliberately Mac waited until he'd taken a few steps in the direction of the door before he turned around again. "Say, you wouldn't happen to know of a ranch about twenty miles south of here, would ya ? A place called Sunset Ranch?"

Fully expecting the same, evasive response he'd so far gotten from the townspeople, Mason surprised him by growling a vicious curse. He spat on the ground, a look of such intense hatred twisting his disfigured face that Mac immediately tensed.

"Reckon I do, and if you're kin to those murdering bastards , then you can have your money back, mister."

Finally Mac had found an ally—one who wasn't afraid to volunteer a little information. He hid his eagerness behind a grim smile. "I'm no kin. In fact, I've got a score to settle with Ned Barlow, and I heard he was heading that way."

Mason, who had doubled his fists and spread his legs in a fighting stance, apparently saw the truth on Mac's face. He visibly relaxed. "You don't want to go out there alone," he warned. "Those varmints don't hesitate to shoot first and ask questions later."

Mac tipped his hat, deciding to wait until he returned to ask for more specific directions. Give West time to cool down. "I'll keep that in mind, and thanks, Mr. West. See you in an hour."

As he headed back to the hotel to say goodbye to Savannah and remind Roy of his responsibilities, Mac wondered if Mason's show of hatred had anything to do with the hideous scars on the man's face. If it did, he didn't blame the man for his reaction.

One more reason—not that he needed another, he had plenty in his opinion—to find Barlow and put him where he belonged. Behind bars.

Back at the hotel, Mac found Savannah pacing the room. She looked agitated. The moment she spotted him, she rushed to him and grabbed his hands, squeezing them so hard Mac felt a rush of alarm.

"Mac, I've changed my mind," she began in a tumble of words he could scarcely follow. "I don't want you to go after Ned. I don't care about the money anymore, or even the necklace! Let's just forget it and head for Angel Creek."

Ned. Not Barlow, but Ned. Mac felt the vicious hand of jealousy squeeze his heart. Attempting to ignore the weak emotion, Mac lifted a mocking brow. "Have you lost faith in me, my sweet Savannah?" The words had slipped out before he could think.

Savannah noticed. "Don't make fun, Mac! Ned's dangerous—he's a bank robber—"

"And catching bank robbers is what I do for a living." He could have added that he also hunted many other types of unsavory characters, such as murderers who wouldn't hesitate to cut a man's throat as he slept, but her frightened expression stopped him. Savannah was *worried* about his safety. Dare he hope that it was more than just friendly concern?

His attempts to reassure her appeared to fall on deaf ears. She jiggled his hands for emphasis. "Please, Mac. I—I don't want you to go!"

"So you just want to give up?" Mac challenged. "After the trouble we've gone through?"

"I can reimburse you when we get to Angel Creek."

"It's not about the money, Savannah." Mac stared into her violet eyes and lost himself again. For a moment he couldn't speak around the lump in his throat. "We're too close to give up now. The man deserves to be put behind bars." Those great, soul-stirring eyes filled with tears. Genuine or not, Mac wasn't immune.

"I can't change your mind, then?" she asked softly.

Mac shook his head, then grunted as she landed against him and flung her arms around his neck. To his further shock, she planted her mouth square against his and kissed him. His reaction was instant and as natural as the breath he drew; he closed his arms around her waist and took control of the kiss, savoring the sweet warmth of her mouth and the tiny whimpers that rumbled in her throat—or was that his own?

Breathless, they finally drew apart. Mac had to ask. "If that was a good-luck kiss, I'll have to leave more often," he teased huskily. Her cheeks were flushed, and her eyes glittered with tears.

"I couldn't bear it if I lost you, Mac," she confessed. "You've been one of my dearest friends for so long that I just can't imagine my life without you."

Friends. Mac closed his eyes before she could see the hurt and pain her words evoked. He let his arms fall to his sides, forcing himself to admit that it wasn't Savannah's fault he was a coward. She didn't know how he truly felt about her because *he* was afraid to tell her.

Afraid of losing her forever.

Well, she had tried.

Savannah leaned into the door and pressed her cheek against the cool wood. Anxiety caused her heart to pound, even as her lips throbbed from his kiss. If something happened to Mac . . .

It would be her fault. *She* had persuaded him to go after Barlow. If not for her, he'd be making his way back to Angel Creek to take over Sheriff Cannon's job. Angel Creek was a civilized town, a safe town, except for an occasional brawl at the saloon and a theft now and then.

Mac wouldn't be in much danger as the new sheriff.

But going after Barlow *would* be dangerous, she knew. What had she done? In her selfish desire to get back at Barlow for not only stealing her money, but also humiliating her, had she unwittingly placed Mac in danger? Granted, Mac was a bounty hunter, but Savannah couldn't forget how cleverly Barlow and Raquel had fooled *her.* Savannah pressed a hand to her hot cheek, recalling how she had confided in Raquel about Jon Paul and his painful betrayal. In return, Raquel had confessed to Savannah that she and Ned had been notified that their parents had passed away earlier in the year, and she and Ned were traveling to Jamestown to collect their younger sibling. She and Ned traveled a lot, she'd said, and had only just gotten the news last week.

Apparently Raquel was an excellent storyteller, because Savannah doubted there had ever been an orphaned sibling. If there was, she doubted Ned and Raquel cared.

Yes, they were dangerous and clever. But then, so was Mac. She had to remain strong in her belief that Mac would prevail. He'd brought in many criminals during his years as a bounty hunter. He would be all right. He *had* to be, because in the last few days she'd discovered that Mac was more precious to her than ever.

Which was exactly why she'd decided that if she couldn't change his mind, then she would disobey him.

She jumped as someone thundered on the door. It was Roy, looking comically secretive as he glanced both ways before slipping into the room.

"Does he suspect anything?" he whispered when the door was closed.

Savannah smiled at the bittersweet memory of their far-from-friendly goodbye kiss. "No, I don't believe he does. We'll give him an hour's head start, then follow him."

Roy thrust his chest out, flipped his coat aside, and showed her the gun strapped to his hip. "Don't be scared. I'm gonna protect you."

"I don't—" Savannah bit her lip, swallowing her spontaneous denial as she reminded herself that Roy was trying to be a man. "Thanks, Roy. I feel safer knowing you're around."

The boy's chest seemed to swell even bigger. With an exaggerated swagger that made Savannah want to giggle, he advanced into the room. His gaze held a youthful scorn as he pointed at her dress. "You gonna wear *that?*"

Nonplussed, Savannah shrugged. "I don't have much choice."

"We'll just see about that," Roy stated. He strode to the door, tripped on his coat, and fell flat on his face. Savannah winced. Before she could reach him, he bounced up and brushed himself off. His hat had fallen forward, but what little she could view of his face had turned red.

"Come with me," he growled, shoving his hat into place again. "I've got an idea."

Resigned to building Roy's ego, Savannah followed him through the door. "Did you get the horses, Roy?"

"Yeah. Got you a beaut of a filly and me a horse by the name of Buckaroo. The man thought I was a fool—tried to get me to pick a mean-looking horse by the name of Buckaroo." Roy scowled at the reminder. "I might be young, but I ain't stupid."

The last word had scarcely cleared his throat before a deafening roar filled Savannah's ears. Slack-jawed with shock, she stared at the hole in the floor inches from Roy's foot, then at the smoking gun dangling from his hip.

"Roy . . ." she began, hesitating to add to his humiliation. His face had darkened from its previous shade to an alarming purple.

Roy's Adam's apple raced to the top of his throat, then back down again as he swallowed hard. He was looking at the hole as if he couldn't believe it was real. "Ah . . . we'd better get going before someone comes to investigate."

"Yes, we'd better." She grabbed his arm and hurried him along the hallway. "When we get clear of town, I'm going to teach you how to handle a gun," she promised him in an undertone. "So that you can properly protect me." To her surprise, he didn't argue.

"Yeah, guess that would be a good idea."

Chapter Twelve

Mac traveled south through the rugged hills and dense forests of West Virginia until dusk. He spent a lot of time thinking about Savannah, wishing she could share the beauty of his surroundings. He could easily imagine her delight in the lush forests, bountiful wildlife, and pure, sparkling streams. What a vision she would make, he mused, sitting astride a horse with the rich sunset of red, orange, and yellow as a backdrop to her incomparable beauty.

It wasn't Mac's first visit to West Virginia, yet he seemed to be viewing everything with a breathtaking new clarity. He supposed being in love heightened one's senses, made one more aware of the wonders of nature.

Cactus snorted as if to mock his poetic thoughts as Mac dismounted near the banks of a creek. According to the directions West had given him, Mac figured he was about three miles from Sunset Ranch. He'd make camp for the night, then head out at first light. Tomorrow he'd spend a few hours observing the ranch and its occupants from a distance.

Until he knew what he was up against, he would not make a move.

After he had taken care of Cactus, Mac ate a cold supper of dried beef and biscuits, washing it down with cold, sparkling water from the creek. With his hunger taken care of, Mac propped his back against a tree and pulled his hat low. His bed was a soft carpet of pine needles; the air was fresh, crisp, and clean. He inhaled appreciatively. Yes, being in love certainly changed a body's prospective, he mused ruefully.

A gentle breeze tickled his nose, bringing with it the scent of mountain earth, pine, and jasmine.

The latter reminded him of Savannah.

A delighted smile kicked up the corner of Mac's mouth as he inhaled again. Yes, definitely jasmine—

"I think we're lost, Roy."

The voice, so dear and familiar to Mac, jolted him upright. For one incredible moment, Mac believed he had conjured Savannah by the sheer strength of his will.

It was the only explanation that he was *willing* to believe.

"We're not lost. I know that he came this way because we passed a pile of horse shit a while back."

And then the sweet, arousing sound of Savannah's voice again, patient yet persistent in her quest for logic. "But how do you *know* the manure belongs to Mac's horse? What if we're following someone else?"

"We aren't," Roy insisted, but Mac thought he sounded unsure . . . and a little frightened? Roy? Frightened? Nah, he had to be dreaming. If Roy *was* frightened, Mac suspected the boy would take a bullet before he would admit anything so unmanly. He smothered a chuckle at the thought.

What Mac heard next sent his heart to pounding.

Savannah shrieked, then there was a heavy thud, followed by uncensored cursing that made *Mac's* ears burn.

"Roy? Are you all right?"

"Damned jackass of a horse!" Roy snarled, sounding breathless and furious. "If I ever find out who swindled me out of *my* horse, I'm gonna shove *Buckaroo* straight up his—"

"Roy! You shouldn't speak that way in front of a lady."

"You don't mind, do you?"

"Well, no, *I* don't, but—"

"Then what's the problem?"

In his dazed mind, Mac clearly imagined Savannah's luscious lips pursed in a stern line. He wasn't surprised when she decided to ignore Roy's impertinent question. That she had developed a soft spot for the brat was an obvious fact. He envied the boy.

"I think we should make camp for the night. We've traveled most of the day. Surely we're halfway there by now? I'm dead tired, and so is Billy. Look at the way her head is drooping."

Halfway? Despite his irritation, Mac had to stifle a laugh at Savannah's naive assumption. Thank God they'd managed to somehow trail him, or they might have run into the ranch before realizing it!

"Besides," Savannah added, "if we keep going we're liable to stumble over Mac in his sleep!"

Roy snorted at that, which was a good thing because it covered the sound of *Mac's* helpless laugh. "We're at least two hours behind him."

In reality, they were on the opposite side of the narrow creek from Mac, making their noisy way through the forest. If not for the encroaching night and Cactus's dark coloring, they would have noticed the horse grazing contentedly along the bank.

"Well, me and Billy are stopping right here. You can go on if you like."

"Fine. I think I will."

A coyote howled in the distance. It was a long, mournful sound familiar to Mac.

But not, apparently, to Roy.

"Maybe I should stay with you," Roy said quickly. "Mac would have my hide if something happened to you."

Mac planned to have Roy's hide anyway, for disobeying his orders. For now he was content to listen to their entertaining conversation and plan just how he was going to let them know he was but a few yards away.

"Why would he be mad at you?" Savannah asked. "It was *my* idea."

The creak of the saddle and a very plaintive groan told Mac she was dismounting. He should have guessed that Savannah was behind their daring adventure. Pit her stubborn nature against Roy's eagerness to become a man, and was it any wonder they decided to follow him? And Roy was riding Buckaroo, which meant they'd made their plans before he returned to the hotel to say goodbye—before Savannah had thrown herself against him and planted a soul-searing kiss on his mouth, declaring she'd changed her mind and begging him—most prettily—to stay.

As painful as the truth was to admit, Mac realized he'd been fooled. Savannah's passionate kiss had merely been a smoke screen to distract him from their plans to follow him.

Mac swallowed a frustrated curse. Once again, when he thought he'd taken a step forward with Savannah, he found he'd taken two steps *backward*.

Duped by an angel.

If she only knew how much power she held over my emotions—and my heart.

She would pity him, Mac decided, forcing himself to be brutally honest. If she didn't pity him, she would be furious at how he'd ruined their friendship by falling in love with her.

"Son of a bitch!" Roy suddenly howled, startling Mac from his unpleasant thoughts. Cactus gave an alarmed snort, which neither seemed to notice.

"What happened?" Savannah demanded.

"That son-of-a-bitchin' horse *bit* me when I tried to take the saddle off of him!"

Roy needed his mouth washed out with soap, Mac decided grimly. At least they needn't worry about curious critters tonight, for Roy's howling had probably frightened everything for miles around.

"Well," Savannah declared, finally beginning to sound irritated with the brat, "if you're through shouting, I'm going to try to get some shut-eye."

"Go ahead," Roy grumbled. "I'll stand guard. Thanks to *Buckaroo,* I don't think I'd be able to sleep anyway. Besides, Mac would expect me to protect you."

"Of course he would."

Savannah's voice had softened; Mac had to strain to hear over the gentle gurgling of the creek water that separated him from his lady love.

"He likes you, Roy. Mac just has trouble showing his feelings. I should know. He has the same problem around me."

Of all the—! Mac had to physically restrain himself from stomping across the creek and jerking Savannah over his knee. After the past week in his company, how could she baldly state that he had trouble showing his feelings? He kissed her at every opportunity. Touched her when he thought he could get away with it. And just last night he'd nearly claimed her virginity!

With a disgruntled sigh and a self-reminder that he'd *never* understand females, Mac settled against the tree again. He marveled anew at Roy's tracking abilities. And was that warm rush of feeling in his chest *pride?* He hardly *knew* the boy! Yet that's exactly what he was feeling; pride in the boy's accomplishment.

He'd tell Roy, too, *after* he taught him an important lesson about disobeying a direct order from his trainer. Maybe then Savannah would realize how terribly wrong she was about him. He had no trouble at all showing his feelings.

"Good night, Roy."

Her sleep-husky voice sent shivers along Mac's spine, reminding him of last night and how close he'd came to making her his in every way imaginable.

"Good night, Miss Carrington. Sleep tight, and don't you worry about a thing. I plan to stay awake all night."

Mac couldn't help but smile. Roy sounded just as sleepy as Savannah. He suspected it would only be a matter of time before he could begin the lesson.

Exhausted, Savannah drifted to sleep to the sweet, lulling sound of creek water gurgling over the rocks.

She didn't stir when Roy began to snore, or when Billy stamped her feet restlessly, but the nearly imperceptible disruption in the steady flow of the creek water brought her instantly awake.

A quiet swish, then silence. Another swish, and silence once again. She lay wide-eyed and still, listening intently. It came again. Swish . . . swish . . . swish.

Someone or something was crossing the creek in stealthy movements, and since she could hear Roy snoring, she knew it couldn't be him. Silently she rose from her bedroll and crept behind the tree she'd propped her boots against. She removed the small derringer from her pocket, heart pounding, mouth dry.

There was a half-moon, but it scudded behind clouds more often than not, leaving her in the dark. She could make out vague shapes—the outline of her bedroll and the indistinct shape of her horse.

And beyond that . . . a bulky shadow emerging from the darkness, advancing steadily in her direction. She swallowed hard yet quietly.

The shadow paused by her bedroll.

Savannah took a deep, quiet breath, wishing the moon would cooperate. The intruder wasn't a bear; she felt certain she would have smelled it or heard it breathing. The only scent she could detect was the aroma of pine needles and creek water. A man, then. It had to be a man. Another thief? Savannah's lips tightened at the thought. She had nothing of value, just a rented horse, a bedroll, and the man's clothing she wore.

But she wasn't prepared to give up her meager belongings to this thief. *This* time she was better prepared.

Her finger quivered on the trigger of her gun. She'd have to be quick. She'd have to step forward as she cocked the hammer and press it against his head before he realized she was behind him.

Above her, the clouds parted. Moonlight filtered through the treetops for a brief moment, shedding enough illumination on her subject to spur her forward.

It was now or never.

A twig snapped beneath her feet. Savannah froze. In a flurry of movement that left Savannah stunned, the man toppled her to the ground and thrust his hand over her mouth. His body sprawled across hers, pinning her down. Her derringer flew from her hand and landed on the ground with a soft plop. Hands roamed roughly along her hips and legs, as if searching for something—a weapon, perhaps?—then up over her breasts.

He became stock-still, one hand returning to cup her heaving breast. Slowly his hand took flight again, moving along her shoulders until his fingers bumped against her thick braid. He explored it like a blind man.

"Savannah?" the man whispered incredulously, removing his hand from her mouth.

Savannah struggled to catch her breath. "Mac?" She gasped, peering at the shadowed face leaning over her. She'd never been so glad to see him in her life! Before she could say more, he placed a warning finger against her lips. He picked her up in his arms and rose, carrying her back across the creek and into the dense forest. She marveled that he could move so easily in the dark—and carrying her, no less!

When she could no longer hear Roy snoring, he sat her on her feet. Savannah leaned weakly against a tree. Her legs were shaking from the aftermath of her scare.

Then it hit her.

Mac was here. Mac was standing before her, watching her intently. Silently.

She struggled to make out his expression. Why didn't he speak? Was he *that* furious? She began to fidget. Of course he was furious. Mac had ordered them to remain in Cornwall.

They had followed him instead, blundering through the forest, stopping to check the temperature of each pile of horse manure they came across.

Belatedly her chin rose. She didn't have to obey Mac's orders. They were friends, not husband and wife. They had a deal, and in making the deal nothing had been mentioned about obeying orders. If something *had* been said, she would have reminded him then and there that she was a grown woman who could take care of herself, make her own decisions.

Besides, other than her fright, nothing serious had happened to her.

Mac stepped closer. Very close. Close enough for her to see the faint glimmer of his eyes and feel his warm breath on her face. Savannah drew in a sharp breath as his hands moved to the top button of the man's shirt she wore. With an expert twist of his fingers, he slipped the button free and moved on to the next one.

"Mac?" She licked her lips, damning the darkness and his silence—which was beginning to unnerve her. "What—what are you doing?"

"I'm doing what any other red-blooded male would do if he came upon a woman alone in the woods," Mac whispered.

Savannah gave a shaky laugh, edging to the side in the hopes of slipping out of the trap he'd made with his arm. He was teasing her, of course, just like he always did.

Her laugh turned into a gasp when he thrust his leg between hers, pressing intimately against her mound and pinning her effectively against the tree. He finished the fourth button and nudged the material to one side, exposing the pale oval of her breast to the night air. Her nipple immediately puckered.

She made a halfhearted attempt to cover herself, but Mac pushed her hand away. "Mac . . . I'm not alone," she reminded him, hating the quiver in her voice. When Mac touched her, *everything* about her was prone to quiver.

"Listen," Mac said.

They fell silent. Through the dense trees and across the gurgling creek, Savannah heard a sound that mocked her attempts to defend herself—and Roy.

It was the sound of Roy snoring.

Chapter Thirteen

"He's just a boy, Mac. I wasn't really depending on him to protect me."

Thank God she had *that* much sense, Mac thought. He leaned in and brushed his chest against her budding nipple. Back and forth. She drew in a sharp breath.

"Why are you doing this?"

"Because this is what someone else would be doing if they had found you," Mac said as sternly as he could muster, considering his voice had grown husky. "But maybe you're right—maybe they wouldn't be so nice. Maybe they'd do something like this."

He bent forward and plunged his mouth over her quivering nipple, suckling hard. She arched her back and moaned; his manhood acted accordingly, lunging against his trousers as if to burst free.

"So this . . . is a lesson," she said breathlessly.

Mac didn't have time to speculate on the reason she sounded disappointed. He was busy working his mouth and teeth over her breast, feasting on her satin skin and the quivering tip that seemed so eager for his attention. He ground his thigh between her legs, making her gasp. Again and again he reminded himself that it *could* have been someone else, and that someone else could not have possibly loved her as he loved her.

Despite his efforts to stay focused, the lesson he'd intended to teach her got lost somewhere between her thigh-clenching reaction and her gut-clenching moan. The desperate fingers she buried in his hair completed his sudden memory lapse.

"What—what else might they do, Mac?"

Her throaty, provocative question made *him* moan. Breathing hard, he drew back to peer at her in the darkness. They were relatively alone, surrounded by ageless trees and miles from the nearest town. Pressed against the tree with her shirt gaping and her eyelids drooping, she had never looked more desirable to Mac.

He knew he should quit this dangerous game before it got out of hand, and if she had reacted in the frightened way he had been hoping for, then he might have been able to turn away right here and now.

But she wasn't frightened, as she should be.

She was aroused, and her curiosity was aroused as well. Mac should have remembered that about Savannah. He should have remembered *before* he was throbbing with desire and she was giving him those come-hither looks and begging to be taken.

The man who won her heart would be the luckiest man on earth.

He desperately wanted to be that man.

Perhaps he *should* make love to her and take his chances. Perhaps if he did he could enslave her with desire, and over time she would come to love him as he wanted her to love him—as he *needed* her to love him. It wasn't his first choice, to gain Savannah's lust before her love, but what if he passed on this opportunity only to discover later that he'd made a mistake?

She made the decision for him, reaching for his hand and closing it over her breast. "Show me, Mac. Show me what you would do . . . *if* you were a bad boy."

Ah, to hell with it, Mac growled to himself. How could a man be expected to think with his hand filled with Savannah's soft, quivering breast and thrusting nipple? How could he be expected to resist listening to the alluring, husky sound of her voice?

To his knowledge, Savannah was innocent, yet she possessed a natural sexuality he knew a courtesan would envy.

And right now it was directed at him.

Mac was a man, and he loved Savannah with all his heart and soul. He of all men could not resist her. Surely God, in His infinite wisdom, would not expect him to?

Squashing his doubts until there was nothing left but a faint trace of anxiety, Mac pushed her shirt aside and filled his other hand with a sweet globe. For better or for worse, he rejoined the game—a game that had started out as a lesson. "I might kiss you, like this," he whispered, nibbling at her lips and forcing her to reach out for him. Finally he closed his mouth over hers, kissing her tenderly, yet with increasing passion.

When he broke free, her eyes were closed.

"Or I might kiss you like this," Mac growled, taking her mouth in a rough, erotic kiss that left them both panting.

Her swollen lips moved. "What—what else, Mac?"

Nobody spoke his name like Savannah, with that lilting inflection that made it sound like a question. Mac loved it, as he loved many, many things about Savannah. Was it any wonder that he wanted to *show* her how much he loved her?

His fingers trembled as he made quick work of the rest

of her buttons. He pulled her shirt from where she'd had it tucked into her trousers, pausing on the drawstring that held them to her slim waist. The trousers hung low, revealing her flat belly and outlining her womanly hips. He took a moment to draw the rough pads of his fingers slowly along her body, from her neck to the top of her trousers.

She hissed between her teeth as his hand moved lower, forcing the material down until his fingers tangled in her womanly curls. He could feel her trembling all over, and the knowledge of her anticipation fired his own desire to an almost unbearable degree.

Wisely he stopped to allow his ardor to cool, watching her reaction and wishing he had built a fire so that he could see her more clearly. But no, he decided, Savannah by firelight would shorten their lovemaking. He would save that pleasure for another time and place.

Please God, let there be *another time and place!*

"Mac . . . show me, *please.*"

No favor had ever been asked of him with such demanding sweetness. Mac obliged. He tugged on the drawstring, catching her trousers before they could slide over her hips. She twisted from side to side, arching toward him, moaning. Mac placed his mouth at the beginning of the trail his hand had made, and kissed her as he moved down. He went to his knees, plunging his tongue into her navel.

His manhood jerked at her sharp gasp of pleasure. She grasped his head with both hands, trying to kneel with him. Mac held her up with his hands on her hips.

"No . . . stay there," he commanded, startled by the hoarse sound of his voice.

"My—my legs are shaky," she whimpered.

"Do you want me to show you?" he taunted, surprised

by his own bold daring. He made slow, sweeping circles with his tongue around her navel, moving lower, then lower still. His manhood could have passed for the tree behind her.

"Yes, yes, but I want to touch you, too."

Her lusty confession nearly drove Mac over the edge. He let her trousers complete their downward destination, and nudged her legs apart. His fingers found the hot, central core of her womanhood.

She was moist and throbbing to the touch, and touch her he did. But not for long.

He had other plans for his sweet Savannah.

Mac inhaled her musky, arousing scent and placed his mouth where his fingers had been. He thrust out his tongue once—twice, before her knees began to buckle and a keening moan rose in her throat. He caught her firm little bottom in both hands and pressed her to his mouth.

Her moan became a scream of pleasure.

Frantically she tugged at his hair, literally hauling him to his feet with a strength that amazed Mac. Her shaking hands unfastened his trousers and pushed them over his hips.

She closed her fingers around his pulsing, rock-hard length and explored him from the glistening tip to the thickened base.

Incredibly the sound of her awed gasp made him swell to greater lengths. Mac had never felt more virile, more desirable than he did at that moment.

Her lips sought his mouth as she whispered urgently, "Show me all of it, Mac. Show me everything."

As Mac struggled to keep from spending himself in her eager hands, he wondered if she could taste herself on his mouth.

It was, quite obviously, the wrong thing to think about.

Anxious to show her before he *really* showed her, Mac braced her against the tree and gently positioned himself between her legs. But instead of doing what he'd dreamed of doing, longed to do for years, what everything that was male in him *urged* him to do, he hesitated.

Something was missing.

And he knew what it was. Not a single word of love had passed between them.

"Savannah, I—"

The explosion drowned out the rest of his confession. Wood splintered from the tree inches from his shoulder— inches from Savannah's shoulder, as well. Stunned, Mac acted instinctively, moving his body to fully protect Savannah.

"Move away from her, mister, or the next bullet will go right through your black heart."

"Roy," Savannah whispered to Mac, her alarmed eyes wide on his face. "Don't move, Mac. He's a terrible shot— he shot a hole in the floor at the hotel."

Mac wasn't a coward, but neither was he a fool. He stood very still, blocking Roy's view of Savannah. Not that Roy could see much in the darkness, thank God!

Raising her voice, Savannah called out to Roy, "Put your gun down."

But Roy remained suspicious. His voice shook with a mixture of fright and fury. "Don't worry, Miss Carrington. I'm a mite better at aiming now, thanks to you. I won't shoot you by mistake, but I promise I'll get *him* if he moves so much as a muscle."

Mac met Savannah's questioning gaze and slowly nodded. They had no choice but to reveal his identity.

"It's Mac, Roy," Savannah said. "Don't shoot."

"He make you say that?"

Stifling a frustrated oath, Mac shouted, "Dammit, Roy, put the gun down! It's me!"

"Mac?"

"Yes!"

"Mr. Cord?"

"Yes!"

"Miss Carrington?"

"What?" Savannah snapped, sounding as exasperated as Mac felt.

"Is it really Mac?"

"Yes, it's really Mac. Put the gun down so that he can turn around and show you."

"All right."

But Mac had something he desperately needed to do before he turned around. He bent over and grabbed his trousers.

"What's he doing?" Roy demanded shrilly.

"He—he dropped something."

Roy didn't believe her. He began to walk forward just as Mac fastened his drawstring.

"He's coming this way!" Savannah whispered, horrified.

"Don't move. I'll cover you."

"What are you two whispering about?" Roy asked, stopping a few feet away. He craned his neck this way and that, trying to pierce the darkness and see around Mac.

"None of your damned business," Mac growled, his fingers working swiftly to button Savannah's shirt. There was little he could do about the trousers around her ankles with Roy this close. "Now back away and give us some space."

The sound of Roy's strangled gasp made Mac groan inwardly.

"Miss Carrington . . . are you—you *naked?*" The second gasp came louder, and obviously stemmed from embarrassment as Roy made a belated discovery. "Oh, Lord have mercy," he whispered, slapping his forehead. "You two were—you two really *are* married, aren't you? Why didn't you tell me?"

Mac turned slowly around, continuing to shield Savannah. He was relieved to note that Roy had lowered the gun. "You never asked. You just assumed, in your arrogant wisdom, that we weren't."

Savannah frantically pinched his back, but Mac ignored her. He wouldn't have Roy thinking the worst about her, and it wasn't as if they hadn't played the game before, was it? Maybe she would see that it was fate that kept throwing them into the pretend role of husband and wife.

"Now, would you mind disappearing so that Mrs. *Cord* can make herself presentable?" Mac grated softly.

"Oh. Yeah, I can do that. Sorry." Stumbling around, Roy crashed through the forest at a dead run.

Mac had a feeling that if faces could glow, Roy would have his own torch to lead the way. When he'd gone, he faced Savannah. She'd pulled up her trousers and was in the process of tying them. Regret, sharp and raw, streaked through Mac.

"I'm beginning to think we *should* get married," Savannah said with a rueful laugh. "Then we wouldn't have to worry about telling lies and getting interrupted. . . ."

Startled to hear her echo his own thoughts, Mac blurted out, "Why don't we?"

Savannah grew still, staring at him in a searching way that caused Mac's breath to hitch hopefully. He suspected he looked agonized as he waited for her response, but he couldn't seem to control his reaction.

Her sudden laughter knocked the breath from his lungs in a painful whoosh. He knew what she was going to say, then, before she spoke the painful words.

"Because we're friends, Mac."

Chapter Fourteen

Her body was exhausted, but her mind refused to rest. How could she when Mac lay only a few feet away in his bedroll?

So close, yet so far.

And Roy, bless his embarrassed little heart, had buried his face in his bedroll by the time they returned to camp; Savannah hadn't heard a peep out of him since. He'd learned *his* lesson all right, and a whole lot more!

She wasn't surprised by Mac's hasty, yet obviously sincere proposal. Mac was that kind of man, a responsible man who would do everything within his power to protect a lady's reputation. Especially a lady he considered a dear friend.

Which was exactly why she'd said no. Well, that and the agonized look on his face had prompted her refusal. She hadn't been able to see the expression in his eyes, but even in the darkness she had seen his features twist in a frown. Savannah knuckled a tear from her cheek and sighed. She loved Mac—and not just in a friendly way— she knew that now. Loved him so much that her body still tingled and ached from his lovemaking. But because of that love, she couldn't accept his proposal.

She would stick to her guns. She would not marry a man whom she suspected loved her money more than he loved her, and she would not marry a man simply for lust. She would also not marry a man because he felt obligated.

Not even Mac, whom she had grown to love in a most passionate way.

She was probably a fool for not taking advantage of the situation, she mused. But she loved and respected Mac too much. Oh, she figured he'd do his best to pretend to be happy if she had accepted his offer, but after a while he'd grow tired of pretending.

Savannah cringed to think what might have happened if Mac hadn't explained that a man could get aroused by any woman. She might have naively believed that Mac's desire was the result of love, instead of lust.

What a disaster that might have been . . . if she didn't know differently, thanks to Mac. She clenched her thighs together as a tremor of desire arrowed through her.

Just thinking about Mac could do that.

He'd brought her pleasure, but she'd wanted more. She wanted to feel him inside her, to know the full glory of Mac's loving. Maybe if she had that memory to have and to hold, she could survive the rest of her life, and perhaps find a small measure of happiness with someone else.

And maybe . . . just maybe, she could convince Mac that she truly expected nothing from him afterward. No hasty offers of marriage, no obligation, and no regrets.

Call her brazen, and he just might think it—but she knew she wouldn't be satisfied until she and Mac could finish what they'd started in the forest.

Because she was afraid the memory would have to last her for a very, very long time.

•   •   •

Dawn crept over the beautiful, rugged mountains, snapping Mac out of a light sleep. He rose and hunkered beside Savannah, studying her flushed, sleeping face in the pinkish light. Her long, golden lashes rested upon her cheeks, and her pouting lips were parted slightly. She slept with one hand pillowing her head and the other tucked against her chest.

She was beautiful.

Casting her one, last longing look, Mac moved to Roy's bedroll and gently shook his shoulders. The blanket flew from the boy's face, revealing his wide, alarmed eyes.

"What is it?" he demanded, glancing wildly around, still befuddled with sleep.

Mac shushed him, pointing to where Savannah slept. "I'm heading out. Can I trust you to look after her?" he whispered, then added sternly, "And to keep her here until I get back?"

Roy nodded, rubbing at his sleepy eyes and reminding Mac that he was just a boy. "Don't worry, Mac. I'll take care of her." When Mac started to rise, Roy grabbed the sleeve of his shirt. "If I had known she was your wife, Mac, I would have tried harder to keep her in Cornwall."

"She's got a mind of her own," Mac agreed, sharing a rare smile of understanding with the boy. The truth was, he was growing fond of the brat. There was something oddly vulnerable about Roy, as if he had suffered more than a boy should have at his tender age.

"I'll tie her up if I have to."

An image of Roy attempting to restrain a determined Savannah made Mac chuckle. He hoped Roy's promise wouldn't be put to the test, or Mac would be nursing the boy's bruised ego upon his return.

"And Mac . . . be careful, will ya?"

Mac nodded, bemused by the lump that filled his throat

at Roy's obvious concern. Impulsively he asked the boy, "Mind if I trade horses with you?"

Roy sat up, his gaze going to the cluster of horses grazing near the creek. He gasped when he spotted Cactus. "So *you're* the one who swindled me out of my horse!"

Grinning, Mac said, "What can I say? I made the man an offer he couldn't refuse."

"But he promised *me* that horse!" Roy argued in a loud whisper. "You just wait till we get back. I'm gonna demand my money back."

"Which reminds me. You never said anything about having money of your own."

"You never asked." Roy's eyes glinted with mischief as he flung Mac's words back at him. "You just *assumed* that I didn't have any."

"A logical assumption, considering you stowed away on the train instead of buying a ticket," Mac reminded him.

"There wasn't time to buy a ticket."

"Hm."

"Well, there *wasn't!*" Roy repeated, angling his sharp chin in a way that reminded Mac of Savannah. "Besides, it's kinda hard to speak up with a gag in your mouth."

He had a point, Mac had to admit. Rising, he approached the horses. Cactus greeted him with a nicker, and the filly eyed him with curiosity.

Buckaroo tried to bite him.

Aware of Roy watching, Mac grabbed the horse's bridle and pulled him in for a close view of his determined face. "Don't mess with me, Buckaroo," Mac growled softly. "Because you won't win."

The horse jerked free and nodded as if to assure Mac that he understood perfectly. Mac saddled him and mounted up, waving to Roy as he guided Buckaroo along the banks of the creek.

Twice the ornery horse tried to buck Mac from the saddle, thankfully out of sight from the camp.

Both times Mac anticipated his move and hung on, slapping the horse lightly around his ears with the tip of the reins. While it wasn't painful, it annoyed the horse. It didn't take Buckaroo long to figure out that Mac meant what he said; he wouldn't win.

An hour later Mac crouched at the top of a hill and looked down into the valley below. It was a breathtaking view. In the far distance cattle grazed on the lush grass. Closer to the sprawling, well-tended ranch house, a dozen or so horses cavorted in a corral. A wide porch ran the length of the ranch house. Huge clay pots filled with flowers dotted the porch. A few chairs conjured images of lazy evenings and family gatherings.

Mac frowned. It wasn't the hideaway he expected to find. This ranch looked like someone's home, not a temporary hideout for criminals and murderers—as Mason had implied. But why would the man lie? he wondered.

Time would tell.

As he settled into a more comfortable position, Mac's thoughts turned unerringly to Savannah and their disastrous ending to what had otherwise been an unforgettable encounter. What if Roy hadn't interrupted them? What if Mac had taken that plunge? Would Savannah have laughed at his proposal of marriage then? Mac shook his head, admitting that Savannah's lusty, enthusiastic response to his lovemaking left him baffled.

Perhaps it was wrong of him to be shocked by her behavior. Perhaps it was hypocritical of him to be both shocked *and* thrilled to discover that the woman he loved was fiery and passionate and unafraid to show it.

The part that shocked him was her casual indifference

to commitment afterward. He'd told her the truth when he had confessed that men were more easily aroused, and he had meant to further explain that lovemaking should happen between two people who love each other. Yes, he'd planned to, but there hadn't been time. And then he'd gone and done it *again*.

Maybe he was the one who was naive, he mused. The women he'd known in the past either wanted money or commitment when they made love. He'd always known Savannah was different, which was one of the reasons he'd fallen in love with her. Yet, should he worry that after arousing Savannah's sexual curiosity, she might turn to other men to satisfy that curiosity?

It was a scandalous, jealousy-inducing thought, and Mac immediately felt disloyal.

Nevertheless . . . the question lingered.

What if she had other friends like him? Savannah wasn't a child, true, but what if *he* was the reason for her sudden eagerness to explore her sexuality?

A burst of carefree laughter cut into Mac's agonized thoughts. He stiffened, focusing on the ranch snuggled in the valley below. It was a child, perhaps three or four years old, running hell-for-leather along the porch. An older child—a girl, Mac thought, noticing the long braids flying out behind her—chased the younger child.

His confusion deepened at the domestic scene; Sunset Ranch was a family home, filled with children and caring adults—judging by the condition of the ranch. He couldn't imagine finding a dangerous outlaw like Ned Barlow and his enterprising sister here. Still, it wouldn't hurt to mosey on down and introduce himself, ask a few questions.

Several yards behind him, Buckaroo whinnied a greeting.

Mac froze midway to rising. The hair at his neck prickled in alarm. He knew before he heard the voice that he was no longer alone.

"This old shotgun's a little contrary," a deep voice began almost conversationally. "Sometimes it hits the mark with a clean shot, and sometimes it scatters. When it scatters it makes an awful mess."

"Mind if I turn around?" Mac began to move slowly even as he asked the question, holding his arms away from his body. He knew from years of experience that showing fear would gain him nothing.

"As long as you keep doin' it nice and slow."

Mac had the presence of mind to hide his shock when he set eyes on the man. He was an Indian, but he spoke like a white man. So well, in fact, that Mac hadn't guessed beforehand. But he understood why he hadn't heard him; nobody could move as soundlessly as an Indian.

"State your business," the man said, holding the shotgun steady. "And move away from the ledge. If I have to shoot you, I don't want my children to see it."

His children. Most likely his ranch, too. The pieces of the puzzle fell into place. Mac would bet his next bounty haul that the man's wife's skin was fair. It would explain the reaction of the townspeople to his questions.

"You're no murdering savage," Mac stated boldly, testing his theory. The shotgun dipped a fraction—the only indication of the Indian's surprise. His face remained impassive. Mac noticed there were streaks of gray in the long braids hanging over his shoulders, and many lines around his eyes, as if he spent long hours in the sun.

From the looks of the ranch, he did.

"There are folks who might disagree with you." The Indian jerked his head in the general direction of Cornwall. "If you came from there, you've met a few."

"I came from Cornwall," Mac admitted. "And I heard talk, but I make my own judgments."

"Then why are you here?"

Mac allowed himself to relax—although the other man didn't. "I'm looking for Ned Barlow. I heard he came through this way."

"You got a name?"

"Mackenzy Cord." Mac held out his hand, continuing in the same bold direction because it seemed to be working. "And your name?"

A tense moment passed. Mac held the man's fathomless gaze without fear. Finally the man lowered the shotgun and took Mac's hand. He gave it a brief shake before he dropped it.

"My friends call me Eye of the Hawk. My wife calls me Hawk. I knew Barlow would bring trouble." He spat on the ground as if the mere mention of his name left a nasty taste in his mouth.

"You know him, then?" Mac asked, tensing. Maybe he was wrong; maybe the peaceful serenity of the Sunset Ranch was just an illusion.

"He's a brother to my wife, Patricia, unfortunately. He *was* here, but he and that harlot of his left three days ago."

"The woman . . . She isn't his sister?"

Hawk's lip curled. "If she is, they have a sickness for one another. My Patricia, she has a soft heart for her brother."

"And you have a soft spot for Patricia," Mac guessed shrewdly.

A rueful smile flashed briefly on Hawk's face. "You are wise, Mr. Cord. May I ask why you search for Barlow?"

Mac hesitated. Although it was obvious Hawk harbored no love for his brother-in-law, Mac had to remember that blood was thicker than water. He chose to tell another truth instead, one he thought Hawk would understand. "There's a woman I love as you love your Patricia. Barlow tricked her into believing he was a gentleman, then took her money."

"You intend to get it back," Hawk concluded with a single nod of understanding. "You look thirsty. Come, we will share a drink, and I will tell you what I know."

Assuming Mac's acceptance, he turned and descended the hill. As he passed Buckaroo, he reached out and yanked his tether free from the branch, then proceeded on without a backward glance. Without looking at Mac, he said, "Don't worry, he will follow."

Mac chose his words with care. "Uh, Hawk? This horse may be a mite different than what you're . . ." He trailed off in amazement as Buckaroo let out a fierce whinny and began to trot after the Indian.

"Well, I'll be damned," Mac muttered beneath his breath as he, too, followed the Indian.

Chapter Fifteen

Mac smelled baking bread when he and Hawk stepped onto the porch of the ranch house. His stomach rumbled, reminding him that he'd had little to eat the night before.

"Patricia, she cooks good," Hawk said, holding the door for Mac.

Before either of them could enter, a young child came hurtling through the door and straight into Mac. Mac steadied her before she could bounce backward.

Only it wasn't a *her*, he realized on closer inspection. The child's long dark braids had misled him.

Hawk squeezed the boy's shoulder. "This is Sparrow—"

"Eagle," the boy interrupted breathlessly. He shot a challenging glance at his father. "My name is Eagle, not Sparrow."

Hawk chuckled. "I told you, you have to earn a name like Eagle. Until then you will be called Sparrow."

The boy thrust his chin out. He was dressed in soft, handmade buckskins, and his face was painted with streaks of black and red. He was tall, but the fullness of his face suggested he was younger than he appeared. Perhaps six or seven years of age.

"Then I will go and earn the name," Sparrow promised, attempting to rush by Hawk.

But Hawk caught him deftly around the waist and held him high. "And how do you plan to do that, my blood-thirsty little brat?"

"By bringing you a prisoner." Sparrow slanted a sly glance at Mac before he added, "A *white* prisoner."

There was a sharp, feminine gasp behind Mac. He turned around to find a woman standing in the doorway. Patricia, he presumed, looking furious and appalled. More amused than insulted, Mac smiled as he watched the domestic scene unfold.

He highly suspected Sparrow was about to get his wings clipped.

"Newton Oliver!" Patricia scolded. "Apologize to our guest and go to your room."

"Mama!" The boy groaned and struggled to get free, clearly embarrassed to be addressed by his Christian name. "I *told* you, it's *Eagle!*"

"Sparrow," Hawk insisted, setting the boy on his feet. "Now do as your mother says."

Newton Oliver, despite the defiant glint in his eye when he looked at Mac, did as he was told. "Sorry, mister." Feet dragging, he disappeared through the doorway.

Patricia watched him go, sighing. She managed a weary smile and stuck out her hand. "I'm Patricia." She nodded toward her shuffling son as Mac shook her hand. "And *that* is Hawk's fault. He fills their heads with wild stories from the *old* days." The look she cast her husband was loving but stern.

"Mackenzy Cord. My friends call me Mac." She was younger than Mac imagined, with thick dark hair and brown eyes. He wondered briefly about the honey tint to her skin. If she was a half-breed, she had obviously been raised in a white man's world, and educated to boot.

"No, Mr. Cord," Patricia said, apparently reading his thoughts, "I'm not a half-breed. I just like the sun . . . and Indians." She sounded amused, which in turn relieved Mac.

He smiled ruefully. "Am I that transparent?"

"Not really. I'm just good at reading faces. Hawk taught me that." She laced her arm through her husband's. "Shall we go inside? The bread should be cool enough to cut, and I need to check on Edmond. He's down for a nap."

Just the mention of food made Mac's stomach rumble again. Hawk and Patricia laughed. Mac didn't think she'd be laughing if she knew the reason he was here.

His gaze met Hawk's for a brief second. A silent message passed between them; nothing would be said about Barlow in her presence.

"So, Mr. Cord, what brings you to these parts?"

As Mac followed the couple into a spacious living room, he put his useful, living-saving talents to work.

He lied through his teeth.

"I'm an artist, ma'am. West Virginia's a beautiful state." Colorful rugs were scattered on the hard plank floor. Blankets in vivid colors of the sunset hung on the walls, among portraits and paintings. It was a warm room, welcoming and homey. Mac found it hard to imagine a man like Barlow in this room, or kin to Patricia, for that matter.

"An artist! Did you hear that, Hawk? Mr. Cord is an artist."

"I heard," Hawk mumbled, clearly uncomfortable with the lie. "Come, Mac. We shall silence your stomach and then take our smokes outside. The smell of my pipe makes Patricia ill."

Patricia blushed and patted her slightly rounded belly. "I think it's a girl this time. With Edmond and Newton, I loved the smell of Hawk's tobacco. Where are you from, Mr. Cord?"

"South Carolina. A little town called Angel Creek."

"You're a long way from home."

"I move around a lot," Mac said, following the couple along a hallway and into the kitchen. Here the smell of baking bread was strong enough to make his mouth water. He and Hawk took a seat at the table while Patricia busied herself slicing bread and pouring tall glasses of lemonade.

Ice tinkled in the glass when she set it before him. Mac's eyebrow rose in surprise. Patricia caught his expression and smiled.

"Hawk built an ice house a couple of winters ago, and my brother brought the lemons clear from Florida. He was just here a few days ago. He travels a lot, too."

Mac kept his expression blank and didn't dare look at Hawk. "Really?" he asked politely. He took a long draw of the lemonade and smacked his lips. "This is delicious." So was the bread, he discovered as he took a man-size bite. He supposed he should feel guilty knowing Savannah and Roy were back at camp, chewing on tough jerky and drinking creek—

"Pa?"

Standing in the doorway was Newton Oliver, breathing hard and looking as if he'd just discovered gold.

"You're supposed to be in your room," Patricia reminded him.

"I was," Newton said, his voice shrill with excitement. "And I was watching the ridge, just like Pa tells me to, and I saw something."

Hawk went rigid. "What was it?"

It was then that Mac noticed the rope in Newton's hand.

The boy gave it a sharp yank. It went taut, but whatever was on the other end was obviously bigger, and more determined than Newton.

Mac had a sudden, awful premonition.

"This! I found this!" He hauled on the rope again, and the object of his excitement fell into view. Literally.

It was Savannah. Her hair had come loose, and there was a good-sized tear in the seat of her trousers—baring to Mac's stunned gaze an enticing glimpse of her smooth buttock—but she looked otherwise unharmed.

"I caught her snooping around on the ridge, spying on us!" Newton let out an earsplitting whoop, danced in a circle, and tangled the rope around him. "So I caught her—I caught me a white prisoner, Pa! *Now* will you call me *Eagle?*"

Patricia gave little warning; she let out a tiny gasp and crumpled. Hawk reached her in time, holding her limp form in his arms. He glared at his errant son, his voice like thunder. "You have gone too far, *Little Sparrow!* Who is this woman?"

Stifling a sigh, Mac found himself saying the all-too-familiar words, "She's my wife."

"But he's so young, Mac," Savannah whispered as Newton Oliver lugged yet another bucket of steaming water into the room and dumped it into the tub. Each time he passed her, he stopped and mumbled an apology.

The sight of his stricken face made her want to weep.

"Don't interfere. He's old enough to rope you and drag you down the ridge."

"Yes, I know, but he explained why—" She broke off as Patricia came into the room. The woman's lips were still pursed tight, but her eyes were warm and apologetic when they landed on Savannah.

"I brought you fresh towels and a cake of scented soap. Thank God Ned travels and visits often, or I'd never have these little luxuries."

Savannah felt her stomach bottom out. "Ned?" she squeaked. Mac gave her arm a warning squeeze, but she ignored him. "Are you talking about Ned Barlow?"

"Why, yes. He's my brother. Do you know him?"

This time Mac pinched her—hard. It was a warning she couldn't ignore.

"Um, yes, I do. I met him on the train on my way to Jamestown."

Newton came in again with another bucket of steaming water. A younger boy, who looked to be about four years of age, followed on his heels, carefully balancing a tin cup between his chubby little hands. When Newton dumped the water and turned away from the tub, the younger one dumped the contents of his cup into the tub.

"I'm sorry, Mrs. Cord," Newton paused to mumble.

The younger boy stepped into the spot Newton vacated. Entranced, Savannah stared down into his big, solemn brown eyes. "Who are you?" she asked softly.

"I'm Edmond, and my brother's sorry he did what he did."

Before Savannah could respond, Edmond turned to follow his brother, mimicking his movements right down to the shuffling feet and bowed head. Although Patricia's expression remained resolute, Savannah saw the love shining in her eyes as she watched her boys march from the room.

"I can't apologize enough," Patricia said. "Hawk wants them to know and remember their Indian heritage, but after what happened today, I'm not so sure it's a good idea."

Savannah felt compelled to defend her little captor. "I don't think he meant any harm."

"No, I'm sure he didn't." Patricia drew in a deep breath.

"But you could have gotten hurt, and that makes his actions inexcusable. He'll make amends."

"It's not necessary—"

"Yes, it is. He'll sleep outside your door tonight, and if you need anything—anything at all—let him know."

One look at Patricia's stubborn face, and Savannah knew any further protests would be useless. While she might feel their actions were a little harsh, she had to remember she was a guest—an uninvited one at that—in their home.

"I'll bring you something to wear so that I can repair your trousers." A smile tugged at Patricia's mouth. "I'm sure Mr. Cord doesn't mind the—er—exposure, but you're probably feeling a little drafty."

Mac chuckled. Savannah poked him sharply in the ribs, which in turn made *Patricia* chuckle. Then, to Savannah's mortification, she felt Mac's hand slip into the tear and cup her buttock. He squeezed.

Her knees nearly buckled. Swearing vengeance beneath her breath, she tried to keep a smile on her face. Thank God Patricia couldn't see what Mac was doing!

"I'll leave you two alone to rest up for supper," Patricia said with a knowing smile.

The moment Patricia shut the door, Savannah danced away from Mac and his naughty hand. Her abrupt movement caused the trousers to rip further. "Mackenzy Cord! You are the wickedest man I've ever met!"

"And you're the stubbornest woman *I've* ever met," Mac retorted, clearly unrepentant. He folded his arms and propped his back against the bedpost, watching her through lazy, hooded eyes. "Aren't you going to take a bath?"

Savannah drew in a sharp breath and backed against the door, determined to keep her bare behind out of sight.

"With *you* watching?" As his gaze traveled slowly along her body, she felt her skin tingle with awareness. *Not now,* she thought, *not here!*

"Why not? I've seen you in the altogether . . . remember?"

"But it was dark."

"So?"

"We have a little boy camped outside our door," Savannah reminded him desperately. She wanted Mac, but not in broad daylight and with people listening!

"We're talking about a bath, Sav," Mac chided. "I thought you might need help washing your hair."

"Oh." She flushed at his mocking look. "In that case, turn around until I get undressed and in the tub."

"Do I have to?"

"Yes, you have to."

"That's a shame."

She waited until he'd turned his back before reaching for the buttons on her shirt. Her fingers shook, and she nearly shrieked when he spoke again.

"Do you . . . have your shirt off yet?"

Damn him and his husky voice. "No—no, I don't."

A full moment passed. Savannah managed to get the shirt off and hastily start on her trousers. She edged toward the tub as she fumbled with the drawstring.

"Are you sure you don't need help?" he asked in a soft, yearning voice that turned her knees to jelly.

Oh, he was good. Very good. If she didn't know Mac's game, she might just believe him. But then, maybe it *wasn't* a game. He'd made it clear that he wanted her, friend or not.

She shivered as she stepped into the big tub and sank beneath the water, bringing her knees to her chin to hide the evidence of her reaction to his teasing. "Okay, you can turn around now."

He did, moving slowly in her direction. He went to his knees beside the tub and reached for the cloth and the soap Patricia had provided.

Savannah's mouth went dry at the look of languid desire in his eyes. "Mac, what are you doing?"

"Asking for trouble," he said softly.

His hot gaze never wavered from her face as he soaped the cloth.

Chapter Sixteen

"Where's Roy?" Mac asked, attempting the impossible, which was to ignore the satin feel of her skin as he soaped her outstretched leg.

With a weary sigh, Savannah rested her head against the back of the tub. The movement brought her breasts to the surface, giving Mac a teasing, tantalizing glimpse of the creamy globes.

"I left him at the camp."

Her eyes were closed, leaving Mac blissfully free to look his fill. He tugged on her other leg, and she absently obliged. "Tied to a tree?"

She gave him a one-eyed dirty look. "No, I didn't tie him to anything. He just said he wasn't going to follow me and get chewed out again by you."

"He didn't try to stop you?"

"Oh, he cursed and begged and pleaded. Then he realized he was wasting his time and gave up."

Mac was surprised; Roy had seemed so earnest in his promise to keep Savannah at the camp. He had expected more of a fight.

"Are you going to tell me about Patricia's dear

brother, or do I have to ask her myself?" Savannah asked tartly.

"What's there to tell? Although it seems impossible, your Ned is Patricia's brother. We missed getting to meet the man by a few days." Inch by slow inch, he worked his hand along her inner thigh with the soapy cloth. She didn't seem to notice. Mac didn't know whether to be insulted or glad. In the end he decided to be glad, because if she began to notice she might make him stop.

And he definitely didn't want to stop.

"He's not *my* Ned, Mac," Savannah protested. "And how could he be kin to that sweet woman? Does she know what a monster he is? Does she know that he not only robbed the bank in Jamestown, he took *my* money as well?"

Agitated, she sat up, dislodging his hand. Mac swallowed a curse; his fingers had been so close to slipping into her tight sheath. Would she have moaned and squirmed with pleasure? he wondered. Or would she have leaped from the tub and cursed him? Now he'd never know. . . .

"Mac, have you been listening to a word I've said? How could you *not* say something to them?"

"Hawk knows. We're supposed to talk later."

She slapped at the water. "So! While you and Hawk discuss the man who took *my* money and my dignity, I'm stuck in this room chewing my nails and wondering what you're talking about." Her look scorched him. "Why am I not surprised? No wonder you're still a bachelor—you're a tyrant!"

Her careless remark stung. Mac dropped the cloth on her flat belly and stood. Belatedly Savannah noticed his rigid expression.

She was instantly contrite. "Mac, I didn't mean—"

"Didn't you?" he asked softly, staring down at her beautiful, anxious face. God, he loved her, but sometimes he just wanted to bend her over his knee and spank her until she begged for mercy!

Or love her until she couldn't move.

"Mac . . . please don't go away mad."

"I'm not mad." And he wasn't. He was hurt, but she wouldn't understand, so there was no need to voice his feelings and possibly leave himself open for more ridicule.

"Why, if we weren't such good friends, I'd marry you myself. You're kind and sweet and loyal and handsome."

"Right." Mac turned and headed for the door. Maybe Hawk had something a bit more powerful than lemonade. He heard water splashing and had to bite his tongue to keep from glancing over his shoulder to see if she was standing.

"Mac?" she called in that lilting way that made his heart skip a beat.

He paused with his hand on the doorknob, struggling with the devil inside him that wanted to march back and carry her, dripping wet, to the bed.

"You—you aren't going to stop being my friend, are you?"

Mac made sure he slammed the door good and hard as he left.

Mac found Hawk with the horses.

He had his back to Mac as he stood at the fence. Without turning around, he said, "Folks in Cornwall, they turn their nose in the air because of my red skin, but they buy my horses."

"Do you have eyes in the back of your head, Hawk?" Mac asked, coming to stand beside the Indian.

Flashing him a grin, Hawk nodded. "Patricia thinks so."

His smile faded abruptly. "She also believes her brother is a good man, that he is just sowing his wild oats."

"By robbing banks and kidnapping women?"

"She doesn't know." Hawk's mouth firmed into a thin, relentless line. "He boasts to me of his deeds, but he is a man of two faces. It would break her heart if she knew."

Mac caught the subtle warning. "Don't worry, she won't hear it from me." He couldn't, however, speak for Savannah. "Do you know where Barlow is headed?"

Hawk turned to look at the ranch house behind him for a long contemplative moment, as if he were envisioning Patricia's reaction to what he was about to say. "He mentioned buying a spread in Virginia, near a town called Paradise."

"How convenient. We're headed that way ourselves." Paradise was a popular town that Mac had visited a time or two. He closed his hands over the top rail and looked at the cavorting horses in the corral. Hawk's lack of loyalty aroused his curiosity. "By the way, what exactly did Barlow do to you to make you hate him so much?" Expecting Hawk to tell him to mind his own business, the Indian surprised him by answering without hesitation.

"Not what he did, but what he *does*. He begs Patricia to give up her life here and go with him. He tells lies about the white man's world to entice my sons from me. He brings Patricia things I cannot buy for her."

"Well, I guess that's plenty of reasons not to like the man," Mac agreed. But Hawk wasn't finished, it seemed.

"And he calls me Chief. I'm not a chief. My grandfather was a great chief, but I'm just an Indian."

"Since you haven't told me to mind my own business, I've got one more question. Do you know a man named Mason West?"

Hawk nodded. "West believes my father is responsible for the deaths of his parents."

"Sins of the father," Mac murmured, then couldn't resist asking, "Was he?"

"Maybe." There was pain in Hawk's voice, making Mac regret his careless question. "My father and I were not close."

"Still, you're not responsible for what your father did."

"There are those that would disagree with you," Hawk said dryly. "Such as West. He has tried to kill me twice. Patricia worries that he will succeed, and does not want me to go into town."

Mac cursed low and long. "A man has a right to defend himself," he began, only to have Hawk's laughter cut him off.

"Mackenzy Cord, you are a good man, but you are blind. I am an Indian of wealth and married to a white woman. If West dies, then I die with him, swinging from the end of a hangman's rope." He spread a hand to indicate the horses and the cattle grazing in the distance. "All that I have, all that I have nurtured with these two hands, would be taken from my sons. Stolen."

Bad as Mac hated to admit it, he sensed that Hawk was right. But that didn't *make* it right.

"Do not let my burdens become yours, my friend. I will protect what is mine. Now, since I have told you my secrets, it is only fair that you tell me yours."

Mac tensed. Did Hawk know—as he seemed to know everything else—his true reason for wanting to find Barlow? Could he have guessed that he was a bounty hunter? He hated deceiving him, but neither did he want to disappoint his new friend.

"She is quite a woman, your Savannah," Hawk prompted.

Smothering a sigh of relief, Mac chuckled. "Yes, she is."

"Stubborn, like my Patricia."

"She is that."

"And almost ready for mating," Hawk added outrageously. While Mac choked on embarrassed laughter, Hawk pointed to the far corner of the corral where a pretty little filly pranced coyly away from an anxious—and obviously aroused—stallion. "Your woman reminds me of that filly. She trembles in eagerness for his huge staff, yet she is afraid to take the final step and let him mount her."

"We're not married," Mac confessed, feeling his face heat. He wasn't shocked—after all, he was a man and could remember a time when *he* had joined in with a lewd comment or two about a past roll in the hay, but this was *Savannah*. "Although I'd like nothing better."

"Then why not marry her?" Hawk asked, clearly puzzled. "She wants you, and you want her. It is plain to see."

"We've been friends a long time." When Hawk merely lifted a questioning brow, Mac added, "A *very* long time. She trusts me."

"Like a child trusts a wolf? When Sparrow was but five winters old, he wandered into the forest and became lost. We looked for him all night, fearing he'd freeze before we found him. It was very cold."

Mac sucked in a sharp breath, imagining their angst and terror over losing their child.

"He was warm when we found him, but his hand was bloody."

Hawk paused, and Mac understood how his children became enthralled with his storytelling abilities. "Well? What happened?"

"A wolf had kept him warm through the long cold

night, but when Sparrow awoke and tried to pet the wolf, the wolf bit him and ran away."

"I would never hurt Savannah," Mac growled, feeling suddenly defensive. "If that's what you're implying."

With a shrug, Hawk pushed away from the fence. "Then if I were you, I'd marry her."

"She loves me as a *friend.*"

"Then make her love you as a man," Hawk stated. He began to walk in the direction of the house. "Make yourself so indispensable she can't imagine life without you."

Frustrated, Mac called after him, "I've tried that. It doesn't seem to be working."

"Then try harder."

"How?" Mac demanded, striding after the stubborn man. "Since you're so full of advice, tell me how!"

Hawk stopped abruptly until Mac reached him. "What does a *woman* do when she wants a man to marry her?"

Mac frowned as he considered the question. "Well, she plays hard to get. Tempts a man. Acts sort of coy, like that filly—" He ground to a halt, turning to stare at the excited horses in the corral. The light finally dawned. Incredulous, he looked at Hawk's grinning face. "You think *I* should play hard to get? Make her—*tease* her into wanting me, then hold out until she agrees to marry . . . me?"

It was brilliant. If it would work.

He supposed the biggest question was, could he do it? Could he resist Savannah long enough to make her want him badly enough to think of marriage? Remembering the heat they'd generated last night, he couldn't help but wonder if they'd already gone too far.

Tonight he could test Hawk's plan, for they'd be sharing a bed since Patricia believed them to be married.

* * *

Savannah had more than enough reasons to want to leave before nightfall. Roy was alone in the woods; she couldn't bear to think about Sparrow sleeping on the cold hard floor, and she didn't think she was strong enough to share a bed with Mac without making a fool of herself. Just the thought of lying so close to Mac without touching him made her break out into a cold sweat.

"I think we should leave now," she whispered to Mac as they helped gather the dishes from their meal. "Roy will be worried, and he's all alone in the forest." It was her first excuse, and, she hoped, the only one she'd need.

Mac balanced a glass and his plate, but dropped his fork. He bent to pick it up, whispering back, "Roy can take care of himself. Besides, he deserves what he gets for letting you follow me—the first *and* second time."

Undeterred, Savannah launched into her second excuse. "I won't sleep a wink knowing poor Sparrow is having to sleep on the floor like—like a *slave,* awaiting my every whim," she whispered, snatching the dishes from his clumsy hands.

"Then don't have any *whims,*" Mac suggested sweetly.

He was leaving her no choice; blackmail was her only card left, because she certainly wasn't going to explain her *third* reason for wanting to leave! "Mac, if we don't leave now, then I'm going to have a talk with Patricia. I think it's about time she found out what a thieving, horrible man her brother is."

It was a bluff, because she'd already decided she could never tell the big-hearted Patricia anything of the sort. She hoped Mac wouldn't see through her bluff.

"What are you two lovebirds whispering about? Or should I ask?" It was Patricia, looking flushed and happy as she swept into the room and began to gather the rest of the dishes.

Savannah seized her chance to taunt Mac. "I was just telling Mac how sorry I was that I didn't get a chance to see Ned again. *And* your sister, of course. Raquel was very nice to me on the train."

Patricia looked surprised. Suddenly, to Savannah's consternation, she burst out laughing. When she managed to catch her breath, she asked, "Whatever gave you the idea Raquel was my *sister?*"

After shooting Mac a look that should have knocked him to the floor, Savannah said, "I must have just assumed."

Still chuckling, Patricia shook her head. "Thank God she isn't. I know Ned loves her, but there's something about her that I can't quite get used to."

Savannah knew exactly what she meant. Unfortunately she felt the same about Ned. Her humiliation deepened as she realized that Ned had only pretended to be unattached so that his charm would be more effective against *her.* She opened her mouth to speak, intending to confirm her suspicions that Raquel was Ned's wife, but Mac hastily interrupted her.

"I think we'll skip that offer of a bed, Patricia, and get going. Savannah reminded me that we left our things at the hotel in Cornwall."

"Did anyone know you were coming here?" Patricia asked anxiously. "Because if they did, they've probably made a bonfire out of your belongings." She didn't sound bitter, just resigned to the prejudice of what had once been her people.

"No, no one knew," Mac said, and Savannah blessed him for the lie. There were kind lies and there were hurtful lies; this one she considered a kind lie.

Hawk appeared in the doorway, looking every inch the proud warrior. Yet his eyes held a gentleness that Savannah failed to see in many of her own people. The realization saddened her.

"The horses are ready," he stated.

"How did—?" Savannah began.

"Not only does he have eyes in the back of his head," Mac drawled with a smile, "the walls of his house have ears."

The tall Indian grinned back. "The filly, she is still dancing away from the stallion."

"And the stallion? Is he ready to give her anything she desires?" Mac asked with barely concealed eagerness.

What in God's green earth were they talking about? Savannah exchanged a bewildered look with Patricia.

"He gave her his share of oats," Hawk said with such smug satisfaction that Savannah wanted to scream her frustration.

"Ah." Mac nodded, obviously pleased. "I'll have to remember that."

Savannah gave up.

Chapter Seventeen

Roy had built a fire, Mac saw as they approached the campsite. He'd also caught a rabbit, which he'd skewered on a stick and propped over the fire. The fat from the rabbit dripped onto the coals and made it sizzle and hiss.

There probably wasn't a coyote or a wolf for a mile that hadn't smelled the cooking meat by now, Mac mused. Which meant he'd get little sleep tonight because someone would need to stay awake to keep the fire going and the critters at bay.

When Roy spotted them, he waved nonchalantly from his comfortable position on a fallen tree. Mac muttered an oath and slid from the saddle, glancing at the dying sun as it sank below the trees. Savannah was right—the kid was too green to be left alone.

"Did you find Badlow?"

"*Barlow*, Roy. The name's Barlow," Savannah corrected, accepting Mac's help from the saddle. "And, no, we missed the varmint by a couple of days. He's headed for Paradise."

Mac held her against him an instant longer than necessary, just to feel her heartbeat. Reluctantly he let her go.

"Damn shame," Roy said, earning a narrow-eyed glare from Mac. He meant to have a talk with the boy about his language. No time like the present, he decided. But first, he had another, more important lesson to teach him.

He grabbed the spit from the fire and tossed the roasted rabbit into the creek.

"Hey!" Roy protested, leaping to his feet. "That was my supper you just dumped into the creek!"

"They're probably surrounding us right now, waiting for us to let the fire go out."

"Who?" Roy demanded, stalking to the creek with the intention of rescuing his supper.

He reminded Mac of a bristling porcupine. "Coyotes. Wolves. Maybe even a grizzly or two, for starters."

Roy froze. He turned toward Mac, his eyes huge in his thin, youthful face. "C-coyotes? G-grizzlies? You're—you're pullin' my leg, right?"

"I'm serious, kid."

With a grunt, Savannah hoisted her saddle from her horse and set it on the ground. She glared at Mac. "Stop scaring him, Mac. He's just a kid."

"I'm not a kid! And I'm not scared!" Roy denied heatedly.

Mac shook his head, weary of trying to convince them of the danger. "Sleep close to the fire, both of you," he ordered, pulling his rifle from the saddle holster. He checked the chamber, then began unsaddling the surprisingly calm Buckaroo. Apparently Hawk had worked his magic on the horse during their short stay at Sunset Ranch. Mac doubted Mason West would thank him for it.

Savannah unearthed a cloth-wrapped loaf of bread and a small jar of pear perserves from her saddlebags. She gave them to Roy. "Here, Patricia insisted that I take this."

Roy grabbed the fare with eager hands, smashing his

nose against the fragrant bread and inhaling deeply. "She's a good cook."

"How do you know?" Mac asked sharply.

"Because I can *smell* the bread. For Christ's sake, Mac, get off your high horse, will ya?"

"And that's another thing. Clean up your language around Savannah. She's a lady, best you remember that."

"But she don't—"

"I don't care what she said, *I* said to clean it up."

"Yes, sir," Roy muttered ungraciously around a mouthful of bread and jam.

Despite the scent of roasting meat that lingered in the air, the night proved uneventful. Mac spent the better part of it thinking about Hawk's advice, and wishing he and Savannah were in that big bed at Sunset Ranch.

His contemplative gaze strayed for the hundredth time to Savannah's sleeping form revealed clearly by the flickering orange flames of the campfire. Her face was soft and relaxed in sleep, her full lips parted slightly. Beneath the bedroll, he could easily follow the curvy lines of her figure.

He swallowed hard.

Perhaps they were *both* better off right here at the camp with Roy for a chaperon and the fire between them.

The hotel staff—what there was of it—didn't burn Savannah's massive trunks or Mac's single bag, as Patricia had feared. Everything was just as they'd left it.

Mac went straight to his satchel containing the wanted posters he carried with him from habit. He had a gut feeling about Mason West . . . a feeling that he'd seen his face before. Of course, he'd had the same feeling about several of the faces he'd encountered in Cornwall, but Mac had a particular interest in West. Perhaps there was something he could do to cool the rage in West toward Hawk.

"My, those are some dangerous-looking faces," Savannah commented softly in his ear.

Tilting his head, Mac looked at her. She was peering over his shoulder, and the movement brought his face close to hers. Close enough to kiss. He cleared his throat. "Um, yes, they are."

"Anyone I know?" she teased.

Mac couldn't stop staring at her smiling mouth. His heart began to thunder. With a shrug, he handed her a pile of posters. "It's always a possibility. Here, have a look."

She came to her knees beside him and began to look through the posters.

"I'm looking for the man who owns the stable," Mac explained in a voice that was betrayingly husky. The fragile scent of jasmine teased his nostrils. Her thigh was only inches from his own.

"He's a criminal?"

"I'm hoping." His lips twisted. "If I can get something on him, maybe I can convince him to leave Hawk and his family alone." He went on to tell her Hawk's story. By the time he was finished, her eyes had darkened with outrage.

"But that's not fair, Mac! It wasn't *Hawk* who killed his parents." She looked at the pile of posters on her lap. "What makes you think he's in here?"

"Because his face seemed familiar, and I've never been to Cornwall."

"Oh." She fell silent, studying each poster carefully before setting it aside. Most of them were nothing more than crude sketches hastily drawn by amateur artists. A few were actual pictures confiscated from the outlaw's relatives or his home.

"Mac. Look at this one!" She held a poster in front of

his nose, her voice rising with excitement. "It's Raquel. She's wanted in Tucson for murdering her husband back in eighty-four."

Surprised by her find, Mac took the poster and studied the faded picture of the dark-haired woman. She reminded him of a gypsy, right down to her dark, mysterious eyes and secretive smile. He didn't recognize her, but he trusted Savannah. "Well, well, well," he murmured. "She's got a hundred-dollar bounty on her. Guess we'll just have to haul her in with Barlow."

"*If* we catch them."

"Oh, we'll catch them all right. Once we reach Paradise, we'll look in every nook and cranny until we *do* find them." Mac looked up to find Savannah's admiring gaze on him. He flushed. "What?"

"You're good at your job, Mac, and I'm thankful to you for helping me. I wonder if I'll ever be able to repay you."

Mac could think of many ways she could repay him. He wiggled his eyebrows suggestively. "Well, you could start by giving me a . . . kiss."

"That wouldn't be payment, Mac," Savannah whispered, angling forward to reach his mouth. "That would be a pleasure."

Their lips met in a gentle, explorative kiss. Each time he kissed her, Mac discovered something new. Like the way she moved her mouth against his . . . and the teasing way her tongue darted in and out.

"Christ's sake, don't you people *ever* give it a rest?" came Roy's disgusted-sounding voice from the doorway.

Reluctantly Mac ended the kiss. He scowled at Roy. "Don't *you* ever knock?"

"I did. I guess you two couldn't hear me over all that heavy breathing."

"Get lost!"

"I came to tell you that they're serving fried chicken tonight." He rubbed his belly and licked his lips. "My favorite. Let's go eat."

As Mac rose to his feet and put his arms around Savannah to give her a hand, his gaze landed on the posters that had slipped from her lap. He reached down and plucked the crude drawing of a man from the pile.

It was West, all right, right down to the scarred face. "You two go eat without me. Since we'll be catching the morning train, I need to get the horses back to the stable." *And have a long talk with Mason West about his penchant for stealing horses.*

"Is it . . . ?" Savannah asked.

Mac nodded, staring at her mouth. Her lips were moist from their kiss. Damn Roy and his habit of popping up in the right place at the wrong time!

"Mac, be careful, will you?"

He thought he might drown in the liquid blue of her eyes. If only her concern stemmed from an emotion deeper than friendship. He prayed Hawk was right, that the attraction they felt for each other would eventually win him the prize he desperately wanted—Savannah's heart.

West met him at the stable doors, and once again Mac got the itchy feeling that his every move was being anticipated. Well, West was about to discover that Mac knew a few things about *him* as well.

When West saw Billy and Buckaroo trailing behind Mac, he didn't look surprised, which meant that someone had probably already informed the stablemaster that he, Savannah, and Roy had ridden into town together, Mac surmised.

"Have any trouble?" West asked, grabbing the reins as Mac dismounted.

Mac jabbed a finger in Buckaroo's direction, then placed a casual hand on his gun holster as he said, "Buckaroo was more than a little feisty, but Hawk straightened him out."

"Hawk?" West's face mottled with furious color. His big, ham-sized fists clenched. "You let that murdering bastard touch my horse?"

"You mean, Buckaroo really belongs to you?" Mac cocked a disbelieving brow. "I thought maybe you stole him."

"Stole—"

"Yes, stole." Mac was overjoyed to get to the good part. "I'm a bounty hunter, West, and I've got a poster with *your* name on it. Says you've been stealing horses and puttin' your own brand on them. You made the mistake of letting someone see your face." By this time West had turned an alarming shade of purple, making Mac wonder if he wouldn't die right on the spot.

"You plannin' on turning me in?" West growled, taking a threatening step in Mac's direction.

Mac drew his gun and cocked the hammer, all in one swift, expert move. "I generally just shoot one foot, but I'm willing to shoot both. That way I don't have to worry about you running. So, unless you're interested in making a deal, we'll get on with it." Mac deliberately aimed his gun at West's foot. He was bluffing, but West didn't know. Just for good measure, Mac added, "I believe the poster said dead or alive."

West seemed to struggle with himself. "What kind of deal?"

"You leave Hawk and his family alone, and we'll forget about having this little conversation."

"He murdered my folks!" West snarled. "What are you, some kind of Indian lover?"

"Hawk didn't murder anybody, and you know it. Leave him and his family be, or I'll take you in right now. The sheriff might be interested in knowing he's got an outlaw living right beneath his nose."

"The sheriff minds his own business."

"For two hundred dollars I think he might be tempted to mind *your* business, West."

"You bastard."

"Hey, I'm not the one stealing horses. I just catch the people stealing them. If that makes me a bastard, then I guess I'm a bastard." Mac dared to smile in the face of West's raw fury. "Do you we have a deal, or not?"

"How do you know I'll stick to the deal after you're gone?"

It was a damned good question, and one he hadn't thought of. "Because I have a cousin who lives here in town," Mac lied. "He knows how to get in touch with me, and if he hears that you've so much as *spoken* to Hawk or anyone in his family, I'll be back for you."

"I could skip town," West threatened.

Mac shrugged. "Then you'd be doing me a favor." He threw a ten-dollar gold eagle into the dust at West's feet. "That should cover the extras. You have a nice day now, you hear?" Whistling, he put his gun away and strolled in the direction of the hotel.

But his ears were tuned to hear the slightest movement from the livid-faced man staring after him. He knew that if looks could kill, he'd be a walking dead man right now.

Chapter Eighteen

Mac knew he should try to get some sleep, but between the rumbling of the train and Roy's constant snoring beside him, he found it impossible. He sighed and tipped his hat away from his eyes.

Savannah sat across from him, poring over an assortment of sketches she'd taken from a slim leather satchel. Mac leaned closer to get a better look. They were hats, he realized, of all shapes and sizes. The sketches were good, too.

"Did you draw these?" he asked, smiling when she jumped at the sound of his voice. Her gaze flew upward to meet his.

"I thought you were asleep."

With a rueful shake of his head, he pointed to Roy. "Not likely." His gaze fell on the sketches. "Mind if I take a look?"

"I didn't think you'd be interested. They're just hats."

Mac pretended to be wounded. "Not be interested? Well, I'll have you know that I *like* hats."

"You do?"

She sounded so hopeful Mac wanted to snatch her onto

his lap and kiss her long and hard. "Yes, I do. In fact . . ." He picked up one of the sketches and studied it, blessing his talent for remembering details. "Isn't this something like the hat you wore last summer at the cotton festival? The gray and black thing with the silver plums?"

"Why, Mac! Yes, yes it is!" She became flushed and animated. "As a matter of fact, I designed that very same hat. I can't believe you remember."

"And this one." Mac plucked another from the pile. "Didn't you wear something similar to the party your father held at the bank this past Christmas? Red . . . and green, with little ornaments dangling from the side." A look of amazement came over Savannah. For a moment, she was speechless.

"Mackenzy Cord! I can't *believe* you remember that!"

Mac glanced quickly around, then leaned in to whisper conspiratorially, "It's not something a man wants everyone to know, darlin'."

"Oh. Sorry." She giggled, then clamped a hand over her mouth. "Are there any other *secrets* you'd like to share with me?"

Taking his time as he studied each and every sketch, Mac finally put them aside. "They're all good, which doesn't surprise me. I've always known you were talented as well as beautiful." He cleared his throat before he confessed in a low voice, "I like fresh flowers." He suspected a lot of men appreciated a good bouquet, but he also suspected they'd die before they admitted it. Maybe *they* had never loved a woman as he loved Savannah.

"Really?"

His voice dropped an octave lower so that Savannah had to lean forward. Was it Mac's fault if her movement revealed to his hungry eyes a fair amount of cleavage? "I also like bubbles in my bath."

"Oh, my." Her eyes were growing rounder by the second.

"But I draw the line at scented soap."

Her jaw dropped open, then snapped shut. "You—you're teasing me."

"I hope so," Roy mumbled, then promptly began to snore again.

Mac tried to look grave. "No, I'm not. I do like hats and flowers and bubbles in my bath. Now it's your turn. Tell me something about yourself that I don't know."

"You mean, like a secret?" Savannah's eyes began to gleam, which should have warned Mac. She flicked a glance at Roy before she whispered, "Sometimes . . . I sleep bare."

The moisture drained from Mac's mouth as if the sun had slipped inside. "You . . . you . . . sometimes sleep bare," he repeated. He didn't dare close his eyes, because he knew what he would see if he did; Savannah stretched beneath the sheets . . . naked. "Any other secrets?" he managed to croak.

She shot him a speculative look, as if trying to decide if he could be trusted. "Well . . . Do you remember the barn dance, oh, seven or eight years ago, when someone laced the punch with corn liquor?"

"And the preacher's daughter—Mattie Owens, wasn't it? She got sick and threw up all over her mother," Mac recalled, grinning at the memory. Suddenly he sobered, gaping at Savannah, who was blushing furiously now. "You? *You* laced the punch?"

She nodded, trying not to smile. "I guess maybe I overdid it a little bit."

"That's an understatement. I had a headache for three days!" Mac laughed outright, startling Roy.

He opened one bleary eye and peered at Mac. "Can you

keep it down, Mac? Christ—Jeepers, a body's trying to sleep here."

They both ignored the grumpy boy. Savannah pointed at Mac. "Your turn."

"Okay. How's this? I was hot on the trail of an outlaw one night down in Georgia. It was dark and rainy, and my tooth was throbbing, so I stopped at a saloon in a mud hole of a little town—really nothing more than a couple of buildings and maybe a church—and drank a few whiskeys, hoping to kill the pain until I could get to a dentist." Mac rubbed his jaw and flashed her a rueful smile, bracing himself for her laughter. "I'd forgotten that I hadn't eaten much that day—because of the tooth—so the whiskey hit me pretty hard. I left the saloon . . . on someone else's horse."

Savannah began to giggle uncontrollably. Finally she burst out laughing, trying to muffle the sound with her hand. It was no use.

Mac sat back, grinning from ear to ear, watching her laugh. It was an amazing, memorable sight. When she quieted somewhat, he added, "I didn't realize that it wasn't my horse until I got to the next town."

"What did you do?" she asked, still gasping for air. Tears ran down her face. She kept wiping them away, but more took their place.

"I went back, but when I got there, *my* horse was gone."

This revelation sent Savannah into fits of laughter again. "You mean—you mean while you were taking someone else's horse, someone—someone else took yours?"

He nodded. "I figured the same thing happened to the other man, so I just kept his horse."

"That's the funniest story I've ever heard," Savannah declared, smiling at him.

"Well, the story about you scaring the getaway horses with your hat was a pretty funny story."

"Oh, you!" She blushed furiously.

"Your turn again," Mac said, enjoying himself more than he had in a long while. Savannah was growing more precious to him with every passing moment. He couldn't imagine ever growing restless with Savannah around.

"Well, let me see . . ." Her eyes grew bright, and she snapped her fingers, causing Roy to jump and frown in his sleep. "I've got it." But instead of telling him, she fell silent again, biting her bottom lip until it was flushed with color. "Or maybe I should think of something else."

Amused by her indecision, Mac prompted, "You've got my curiosity aroused now, Sav. It wouldn't be polite to leave me hanging. What is it this time? Did you ride naked down the street with only your hair for cover?"

Savannah gasped as if shocked, when Mac knew she was nothing of the sort.

"I would never!" Her impish grin stole Mac's breath as she added, "Unless no one knew me."

"I'm waiting."

"So you are." She drummed her fingers on her knees, then stuck her nail in her mouth for a quick, nervous nibble.

Mac challenged her with a lift of his brow. It was all she needed to spur her onward.

"All right. I'll tell you, but"—she flashed the sleeping Roy a long hard look—"you have to promise never to tell another soul."

"*All* of your secrets are safe with me, Savannah," he said on a decidedly husky note.

"You won't think I'm brazen?"

"I *love* your brazenness," Mac stated boldly. To his delight, she blushed and lowered her eyes.

"One night—years ago—I followed you home, intending to ask you if you would accompany me to church the following Sunday. You—you'd already gone into your house by the time I got there. I knocked, but I guess you didn't hear me, so I—I went to your bedroom window."

Hot tendrils of fire licked a pathway down Mac's spine as her voice became hushed. Everyone around them seemed to disappear—including Roy, who was still snoring beside him.

"You—you had already started undressing, and instead of leaving, like any decent girl would do, I just stayed there . . . watching you," she finished in a whisper.

Mac had but one problem with her story—other than the fact that it had caused a raging erection. "Sav, my bedroom was upstairs. The only way you could have watched me was if you had climbed the tree outside my window."

Savannah looked at him then, and she was smiling the most mischievous smile Mac had ever witnessed on a woman.

"Now you know how I *really* broke my wrist that summer."

He was so astounded by her confession that it took him a moment to breathe. "You—you fell out of the tree?"

"Yes."

"Watching me take off my clothes?"

"Yes."

"And never told a soul how it really happened—until now."

"Right." Her lips twitched, and her eyes brimmed with mirth. She was trying not to laugh. "I told Daddy that I tripped on the way to the outhouse."

"I can't beat that one," Mac said, chuckling at the image of Savannah hanging on a limb outside his bedroom window—*watching him undress*. It was an arousing thought.

Extremely arousing. Not that he needed further encouragement!

"I didn't think you could."

It was an undeniable challenge she issued, and Mac knew it. He thought about blurting out how long he'd loved her, how much he yearned to make her his wife, but he was afraid she'd find his confession as amusing as she'd found his stories. Instead, he took shameless advantage of the conversation to test Hawk's advice.

He rose and joined her on the seat, sitting very, very close. Leaning close to her ear, he whispered, "Since that night in the forest, I've thought of little else, wondering what it would be like to love you fully . . . to press deep inside you." She shivered, and he smiled, a crafty smile he was confident she couldn't see. "What would have happened if Roy hadn't stumbled upon us, I wonder?" He deliberately let out a sigh of regret as he added, "On the other hand, I'm glad he *did* interrupt us."

"You—you are?" she whispered, turning slightly.

Her mouth tempted him—only inches away. Mac resisted, but it wasn't easy. Instead he trailed his lips along her jaw, pausing near her ear again as he whispered, "Yes."

"Why?"

"Because we're not married, Savannah. Making love is a serious matter between a man and a woman."

"It is? I mean, yes, yes, it is. But—"

"Oh, yes, it's most certainly a serious matter," Mac continued, tracing the delicate shell of her ear with his tongue. She shivered again, but didn't pull away.

"But, Mac, I don't see what harm can be done if both parties agree."

Mac managed a convincing groan of self-disgust. "See? I've given you the wrong impression, haven't I? I should be horsewhipped. What we did—what we *almost* did—was wrong."

"Wrong?" Her voice was but a faint squeak of disappointment.

"Yes. You should save yourself for your husband."

"And if . . . I never marry? What then?"

"Oh, I can't imagine you not marrying, Savannah. You're intelligent, beautiful, and by far the most enchanting woman I know."

"But what if I don't marry?" she persisted. "I'm supposed to live like a nun the rest of my life, and never experience . . . experience making love with a man?" She shook her head. "No, Mac. That's not fair."

"That's life. You're a lady and you have your reputation to worry about."

"I'm a grown woman and I have a mind of my own," she informed him tartly. "If I want to sleep with you, then I will."

Mac chuckled. "Do I have a say in this matter?"

"Certainly." She turned her head until her lips brushed his in a sweet, all-too-brief kiss. "Say whatever you want, Mac," she whispered seductively against his mouth.

She was taunting him, Mac realized, very pleased with himself. Maybe there was some merit in Hawk's theory that if he ran, she would pursue. Or should he say, *appear* to run?

Time would tell. He couldn't wait to get to the next town, because, thanks to Roy, they would be forced to continue their pretense as husband and wife.

Which meant sharing a room—and possibly a bed—with Savannah again.

Chapter Nineteen

A fter two days Savannah was more than ready to get off the train as they approached Paradise, Virginia. Her eyes felt gritty from the smoke that filtered in through the open windows, and she couldn't wait to soak in a hot bath and put on fresh clothes. They'd taken turns sharing a sleep bunk—really nothing more than a hard shelf built into the wall, with a green curtain instead of a door. She was shamelessly anticipating spending another night with Mac some place more private.

Mac, she discovered, had other ideas.

"I want you to put on these clothes and wear this hat."

Savannah stared at the men's clothes and the ugly brown hat Mac held out to her. "Mac, you're not serious!" Wearing men's clothing to ride comfortably in the wilderness was one thing, but in *public?* She shuddered at the thought, then quickly glanced around to see if anyone had heard her outburst. Roy had muttered something about being hungry and disappeared in the direction of the dining car, and most of the other occupants were dozing.

"I can't take a chance on Barlow spotting *you* before we find *him.*"

She eyed the stubborn jut of his chin and realized her arguments would be useless. When Mac was determined about something, he exceeded her own stubborn persistence, she had discovered. She relented ungraciously. "Just until we get checked into a hotel."

Mac nodded. "We'll get you changed in the bunker."

"We?" Savannah licked her suddenly dry lips. "You— you're going in there with me?" Silly, she thought, to be embarrassed about Mac helping her change when all she could think about was making love with him.

"You'll need help hiding your hair beneath your hat." He studied her so hard Savannah began to squirm. "Although I'm not sure this disguise is going to work. Your breasts are too big."

"Too . . . big?"

"Well, not too big in *my* opinion," Mac hastily corrected, casting her bosom an admiring glance. "But too big to hide successfully. Maybe I can bind them with something."

The more he talked, the hotter Savannah became. She had a sneaky suspicion that Mac knew it, too. Why would he continue to tease her after he'd declared he regretted what they'd nearly done? Savannah's eyes narrowed speculatively at his innocent-looking frown. Was he that confident he could resist her?

It was a challenge Savannah couldn't ignore.

"I have to say you make a beautiful man," Mac stated sincerely, stepping back to admire her. Her height lent the disguise credibility, and Roy's coat helped hide her telltale curves. "Keep the coat closed, and maybe nobody will notice your—er—chest."

"You keep mentioning my—my bosom. Don't you like it?"

What the hell kind of question was that? Mac wondered. "Of course I like it." His voice lowered an octave. "I like it a *lot*." Too much, in fact. It had been sheer torture binding her with a strip torn from her petticoat without touching her, without filling his hands with the firm, full globes. Without nibbling, licking, and sucking in a frenzy of passion.

But somehow, he'd done it. He'd passed the first temptation test. He was breathless and hot and nearly insane with desire for her, but *he'd done it*.

Of course, the hardest test would come later at the hotel. Mac swallowed hard and tried not to think about sleeping next to Savannah and not touching her. He could do it. He had to, because Hawk's plan seemed to be working, and Mac was desperate.

"I don't think Barlow would recognize you at first glance," Mac said. He held out his arm. "Let's put our disguise to the test, shall we?"

Savannah grinned, guessing his thoughts. "Roy?"

"Yes, Roy."

Arm in arm, they returned to their seats. Roy had returned from the dining car and was glancing idly through the sketches Savannah had left on the seat.

Her eyes glinting with mischief, Savannah settled onto the seat beside Roy and threw her arm casually over his shoulders. Roy gave an alarmed squeak and gaped at her. The sketches fell to the floor.

"What the hell?" he shrieked, plastering himself against the window. "Hey, mister, get your filthy hands off me!" He cast Mac a wild, disbelieving look. "Mac, ain't you gonna *do* somethin'?"

But Mac was too busy laughing at Roy's expression. Savannah spoiled the game by giggling. No doubt about her gender now, Mac thought, watching them.

"You—Mrs. Cord? Is that you? But what the he—heck are you doing wearing my coat, and that ugly hat—"

"Shh. Keep your voice down," Mac instructed, still chuckling. "We're just making sure Barlow doesn't recognize her. If he does he might bolt or attempt to carry out his original plan to kidnap her." His voice hardened as he added, "Not that he would get away with it."

Roy continued to look dazed by the transformation. "Good idea . . . I guess."

Mac reached beneath his seat and retrieved his satchel. He took the picture of Raquel out and handed it to Roy. "I want you to scout out the hotels and see if they're registered. Paradise is a fairly large town, and the conductor says there are two hotels. The Empress and the Paradise Hotel." He tapped the picture. "I don't have a picture of Barlow, but that's his lady friend."

Roy sneered at the photograph. "She don't look like no lady to me. She looks like a saloon whore." When Mac growled a warning, Roy hastily apologized. "Sorry, Mrs. Cord. With you dressed like a man and all, I forgot to watch my mouth."

"We'll wait at the train station until you get back," Mac said. He glanced out the window, spotting a church steeple in the distance. "Looks like we're here. Get going, and don't dawddle. If you see them, don't do or say anything, just get back here."

"I don't *dawddle*," Roy declared indignantly. "What are you going to do when we catch 'em?"

"I'm going to get Savannah's money back and turn them over to the sheriff."

"What about the bounty money?" Savannah asked.

"I'll collect it later."

Her lips curved in a surprisingly bitter smile. "Oh, I forgot. What's a few hundred dollars compared to the five thousand waiting on you in Angel Creek?"

Roy whistled. "Five thousand dollars! Who—"

"None of your business," Savannah and Mac said simultaneously.

Mac fought the urge to wipe that bitter smile from her beautiful mouth by telling her that he didn't intend to collect her father's offer. But he refrained, because he wasn't quite ready to risk telling her the truth. Let her go on believing the worst for now. Sooner or later she would find out that the last thing on Mac's mind was money.

God willing, by that time she might love him just a little, and the knowledge wouldn't send her running.

"Mac, what are you going to do about Roy?" Savannah asked as they stood guard over her mountain of trunks and hatboxes the porter had stacked on the depot platform.

Mac shifted restlessly at her question. He'd been lost in a pleasant fantasy that involved a big feather bed and a naked Savannah. "I'm not sure what you mean."

"Well, someone is bound to be worried about him. Who does he belong to? Where are his parents? Where is he from?"

"He hasn't told you anything about his past?"

Savannah shook her head, pacing from one trunk to the next. Mac was glad the station had emptied quickly, because she did not move like a man. She didn't frown like one either. Hell, there wasn't *anything* manly about Savannah. She was pure femininity.

"No, nothing. I've asked him, but he just clams up and gets that stubborn look in his eyes. I'm afraid for him, Mac."

"I'll look after him, don't worry. Eventually I think he'll grow tired of tagging after me."

She paused and braced her booted foot on a trunk, her

expression now thoughtful. Her long coat fell to the side, revealing a curvy length of her leg encased in his trousers, and an interesting amount of her bottom. He'd been a fool to think his clothes could hide her lush curves. . . .

"Mac?"

"Hm?" Mac blinked and forced himself to focus on the hatbox at his feet. One of many. He felt a surge of pride as he remembered that Savannah had designed each and every one.

"Do you think Daddy might be interested in adopting Roy?"

He pictured George Carrington's florid complexion, remembering how ill he looked. For a moment he thought about mentioning his suspicions to Savannah, but changed his mind. She'd probably think it was a plot he and George concocted to gain her sympathy. "It's worth a shot, I suppose."

"Will you talk to him about it?"

Mac could deny her nothing. He nodded, relieved to see Roy approaching them at a fast clip. "Well?" he demanded as Roy joined them on the platform.

Roy braced his hands on his knees and sucked in air as if his life depended on it. "He's registered at the Empress," he finally gasped out.

"Get us a carriage for Savannah's trunks," Mac ordered, slapping a few coins into Roy's hand.

Groaning, Roy trotted off to find a carriage.

Mac turned to find Savannah watching him. "I want you and Roy to check in at the Paradise Hotel and wait for me there."

"I want to go with you."

"No."

"Why not?" She indicated her disguise with a wave of her hand. "He'll never recognize me."

"Maybe not, but Raquel might if she sees you up close."

"Then take Roy," Savannah pleaded. "I don't want you going after Barlow alone."

"Your faith in my ability never fails to amaze me," Mac drawled.

"Mac, I know you're good at your job, but I worry about you."

"Then you know how *I* feel."

"Don't change the subject."

Mac sighed. "Roy isn't experienced enough to be of help, Sav. Surely you know that."

"I guess you're right."

He feigned amazement. "Did you just admit that I'm right?"

Her lips twitched, although she tried to look forbidding. "Don't rub it in, Mac."

"Come here and give me a good-luck kiss," he growled, feeling an uncontrollable urge to have her against him, if only for a few seconds.

"A kiss? Shouldn't we get married or something first?"

"Or something," he muttered, pulling her unresisting body into his arms. "Sarcastic minx."

She fell against him, giggling. "Mac . . . if someone sees us, they'll think you're kissing a *man*."

"Who cares? *I* know what's beneath those clothes, remember?"

Her eyelids drooped, and her voice grew husky as her mouth inched closer to his. "Yes, I *do* remember, and I'm not likely to forget."

Good, Mac thought as his lips met hers, because he knew that he would never forget. He hoped he wouldn't have to. And tonight, after Barlow and his lady friend were safely in jail, he intended to add a few more memories.

Chapter Twenty

The door to Barlow's hotel room wasn't locked, and Mac soon discovered why.

It was empty.

The only indication that they had been there was the still-rumpled bed and the stench of urine rising from the chamber pot. So, they hadn't been gone long enough for the hotel staff to clean the room.

Mac slammed his fist into his open palm. Damn! This time they'd been so close. Who had warned them? Had Barlow known they were coming, or was his leaving just a coincidence? If only he hadn't stopped at the sheriff's office on his way to the hotel to inform the sheriff of Barlow's presence in town! The delay had been a waste of time anyway, as the sheriff had not been in.

Well, the time of Barlow's departure was one mystery he *could* solve, Mac decided, returning to the hotel desk clerk. "I'm looking for Ned Barlow in room twelve . . . but no one answers. Has he checked out?"

The hotel clerk consulted his ledger. "Yep, he did. You just missed him by about fifteen minutes, sir." As Mac turned away in frustration, the clerk called after him.

"Oh, he left a package. Are you perchance Mackenzy Cord?"

"Yes, I am." Mac tensed, his eyes on the package the clerk held out to him. With a bad feeling in his gut, he took it and tore away the brown paper wrapping.

It was a heavy gold locket, about an inch in diameter, and Mac knew instinctively it was the locket Barlow had taken from Savannah on the train. Barlow was taunting them, letting Mac know by leaving the locket behind that *he* knew they were following him.

Ignoring the curious clerk, Mac opened the locket. He recognized the tiny likeness of a younger George Carrington on one side. On the other side was a beautiful blond woman who looked remarkably like Savannah. Her mother, Mac presumed. No wonder she treasured the locket. It was possibly the only picture Savannah possessed, since Sylvia Carrington had died when Savannah was very young.

He snapped the locket closed, then curled his fingers around it. Barlow would rue the day he thought to laugh in Mackenzy Cord's face. The man might be clever, but he couldn't outfox Mac. But first . . . First he needed to get Savannah to Angel Creek and out of danger. Mac wasn't so foolish that he didn't recognize a worthy foe.

After Savannah was safely settled, he would find Barlow and his clever little lady friend and help put them behind bars where they belonged.

It would be his last job as a bounty hunter.

Confident in her disguise, Savannah watched from her position across the street as Mac emerged from the Empress Hotel. He paused on the boardwalk, looking left and right, but she was thankful, he never glanced in her direction. He'd have her hide if he saw her, she knew. Nevertheless, she melted into the shadows of the porch in front of the saloon and pulled her hat low over her face.

She watched him stride off in the direction of the Paradise Hotel, wondering why he was alone and what could have happened. Where were Barlow and Raquel? She hesitated, torn between the urge to take a look for herself and sticking to her original plan to beat Mac back to the hotel. He would not only be furious to find her gone, but also he would be worried.

And yet curiosity was killing her!

Another figure emerged from the doors of the hotel and fell in behind Mac, snagging her attention. Recognizing the deputy from Jamestown—the one who had accosted her outside the hotel when she'd tried to sneak away from Mac—Savannah gasped. She quickly smothered it, reminding herself that she was supposed to be a man. The last thing she needed to do was draw attention to herself—

"If it's a shoulder you need, mine's for sale, sweetheart. And for you I'm half price."

Too late, Savannah thought, cringing inside Roy's stifling coat at the sound of the soft, sultry voice behind her. She lowered her chin to her chest, attempting to hide her face. In a low growling voice she hoped sounded convincingly masculine, she said, "No, thanks." She hoped it would be enough to—

"Don't be frightened, sweetie," the feminine voice crooned somewhere close to her ear—too close. "If it's your first time, Alissa will teach you everything you need to know about pleasin' a woman."

Savannah could feel her face heat up and her ears catch fire. Apparently the whore had mistaken her mortification for shyness. She opened her mouth to respond with a more vigorous refusal when the whore's words sank in and sparked an idea. It was an outrageous, brazen . . . and very, very naughty idea.

Mac would kill her if he knew she was even *contemplating* such a thing. So she wouldn't tell him, of course.

Slowly Savannah straightened and faced the woman. She took her time looking her over as she gathered her courage. Surprisingly . . . and sadly, Savannah realized the woman wasn't much older than *she* was. Shorter, with red hair and arresting green eyes, Alissa boldly displayed her wares in a bright green dress that revealed a shocking amount of bosom. Against the whiteness of her powdered face, her red lips and equally red cheeks made a garish contrast.

Beyond the woman's flagrant display of sexuality, Savannah saw her desperation . . . and desolation. Granted, Savannah had wealth on her side, but she, too, had felt desolate at times. She took a deep breath. Perhaps they could help one another.

Thrusting her hand out, Savannah stated boldly, "You said you could teach me how to please a . . . woman." She took another deep, fortifying breath, inwardly cursing Mac for binding her chest too tightly. "Could you teach me how to please a *man?*"

Alissa's jaw dropped. She closed it. Her green eyes narrowed to mere slits. The flaming spots on her cheeks darkened. "So you're that way, are you? I should have known a pretty boy like you—"

"No! I'm not—" Savannah put a hand to her scalding cheek and looked quickly around her. The boardwalk in front of a saloon was *not* the place to be blurting out that she was a woman! "Can—do you have a place where we can talk in private . . . Alissa?" When the woman looked as if she would refuse, Savannah added, "Please? I'll make it worth your while, I promise."

"All right. Follow me." Alissa turned and started through the doors of the saloon.

Savannah's gaze widened on her retreating back as she realized where Alissa was headed. "Wait! Alissa, we're not going in there, are we?"

Alissa shot her a pitying look over her shoulder. "Honey, if you plan on making a living on your knees, you'd better get used to saloons." She jerked her head toward the swinging doors. "This is where I work and this is where I live. Unless you can afford a hotel room . . . ?"

"Um, no. I'm—I'm fine." Savannah swallowed hard and forced her numb legs to move.

Mac was going to kill her.

Mac was going to kill Savannah.

"Tell me one more time."

"I've explained it four times, Mac!" Roy protested, shaking loose from Mac's iron grip on his shoulder. "I don't know how to say it any plainer."

When Mac continued to glare at him, Roy heaved a great, long-suffering sigh.

"Okay, okay. You left after we loaded the trunks onto the wagon, right?"

"Right."

"The moment you disappeared, Savannah made the driver stop and let her down. She said she'd be back before *you* got back, so I shouldn't worry."

"And where was she going?"

Roy scratched his head. "Something about finding a hat shop . . . and checking out the competition, just like I said *four* times before."

"Don't get sassy," Mac growled, so frustrated he felt as if he could blow any moment. Barlow had eluded him, and now Savannah was gone. For all he knew, Barlow *had* Savannah! Icy beads of sweat peppered his brow at the possibility.

"Why in the *hell* did I have to fall in love with such a stubborn, pigheaded—" he began to mutter.

"Because she's *not* like all the rest of the women you've known," Roy said, surprising Mac with his perception.

Roy was right, of course, but in his present mood, Mac wasn't inclined to tell him.

"She's one of a kind, is our Mrs. Cord," Roy added sagely. "Not your usual, run-of-the-mill simpering miss, let me tell you. She's bright and talented—"

"All right, all right," Mac interrupted. "Maybe I won't wring her neck. Maybe I'll just bend her over my knee—"

"Now you're talkin'!" Roy stood on his toes and clapped him on the back. "Come on. I'm sure we'll find her drooling over one of those feathered—feathered *things* the ladies wear." He grimaced. "I wouldn't say it to her face, you know, but I can't understand why they'd want to walk around with those ugly things on their head."

"Hats, Roy. They're hats, not things."

Roy shook his head vehemently. He removed his hat, revealing a thick mop of dark hair. There was a round, darker line where his hat had been. He pointed to the silver band, then ran his fingers lovingly around the brim. "No. *This* is a hat," he explained so seriously Mac's lips twitched despite his efforts to remain straight-faced.

"So it is," he agreed softly, sensing the hat held a sentimental value to the kid. "Was it your father's?"

"No!" Roy's lips tightened, and a hard glint entered his eyes, reminding Mac that for Roy adulthood was just around the corner. "It belonged to the man who raised me—who was *nothing* like my father."

Mac wisely dropped the subject. It was the first time Roy had even hinted at his past, and he didn't want to push him. "Let's go find a hat shop. There's got to be one in a town this size."

They found the hat shop, but no Savannah. An hour later, with the sun sinking fast in the sky, Mac and Roy had looked in every window, peered in every shop from the dry-goods store to a shoe shop, with no luck.

Mac was seriously worried, and judging by the grim look on Roy's face, he wasn't alone. They paused in front of a saloon to decide their next move.

"Maybe she's back at the hotel by now," Roy suggested, trying to sound optimistic and failing miserably. He yanked off his hat and began to twist it around and around.

Up and down the boardwalk, shops were locking up for the night. Soon Mac knew the only places left open would be the saloons. Behind him he could hear laughter and the tinkling of a piano.

The saloons were the only places they *hadn't* looked.

His gaze met Roy's in silent question. "She wouldn't be in there."

"No. Of course not."

A worried silence fell between them. In the saloon the piano began another lively tune. There was a shout of drunken laughter, then someone began to sing in a wobbly, off-key voice, nearly drowning out the sound of the piano.

"I sure could use a drink, though," Roy mumbled. When Mac shot him a sharp look, he added quickly, "Of water, that is."

Mac rubbed his jaw and nodded. The possibility of finding Savannah in a tavern was ludicrous, of course, but they *were* thirsty. They could grab a drink and continue their search. Maybe she *did* find her way back to the hotel and was now fast asleep.

He certainly never considered for one moment that he would find Savannah in the saloon. She was a refined lady through and through. Wild horses couldn't drag her into a disreputable place like . . . a . . . saloon.

With a muffled curse, Mac whirled and pushed through the swinging doors. Roy stumbled into his back as he halted abruptly just inside the room. Mac scanned the crowd, an odd assortment of lumberjacks, cowboys, shop-keepers, and the ever-present whores. Nothing remotely resembling a tall, pretty woman dressed in men's clothing, he noted with a relieved sigh. "See?" he said, turning to Roy, breaking their vow of ignorance. "I knew she wouldn't be . . ." He trailed away as his gaze landed on Roy's face.

The kid was staring, mouth agape, at something across the room.

Mac forced himself to follow Roy's gaze, knowing by Roy's expression that he wasn't going to like what he saw.

And he didn't.

Strolling downstairs was Savannah on the arm of a whore. Unaware of their presence, she was laughing and chatting to the painted, nearly bare-breasted woman as if she'd known her half her life, when in fact Mac would bet his life savings that Savannah had never been within shouting distance of a woman of ill repute. If she had, he doubted that she would have known it.

Or . . . would she? Frozen to the spot, Mac resisted the insidious thought, but it forced its way into his mind de-spite his best efforts. Maybe he *didn't* know Savannah at all. Maybe she wasn't as innocent as he believed. She cer-tainly hadn't been frightened by his lust, he had to admit. In fact, she had embraced it eagerly, leaving him with the impression that he could have taken her any number of times.

Now she was chatting with a whore.

Not that he was a saint, or pretended to be. But that was the way of men . . . not *ladies*. Yet he remembered Savannah had argued this theory very forcefully, stating that it wasn't fair that a woman had to marry to experience love-making, while a man could slake his thirst without fear of ruining his reputation. Had she been speaking from experience? he wondered. Had he, blinded by love for her, failed to see that she wasn't the innocent angel he envisioned? These disturbing questions that ran swiftly through his mind as he watched Savannah descend the stairs raised an even bigger question. If he discovered that Savannah—his sweet Savannah—wasn't a virgin, would it matter?

As if she sensed him watching her—boring holes in her, rather—she glanced up and saw him. Her first reaction was spontaneous delight, which went a long way in melting Mac's anger over the fright she'd given him by disappearing.

But the shame and embarrassment that quickly clouded her expression heightened his suspicions, twisting his gut into knots. If he was wrong about Savannah in this—what other matters could he be wrong about?

Someone had warned Barlow, and by Roy's own words, Savannah had disappeared shortly after Mac left them. Since he'd made a stop along the way, Savannah would have had time to reach the hotel before him. It didn't explain the locket . . . unless it was a clever and deliberate ploy to divert suspicion from Savannah.

None of his chaotic thoughts made sense, and as Savannah approached them with the woman, Mac pushed them from his mind. Later, when he didn't have the distraction of Savannah's big blue eyes begging him for understanding, he would mull it over.

"Mac . . . Roy. This is Alissa. Alissa, this is my *best* friend Mac, and my other friend, Roy Hunter."

Rudely ignoring the introduction, Mac took Savannah's

arm and hauled her backward through the swinging doors. He marched her along the boardwalk, hardly aware that Roy was behind them. He knew he wasn't acting rationally, but he'd had too many scares and too many shocks in the past hour to feel rational.

He'd found Savannah in a saloon, after spending a harrowing hour searching for her . . . thinking she'd been kidnapped by Barlow. And now . . . *now* she'd gotten him to wondering if Barlow had ever been a threat at all!

Savannah struggled against his tight grip. Finally she dug the heels of her boots into the boardwalk and threw her weight backward, forcing him to stop. She was breathing hard, and her eyes sparkled with anger. Glaring at him, she dusted her sleeves and turned to where Alissa stood watching them from the boardwalk in front of the saloon.

"I won't forget my promise, Alissa!" she shouted. "And don't worry—he's really quite harmless."

When she turned back around, Mac made sure they were nose to nose. "I wouldn't bet on that last part, Sav. You've scared ten years off my life."

Her chin angled up, nearly brushing his own. "I'm not made of glass, Mac. When are you going to realize it? Obviously you don't know me at all!"

It was eerie how she echoed his very thoughts.

Chapter Twenty-one

The moment they stepped into the hotel room, Savannah dropped Roy's coat to the floor. The vest Mac had given her to wear over her shirt quickly followed. When she began to unbutton her shirt, Mac forcibly turned from the provocative sight and tried to sound angry as he demanded over his shoulder, "What are you doing?"

"I'm undressing, Mac. What does it look like I'm doing?" She snorted. "Does this conversation sound familiar to you? Let me see . . . What comes next? Oh, yes. We've been friends forever, right? The sight of me undressing shouldn't bother you."

"Maybe it shouldn't, but you know that it does," Mac said without thinking. He gave his forehead a mental slap. The woman was driving him insane!

"Calm down, Mac. I'll be finished in a moment. Although these trousers are comfortable, I feel . . . naked in them."

She looked naked in them, too, Mac recalled, willing moisture back to his mouth. His lips tightened in annoyance. If he didn't know better, he'd think Savannah had deliberately set out to distract him. With extreme effort, he concentrated on counting the colorful squares on the quilt covering the bed.

He gave up after the third one, because looking at the bed reminded him that he and Savannah would be sharing it later. Maybe he'd just take the floor again. . . .

"Since you obviously followed me to the Empress Hotel, you probably already know that Barlow and Raquel weren't there."

"I figured as much when you came out alone." There was a rustling sound behind him, a heavy sigh, then: "You can turn around now. I'm dressed."

Slowly Mac turned. Gone was the pretty boy, and in his place was a goddess. Her golden hair fell in a single thick braid over one shoulder, bared by the cornflower blue dress she now wore.

And wore well. Extremely well. Mac frowned. In fact, he couldn't remember seeing her in the dress before. It was more . . . revealing, with a lower neckline and an off-the-shoulder style. It dipped in tightly at her waist, flared gently over her hips, and gathered fullness as it reached the floor.

Blue looked good on her. It not only matched her eyes, but also brought out the color in her cheeks and made her breasts appear even— Mac swallowed hard, putting a halt to his arousing thoughts. He pulled another convincing frown.

"Something wrong?" she prompted.

"You look lovely," Mac growled. And it was nothing but the truth. Lovely, tempting, edible . . . "But I don't remember you wearing anything so revealing before."

Savannah tilted her head, a slight smile on her mouth. "Maybe you just never really noticed *before*."

"Before what?"

"Before we became aware of each other as a man and a woman."

As a bounty hunter, Mac had traveled far and wide. He'd met many people along the way and knew just about every ploy and trick in the book. Before he'd found Savannah in the saloon, he never would have suspected what he suspected now; that Savannah was deliberately distracting him. Normally he would delight in the knowledge . . . but now he questioned her motives.

Voicing his suspicions turned out to be one of the hardest things he remembered having to do. If he was wrong—and he fervently hoped he was—it could cause a serious setback in his pursuit of Savannah. Yet if he was right, he'd know he'd never had a chance anyway.

There was no subtle way to say the words, so Mac just blurted them out, his heart already thumping painfully. "Why are we really looking for Barlow?"

Her brow furrowed. "You know why, Mac. He took my money and my locket. He also stole a lot of money from the bank. He's an outlaw."

She sounded convincing, but Mac knew he couldn't trust his instincts where Savannah was concerned. "If I could give you the locket and replace the money he took from you, would you be willing to forget about Barlow?"

"What are you saying?" Her confusion deepened the frown between her eyes. "*Did* you find the locket—and my money? And why would Ned leave those items after going to all that trouble to take them?"

Mac searched for hope in her big blue eyes, wondering at its absence. "Answer my question, and I'll answer yours." Slowly he approached her, hoping to get a better look at her eyes. Her eyes would tell him if she lied.

"Yes, Mac. If I had my locket and my money, I would be willing to forget about Ned." She gave her head a bewildered shake. "Although I have to say I'm bursting with curiosity! Why would you ask such a thing? I begged you to give up the chase before you left for Sunset Ranch."

"Wasn't that a ploy so I wouldn't find out you were going to follow me?" The guilty color that flooded her cheeks told its own tale. Mac's heart sank.

"No, it wasn't! At least, if I could have convinced you to stay, it would have been better! Oh, you're confusing me, Mac. What I mean is, I wanted you to stay but I knew that you wouldn't, so, yes, I was hoping you wouldn't suspect that I planned to follow you." She reached out a hand as if to touch his chest, but let it fall short. "I've answered your question—*questions*—now you answer mine. Do you have the money and my locket? And why are you looking at me so suspiciously? What *is* it, Mac, that you're thinking I've done?"

"One more question. Why didn't you tell the sheriff where Barlow was going?" Mac had to hand it to her—she didn't hesitate in her answer.

"Because if I had told Sheriff Porter what I knew, he would never believe that I had nothing to do with that bank robbery." Her chin angled defensively. "Now I want to know why you're questioning me as if I'm some—some kind of criminal."

"Someone tipped Barlow off. He checked out fifteen minutes before I arrived at the Empress."

Her eyes grew frosty. "And you think it was me?"

"I didn't accuse you."

"No, you didn't. But you implied."

She sounded hurt, and Mac could hardly blame her. He could find no fault in her explanations, which told him he'd been wrong.

"Maybe it was that deputy from Jamestown. He was following you when you left the hotel."

Mac looked at her sharply. "What deputy?"

"The one who stopped me as I was sneaking out of the hotel that night."

"You saw him here—in Paradise?" Mac demanded.

"Yes."

"Are you certain it was him?"

"Yes. I was standing across the street in front of the saloon when you came out of the hotel. He came out after you."

"Did he see you?"

Savannah nodded at the pile of men's clothing that she had removed. "If he did, he didn't recognize me, remember? No, I'm certain he didn't see me. Maybe *he's* the reason Ned left town in a hurry. Maybe it didn't have anything to do with us at all, Mac."

Although her theory made perfect sense, and made him realize that he'd been wrong about her, Mac knew that Barlow had known they were coming; he had the proof in his vest pocket. He withdrew the locket and held it out to her. "He left this at the hotel desk . . . for me."

"My locket!" Savannah cried, snatching it from his hand. She quickly opened it, letting out a relieved sigh when she saw the pictures inside. She looked at Mac. "And my money? Did he leave it, too?"

Mac shook his head. "No money, but when we get to Angel Creek, I'm going to replace it." He took a deep breath, determined to sound sincere as he added, "So you can open your hat shop when you get back to Jamestown." He meant every word of it, but he still harbored a faint hope that she would change her mind and stay in Angel Creek. Marry *him*. Have *his* babies. Grow old with *him*. Without her, the money he'd been saving for *their* future lost its appeal.

"I couldn't take your money, Mac," she said gravely. "It wouldn't be proper."

"Proper?" Mac almost laughed, but caught himself in time. She was serious. Dead serious. "You're worried about proper after . . ." Hm. Judging by her narrowed eyes, he decided he should stop while he was still standing. He cleared his throat and tried a different tactic. "There's nothing wrong with a little loan between friends. When you get on your feet and start making a profit, you can pay me back."

She fell silent as if she were considering his offer. Finally she nodded. "In that case, I'll think about it. But it would be a *loan* only, understood?"

"Understood."

"We should go downstairs. Roy's probably fainting with hunger by now."

Mac chuckled. "More than likely he's eaten seconds and *thirds* by now." As she laughed and turned toward the door, Mac drew her back and into his arms. She tilted her face to his. He gazed down at her, his love for her so fierce it nearly choked him. "I'm sorry, Savannah."

As always, she didn't pretend not to understand. "Accepted." She rubbed her palm against his chest in an oddly tender gesture of assurance, her smile whimsical. "We have a lot in common, you know. Daddy tells me I have a suspicious nature, too."

His smile was wry. "In my line of work, it *pays* to be suspicious." He hesitated, then added with genuine regret, "But I should never have been suspicious of *you*."

"Nobody's perfect."

"*You* are," Mac argued softly. Her fingers slid between the buttons of his shirt; her unexpected caress made him jump.

"No, I'm not." Mischief danced in her eyes. "And later, I'm going to prove it to you."

After delivering that tantalizing remark, she pulled free of his embrace and opened the door. Mac stared after her, torn between temptation and dismay. *He* was the one who was supposed to do the luring, not Savannah.

"So what do we do now?" Roy asked, tearing a huge bite of meat from the chicken leg clutched in his hand. A pile of chicken bones sat at his elbow, testifying to his earlier declaration that this meal was his favorite. "We don't know where he's going from here, do we?"

Savannah absently swirled gravy into her mashed potatoes with her fork, considering Roy's question. What *was* her next move? Should she keep good her promise and return to Angel Creek, make amends with her father? She cringed at the thought. She knew her father better than most, and she could believe that he was sorry she'd left, but she didn't trust him to drop the subject of marriage. He was a shark of a businessman. He'd wait a few weeks . . . lull her into believing he accepted her decision to remain independent, then he would move in for the kill.

Who would it be this time? she wondered, only half listening to the conversation flowing between Roy and Mac. There were a number of men in Angel Creek who would love to marry her . . . for her money. Like Jon Paul De-Ment. She had known she wasn't in love with Jon Paul, but she had convinced herself she could eventually grow to love him, and she thought he loved her. How many times had she heard his smooth tongue declare that he wouldn't care if she were a pauper?

Then she'd found out the truth, and the truth had left her eyes wide open.

Her gaze lingered on Mac's face. She wanted a fine,

honest man like Mac. He would never marry for money, but he would marry to protect a lady's reputation.

Yet honor wasn't enough.

She loved Mac, but she wanted to be loved in return.

Her mind returned to the question at hand. Where to go from here? Should she sneak away and head back to Jamestown, ask her father to send money? George Carrington would, she knew, because deep inside his stubborn heart, she knew that he loved her.

Mac would be furious if she left. Savannah almost smiled as she imagined his reaction. He'd probably come charging after her with every intent of hauling her back to Angel Creek again.

The possibility wasn't an unpleasant one, Savannah realized, trying not to blush lest Mac notice and become suspicious. If she decided to continue the journey to Angel Creek, she would have more time with Mac, which was a strong lure. Once there, she could stay in town long enough to get more money for her business venture, then catch the train out again.

Away from her father and Angel Creek.

Away from Mac.

Savannah took a bite of her cold mashed potatoes and nearly choked trying to swallow the food. The thought of not seeing Mac again caused a painful constriction in her throat *and* her heart.

It also made her more determined than ever to make the coming night unforgettable.

Chapter Twenty-two

S he was plotting something.

    Mac could feel it, sense it, and damned near taste it. All through dinner Savannah had been as quiet as a mouse, eating little, talking less, and staring at him as if she were trying to memorize his features. Once he'd caught her blushing.

Now, back in their room, she was undressing behind the screen like a demure virgin instead of taunting him as she had done earlier. Had something changed? Mac thought back as he quickly shed his boots and shirt before climbing into bed, but couldn't think of anything that he might have said to offend her.

Maybe she'd had time to think about her teasing comment, and now regretted it. Maybe right at this moment she was attempting to figure out how she could retract her promise without losing face. His glance strayed to the bathing screen. She certainly appeared to be delaying the moment she had to climb into that bed with him.

Warming to his theory and plotting his revenge, Mac grinned wickedly. He kept his eye on the shadow moving behind the screen as he threw the covers aside and rose from the bed, wincing as the springs creaked. He shed his trousers, then quickly slid beneath the covers again.

Completely naked, and as always when he was around Savannah, completely aroused.

"Mac?"

He tensed, watching the outline of her figure behind the screen. "Yes?"

"Could you turn out the lamp for me?"

Her hesitant, shy request confirmed Mac's theory that Savannah was having second thoughts. Mac leaned over and twisted the wick, plunging the room into darkness. He fell back onto the pillow and propped his hands behind his head as he waited for Savannah to finish her toilette.

Perhaps she'd taken his lecture about waiting for marriage to heart, he mused, anticipating her reaction when she realized he was naked. He would assure her that she was safe, and let her relax.

Then he would casually curl up behind her—not touching her—just simply holding her like the trusted friend she kept insisting he was. With any luck she would get little sleep, thinking about what might have been. Perhaps she'd then start thinking about him in a new light . . . a *matrimonial* light.

The bed dipped, startling him from his devious thoughts. Just knowing she was now sliding beneath the covers next to him caused a dramatic leap in his erection. For his plan to work, he had to control his own raging impulses.

No small feat!

Her hand—or something—bumped against his hip. Mac started to smile, thinking she'd head for the edge of the bed for certain now that she probably realized he was naked.

He was wrong.

Bold fingers grazed his hip bone, curled around his

pulsing manhood, squeezed gently, then moved down. And up. And down. No mistake, no accident, but a conscious, deliberate sliding motion designed to drive him wild.

Mac sucked in a sharp breath of disbelief and raw lust. He let it out as slowly as he could, only to draw another one as she rolled over until her body came into contact with his.

Savannah was naked. Savannah was *naked,* as naked as he was. Gloriously, wondrously—and alarmingly—naked. Her breasts were flush against his side; he could feel her hard nipples as if they were stones.

She'd wanted the light out so that he wouldn't know she was naked until it was too late.

The realization made Mac groan in agony and defeat. Damn Hawk! He'd mentioned nothing about the possibility of a temptation such as this.

"Mac?" she whispered throatily, pressing closer, squeezing him tighter.

He swallowed hard, rigid as a board. Everywhere. Even his fingers were rigid as he dug them into the headboard to keep from touching her. "What?" It was nothing more than a hoarse whisper of a sound, but she obviously heard him.

"I've been thinking about you . . . *us,* a lot."

He could believe it. Oh, could he believe it! His chest felt tight as he struggled not to pant. Her fingers were hot and smooth as silk as she slowly stroked him. He was ever aware of her breasts brushing against his side as she moved her hand up and down.

It was agony.

It was bliss.

"Do you think . . ." Her seductive whisper in the darkness added to Mac's agony. "Could we just do it and not worry about tomorrow? I want to be loved by *you,* Mac, and no one else."

How could a man deny such a request?

"I think I might die if we don't."

He couldn't have her death on his conscious, could he?

Mac pried his fingers loose from the headboard, one by one. He forced himself to take deep, steady breaths, but they came out all shaky.

He realized he was trembling from head to toe.

Savannah was doing this to him. She was offering him something he'd craved for a very long time. True, she was offering her body and nothing else . . . but what if this offering were all he'd ever have of her? What if he managed to turn away from her now—as if he could!—and she never fell in love with him? He'd never stop cursing himself for missing out on having this one incredible night with her.

Yet if he gave in, if he let himself live for the moment, then Savannah's own craving would be satisfied, and the chase might be over before he won the prize.

"You started the fire, Mac." Her warm, moist mouth closed around his nipple; her tongue felt like tiny flickering flames as it darted in and out. "And now I'm burning."

Her provocative accusation prompted a guilty wince from Mac. She was right, and he knew it. He was the cause, which left him with a responsibility to douse the flames.

Or fan them into a roaring blaze.

Savannah took the decision out of his hands. In one startling, sensuous move, she rolled on top of him and sat up, pinning his erection between her warm, silken thighs.

Like before, only this time the barrier of his trousers was absent, her heat against him shockingly intense as it mingled with his own stick of fire. She placed her hands against his flat nipples and slowly drew her nails along his

chest, down across his belly, until her fingers rested lightly
on the tip of his arousal.

With a scoot that made him gasp, she moved so that she
could grasp his throbbing length with both of her clever little hands.

"If I force you, you can't feel guilty," she suggested
huskily, obviously sensing his hesitation.

Mac tried to chuckle at her naive threat, but moaned instead. If she'd only be still, maybe he could think! "You
can't force a man, Sav."

After a tiny silence, she demanded, "Why not?"

What could he tell her? That a man has to be willing,
and if he's willing, then there would be no force involved?
Shaking his head, Mac gave up. Explaining would waste
too much precious time.

He'd much rather show her. He slid his hands along her
smooth thighs, cupping her hips. "Savannah . . . are you
certain you want this?"

Instead of answering right away, Savannah took his
hand and placed it against her burning core. He could feel
her throbbing, and she was moist. Very moist.

"I'm sure, Mac," she whispered, arching her back as he
began to move his thumb back and forth. "I'm very sure."

With a low growl, Mac picked her up and laid her beside him. She protested, winding her arms around his neck.
He laughed and bent his mouth near hers. "I'm not leaving
you, just getting you into a better position."

"Oh." She sounded perplexed. Her hand came up and
cupped his chin. "Wasn't that a good position?"

"Yes, but the first time . . . The first time will hurt, Sav."

"I know."

Surprised, he drew back, trying to visualize her expression in the dark. "You do?" She didn't *sound* frightened at
the prospect.

"Alissa told me," she confessed. "She also told me that a man liked a woman to—to be on top of him."

Mac gave in to temptation and brought her breast close to his hungry mouth. He flicked his tongue over her nipple very lightly, then paused, allowing his breath to follow in its wake. "What else did she tell you?" he asked in a low voice, rejoicing when she shivered.

"Mac, kiss me there, please!"

But Mac delayed her pleasure long enough to demand roughly, "If I do, will you tell me?"

"Yes, yes!"

He nipped her with his teeth, darting at her nipple with his tongue as she had done to him. She moaned and arched into him.

Breathlessly she asked, "May I show you, instead?"

It was too great an offer to refuse. And Mac had to be honest with himself—he *was* curious. "Yes, you may show me . . . if you're certain?"

"I've never been more certain of anything in my life," she answered.

Mac allowed her to push him onto the pillows again. He tensed, wondering at her next move. Her hair brushed teasingly across his chest, then the silken swathe feathered his belly. Had she infiltrated his dreams? How else could Savannah know that he'd dreamed of her pale, glorious hair spread across his chest? Rigid with anticipation, Mac buried his hand in her thick hair and held tight.

Something warm and wet closed over the tip of his erection.

Her mouth, he realized an instant too late.

He jolted upright, grabbing at her shoulders. "Ahhhh! Savannah—"

"No, Mac." She pushed him forcefully down again with the flat of her hand. "You said I could show you."

But he hadn't known, hadn't dreamed she would do this. To go from sweet innocence to the most intimate act Mac could imagine in his wildest fantasies, was a shock to his mind *and* his system.

He halted her progress again. "You—you shouldn't," he said with effort, not understanding exactly why he didn't want her to continue. It was sweet torture, he couldn't deny. Yet . . . yet this was *Savannah!* His lady love, the woman he yearned to make his wife. She wasn't a practiced whore—

"Why not, Mac? Why can't I? You touched me . . . there with your mouth."

The image she evoked made Mac's mouth go dry. How to argue against such irrefutable logic? How to explain without sounding ridiculously prudish? He cleared his throat, his hands still holding her still. "We—we don't know each other that well, Sav—" he began lamely.

Her husky laughter sent chills rolling down his spine.

"Oh, Mac! You and I know each other *very* well. We've been friends forever, remember?"

Desperately, Mac tried another tactic, one that was also the truth. "If you continue, then my release will come early." He felt her grow very still beneath his hands, and stifled the urge to laugh. Finally, he'd gotten her attention! He fought to keep it. "Let *me* love *you* this first time." His voice lowered, became huskily persuasive. "Let me love you good and proper."

"Well, I don't know about *proper*," she teased, thankfully moving away from his throbbing erection. "But I certainly want you to love me."

Mac felt a quiver rush through him at her words, wishing she meant them literally. But he knew she didn't, and the knowledge pained him. "Come here, woman," he commanded. Savannah didn't love him, but after tonight, surely she would know that he loved her. He couldn't say the words, but he could show her.

She twisted around and rested her elbows on his chest, her soft breasts temptingly close to his mouth. They were nearly nose to nose, and he could feel her warm breath against his face. "Mac, I want you to know that I don't expect—" she began.

His finger against her lips shushed her. He replaced it with his mouth, kissing her with all the pent-up longing that swirled inside his chest. He kissed her with passion and with dominance; he kissed her with desperation and fear, because she didn't love him.

Most of all, he kissed her with love.

Tenderly he rolled her to the side and began to love her good and proper, sweeping his mouth along every exposed inch of her. Tasting, nibbling, licking, and sucking. He gorged himself on Savannah, vowing she would never forget him after this night. She was a delicious banquet, a feast to his starving soul, and he feasted.

She responded like the angel she was, moaning and clutching him, gasping when his lips found an extremely sensitive spot, stifling a scream when he plundered the hot core of her with his fingers. She was wet and tight, and Mac groaned, anticipating and fearing the moment when he would sink himself into her.

He'd had his share of women—mostly whores who knew how to please—but he'd never lain with a woman he loved. If he had known what an incredible difference it made, he might have remained a virgin until this time.

"Mac, I'm burning up!" Savannah whimpered.

"I am, too, sweetheart." Mac had never been more sincere. Still, he hesitated. "It will hurt—"

"I don't care!"

He smiled at her panting, vehement response, damning

the darkness that kept him from watching her beautiful face. He imagined it instead. Her cheeks would be flushed with desire, her eyes glazed and heavy. And those lips . . . those luscious lips would be parted with anticipation.

Gently spreading her legs, Mac rose above her arching, restless body. She was open and ready, waiting for him, wanting him. Her hands clutched his arms, urging him forward. Her hips bucked against him, reaching for him.

It was all he could do to keep from plunging ruthlessly into her, claiming her in one fell swoop as he cried his release in a primitive howl.

But he didn't, wary and mindful of her innocence. He gritted his teeth and sank into her inch by careful inch. Full and throbbing, pulsing and aching, he claimed Savannah as his own, if only in his heart.

She embraced him as if she knew it.

Then she grew still, but Mac sensed it was an expectant stillness . . . a waiting one. He continued to ease into her, glorying in the sensations that coursed through his body. Fire and ice mingled in his veins . . . roared through his head and into his heart.

He wondered if she felt the same.

"Mac," she whispered. "Oh, Mac. It's everything I expected. Don't stop now. Please don't stop!"

He didn't intend to. He couldn't. When he met resistance, he hesitated but a second before he pushed through it and buried himself to the hilt.

Savannah began to move again before he could begin to wonder how much she hurt. Her hips rose then fell as if she couldn't get enough. Her nails dug into his arms, pulling his weight onto her. Chest to breasts, their mouths met unerringly in the dark. Tongues clashed in a fever of rising desire. Mac drank her mouth as if it were wine, and became light-headed.

Exhilarated by her response, he set a slow, sweet, agonizing pace, and each time he thrust into her, he felt as if he claimed her anew. This was his woman, his life mate. Why else would he feel this glory, this unearthly pleasure in loving her?

"Savannah, oh, God, Savannah," he whispered, his throat aching with unmanly tears. He buried his face in her neck and inhaled her rich scent. She was *his*! She *had* to be his!

Her hands roamed urgently along his back and shoulders, down to his buttocks. She kept them there, and with each thrust, she clutched him tighter to her, urging him closer, deeper. She had begun to whimper, her head tossing to and fro on the pillow.

Sensing that her release was near, Mac rose slightly and captured her thrusting nipple with his teeth. He suckled hard, feeling the blood rush to his manhood as his own pleasure crested. A low moan warned him just in time to close his mouth over hers, capturing her scream.

He tumbled with her over the edge, his entire body rigid with the strength of his release. It seemed to last forever, as if time stood still just for this precious moment. The sound of their harsh breathing receded until there was nothing left but the pounding of their hearts.

Mac was stunned at the miracle he'd experienced in the arms of the woman he loved. He rolled to the side and held her close to his heart. His lips trailed over her damp forehead as he mouthed the words *I love you.*

Chapter Twenty-three

Savannah awakened as dawn began to filter through the curtains, bathing the hotel room in its fragile new light.

She felt fragile and new. Fragile because of the burgeoning ache in her heart, and new because Mac had made her complete. He had unveiled the mystery of love.

He lay curled behind her, spoon fashion, one leg flung over her own, his arm draped over her hips in an unconsciously possessive gesture that made Savannah smile. When he awakened, would he realize she had deliberately seduced him? Would he know that she had come to bed brazenly naked in the hopes of making him forget his honorable vows?

She could not tell him why she'd made such a bold move. She couldn't explain to Mac that she loved him, and wanted to have this one night of making love with him to carry her through the rest of her life. If she told him, Mac would insist on doing the honorable thing; he would want to marry her. And when she protested, he would claim he loved her.

Savannah knew that he didn't, not as a woman, not as a man should love a wife. He *wanted* her—yes. Respected her—no doubt. Cared for—it was obvious. They were dear friends. Perhaps for some women those important factors would have been enough. Maybe she was just being self-ish in wanting more.

She was a lot wiser after spending a few hours talking to Alissa. She'd learned how to tempt a man beyond rea-son. Alissa had also confirmed what Mac had told her; that both love and lust did not have to be present to experience the joy of coupling, at least for a man. Since Savannah loved Mac, she couldn't say if it could be the same for a woman.

Loving Mac had made their joining unforgettable.

Against her back, Savannah became aware that Mac's breathing had changed. So, the coming of dawn had awak-ened him, too, she mused. What was he thinking as he lay next to her? Was he struggling against his conscience at this very moment as he recalled their fiery night? If she knew Mac at all—and she thought she did—he would be rehearsing his guilt-prompted proposal. Mac was a con-vincing liar, and loving him as she did, she knew that it would take tremendous willpower to remember that it was the honorable Mac speaking and not Mac the man.

He spoke, his voice husky from sleep. "Did you sleep well?"

Savannah smiled. She could feel his manhood stirring to life against her back. Her breasts grew taut in response; her nipples sprang to life. Maybe she could distract him, postpone the inevitable speech, the inevitable ending. "*Very* well. And you?"

"Mm. We've got an early train to catch," he reminded her. Yet, instead of rising, he pushed her hair aside and began nuzzling her neck. The rough pads of his fingers drifted over her stomach, searching and finding proof of her alertness.

She sucked in a sharp breath as he began to roll her nipple between his thumb and forefinger. Her words came out slightly strangled. "We've got another hour or two. Perchance we could . . . ?" His chuckle rumbled through her body, clear down to her toes.

"Aren't you sore, sweetheart?"

"Yes. No." Savannah licked her dry lips and slowly, languidly, stretched her body. "Why don't we find out?" she asked, turning into his arms so that she faced him. His arousal throbbed hotly against her belly, shooting a thrill straight to her toes.

She gazed into his desire-laden eyes. They were the color of moss in the dawn light, framed by thick auburn lashes. His lips were tilted slightly, revealing a disarming dimple she hadn't noticed before. "We—we should take advantage of the time we have left, don't you think?"

Amusement further darkened his beautiful eyes to a rich forest green, but he made no protest when she boldly rose and straddled him. She bent forward, her hair falling around them, enclosing them in a cocoon of hushed silence. Their mouths met in a sweet kiss of remembrance.

The sweetness lasted but a moment. Savannah gasped as Mac thrust his hand through her hair and clutched the nape of her neck, deepening the kiss with unrestrained passion. He made a low, growling noise in his throat when she opened her mouth under his.

His manhood throbbed and pulsed between her legs, reminding her of last night's pleasure. Without thought, Savannah lifted her hips to take him inside her. She would make for herself one last memory. . . .

"No." Mac's throat felt raw, as if he'd had to rip the word out. And he damned near did. He didn't want her to stop.

Of course he didn't. What was he thinking when he stilled her hips and told her no?

But he knew. Mac knew *exactly* what he was thinking. It was a selfish thought. How could Savannah think loving thoughts when lust clouded her vision? How would she ever see him in a matrimonial light if he was constantly giving in to her desires without asking for a commitment?

Mac recalled something he'd once heard his grandmother say; *Why buy the cow if you can get the milk free?* His grandmother had been talking about a girl who'd gotten into trouble by giving herself before marriage. Her intended had broken the engagement and moved on to greener pastures.

As ludicrous as it seemed, Mac understood his grandmother's sage cliché far better now, at this moment with Savannah poised above him. There was no guarantee that Hawk's plan would work, true. Savannah was a woman— a unique woman, granted—but she didn't think like a man. Yet what did Mac have to lose by trying to tempt her into marriage by any means possible—including the strong lure of desire?

Last night she'd caught him off guard, climbing into bed naked and rattling his brain by taking the initiative. But he was alert now, on his guard against her persuasive treachery.

Or so he thought.

He gazed into her bewildered face, her raw, natural beauty silhouetted in the dawn's early light. Her breasts were firm, her waist tiny, her hips flaring gently. A ball of pain and regret formed in his throat, preventing speech. Helplessly he watched her luscious lips move.

"Mac . . . what's wrong? Why can't we do it one last time?"

Mac swallowed hard, quivering from the effort of holding her away from his pulsing need. "And afterward?" he rasped almost angrily. "Do we then go back to being friends?" Voicing the burning question escalated Mac's anger. "We pass each other on the street as if this never happened? Can you truly do that, Savannah?" She squirmed restlessly. Mac gasped and gripped her hips tighter to hold her still, to keep her from swallowing him, and to stop himself from plunging savagely into her.

Despite his anger, he wanted her no less than before.

"Do you truly think that I can waltz back into Angel Creek, stand before your father, and look him in the eye knowing I've taken advantage of his daughter? He expected me to *protect* you, to bring you home safely!"

There was an answering spark of anger in Savannah's eyes as she said, "We made love by *mutual* agreement, Mac. You did not take advantage of me! If anything, I tempted you, so if you insist on bringing guilt into it, then I'm just as guilty." She tossed her head, sending her hair flying over her shoulders. Her chin thrust forward, nearly bumping his own. Contrary to her expression, her voice lowered to a familiar, seductive whisper. "If you're going to feel guilty, Mac, then at least do something to feel guilty about."

She kissed him then, smothering any further protests, and scattering Mac's resistance to the wind. With their mouths locked together, she took his hands from her hips, braced her own hands on the mattress, and slowly enveloped his manhood with her heat. She took all of him inside her in one single earth-shattering stroke.

Mac was lost. He made a halfhearted effort to dislodge her, but she held fast to his hips.

She began to rock against him, slowly at first, revealing her uncertainty, reminding Mac of her innocence. Her hesitancy struck a tender cord in Mac. With a moan of surrender, he twined his fingers with hers and began to guide her forward strokes.

He watched her abandonment, awed and amazed at the sexuality that literally seeped from her luscious body. She was a goddess to love . . . and he was her slave.

"You are beautiful," he murmured.

She gave him a heart-stopping smile as she rode him good and proper. "So are you, Mac. So are you." Her breath hitched, and her facial muscles began to grow taut. Her grip on his hands tightened. "You—you fill me so completely," she added breathlessly.

"You enjoy this . . . very much," he observed, his breath quickening as his own release drew near.

"Yes."

"If we were married," he gasped out desperately, "you and I could enjoy it often."

He'd waited too long; Savannah didn't hear him. She arched her back, her movements frenzied now, her mind not on his words, but on the pleasure that was engulfing her. A keening moan rose in her throat. Her grip became a death grip.

"Maaaaac!"

She stiffened, and Mac could feel her inner muscles convulsing around him. It was the catalyst that toppled him after her. He spilled his seed into her with a low growl of primitive satisfaction, bringing her forward to cover her mouth with a savage kiss of gratitude and love.

The sound of their harsh breathing filled the room for several moments. Mac rolled sideways, cuddling her close as they continued to catch their breath. He swept her damp hair away from her face and planted a tender kiss on her forehead.

"Marry me," he said. She buried her face in his neck, but he heard her muffled "no" clearly. Instead of asking why and getting the same painful answer, he argued, "Yes. You *will* marry me."

"No, Mac. I won't marry you, and you know why."

He did. But he'd rather forget it and he didn't agree. "What if we've made a baby? What then? Will you still say no?" It was a nasty thrust, but Mac was a desperate man.

She shrugged, lifting her face slightly away from his throat. But she didn't look at him, leaving him to wonder what she might be hiding.

"If I discover that I'm going to have a baby, then when I reach Jamestown, I'll be the sad widow Carrington," she said evenly. "Nobody will be the wiser. Anyone who remembers me will also believe I was married to you."

If she had slapped him, Mac could not have been more insulted and hurt. Savannah would rather live a lie than to marry him. She couldn't have said it any plainer. She didn't want him—couldn't bear the thought of marriage to him. What she felt for him was nothing more than friendship . . . and lust.

He had lost.

A pounding on the door saved Mac from further humiliation. It was Roy.

"Get up, you sleepyheads! They're serving breakfast, and our train leaves in an hour!" Without waiting for them to respond, Roy pounded on the door a second time. "Mac? Mrs. Cord? You two up yet?"

"We're up!" Mac shouted, cursing as he flung back the covers. The brat was as irritating as a mosquito sometimes.

Savannah caught his shoulder before he could rise. He looked into her luminous, crystal blue eyes and waited, knowing it was useless to hope she had changed her mind.

"We'll have to explain to Roy before we reach Angel Creek," she said softly.

Roy believed they were married. Of course. Mac managed a smile, although it felt tight and insincere. "I'll speak to him." Her brow furrowed, and Mac successfully fought the urge to kiss her troubles away. Was there nothing the woman could do to make him hate her, to help ease his pain?

"Do you think he'll understand? He saw us in the forest . . . and he's so young."

"He already loves you." *As I do.* "He'd never think badly of you."

She clutched the covers to her chest, sighing. "I hope you're right, because I've grown fond of him as well."

Mac rose from the bed and began to dress. Gruffly he said, "You could always tell him what you told me, that you never intend to marry."

"I never said that I wouldn't marry, Mac. If I could find someone like—"

When she bit off the words with suspicious haste, he turned a narrow-eyed gaze on her. Jealousy nearly ripped his heart in two. "Like who, Sav?" he demanded softly. Her bright gaze slid away from his. *Barlow, perhaps?*

"Never mind."

"Sav—"

"I'm *starving* out here, people!" Roy thundered, pounding on the door again. "I've lost ten pounds just standing here!"

Mac scowled at the door, tempted to jerk it open, haul Roy up by the seat of his pants, and shake him until his teeth rattled. "Go ahead without us!" he snarled. He turned back to Savannah. His breath froze in his lungs.

She had risen from the bed in all her naked glory, unaware that he watched her as she began to get dressed. God, she was so beautiful, so achingly beautiful.

Resolutely Mac dragged his gaze away and finished dressing. It didn't matter how wonderful, how talented, how sweet and unselfish, how beautiful, how lusty Savannah was. She wasn't his and never would be. What made him think God would allow him such an angel for his own?

Ten minutes later Mac opened their hotel door and stepped into the hall with Savannah on his arm. He reached behind him to close the door just as the door down the hall opened. A couple stepped out, a younger woman with an older man who looked vaguely familiar.

"Mackenzy Cord? Is that you?" the older man called out, a huge, welcoming grin on his face. "I haven't seen you in church in ages."

Mac remembered the face, and he knew by the way Savannah gasped and tried to hide behind him that she had recognized the preacher, too. The younger woman with him was Mattie Owens, his daughter.

"Mac!" she whispered fiercely. "It's Preacher Owens! *Do* something!"

For the first time in his life, Mac couldn't think of a quick, convincing lie. There wasn't much chance that the preacher and his daughter hadn't noticed them emerging from their room.

Together.

What *could* he say? Savannah was a young, unattached female with a pristine reputation. Her father was a pillar of the community, her family name one well remembered and revered in the small town of Angel Creek.

He was a bounty hunter, and although he was well liked by most, he was a bachelor and most likely considered dangerous to unattached females due to his unusual occupation. Being seen in public with Mac might raise a few eyebrows and generate a few whispers; getting caught coming out of a hotel room was quite another matter entirely.

Mentally bracing himself as Preacher Owens and his

daughter sauntered toward them, Mac grabbed Savannah's arm and yanked her to his side. Didn't she realize that hiding behind him would only deepen suspicions?

When Mattie saw Savannah, her eyes widened. She wasn't a pretty woman, but she had an interesting, lively face that detracted from her sallow skin and lackluster hair.

"Savannah Carrington! Imagine bumping into you here!" Mattie cried. "And that *is* Mackenzy Cord, Father. Larger than life."

The preacher noticed what his daughter had overlooked, Mac saw. The older man's gaze strayed from Savannah, to Mac, then to the hotel door they had just emerged from. When a suspicious frown settled on the preacher's lined face, Mac's heart sank. He felt Savannah's grip on his arm tighten to a painful degree.

"Miss Carrington," Preacher Owens acknowledged with a brief nod as he reached them. His frown deepened into open disapproval. "I hope you're on your way home. Your father has worried himself sick since your . . . disappearance."

Mattie's mouth formed a perfect O. "I'd forgotten!" she blurted out, then blushed furiously. "Sorry, Savannah. Father says I don't think before I speak sometimes."

Mac heard a tiny squeak from Savannah, but nothing more. Apparently she was speechless. He didn't blame her. "As a matter of fact, we *are* on our way home," Mac informed him cordially.

"Ah, yes, George mentioned that he'd sent someone to fetch her." Preacher Owens gazed at him with such intensity that Mac had to fight the urge to squirm like a naughty schoolboy caught peering up the teacher's dress. "I trust you've taken good care of her?"

His gaze strayed to the hotel door, leaving Mac in no doubt of his meaning. Resigned to play out yet another charade, Mac said, "*Very* good care of her, sir. In fact, you and Miss Owens might as well be the first to hear our good news." He took a deep breath and prayed that he was doing the right thing. Surely Savannah could see that there was no other way?

"What good news is that, pray tell?"

"Savannah and I got married," Mac announced, pasting a proud smile on his face.

Chapter Twenty-four

The moment she heard Mac say the words, Savannah began to pray she'd heard him wrong.

"Got married?" Preacher Owens repeated as if he, too, couldn't believe his ears.

Unfortunately he confirmed Savannah's worst fears; Mac *had* said the damning words! She moaned and buried her face in his shoulder. Did Mac have the slightest idea what he'd done? This wasn't a nameless face they'd never see again—this was her *pastor!*

Forcing a chuckle, Mac gave her trembling back a comforting pat. Savannah wanted to snatch up his lying hand and sink her teeth into it.

"You'll have to excuse my wife," Mac said cheerfully. "She's rather tired from last night."

Savannah risked a peek from between her fingers, and what she saw made her groan again. The preacher's face had suffused with embarrassed color. Mattie stood with her mouth agape, her eyes round saucers of maidenly shock.

Mac had gone too far! Rousting herself, Savannah lifted her face from Mac's shoulder and faced the couple in front of her. She knew her face was flaming, but there was noth-

ing she could do about the telltale color. With what little
dignity she could muster, she sought to undo the damage
Mac's wicked remark had caused. "What Mac meant was
that I spent most of the night rehearsing my speech to
Daddy. He's going to be understandably surprised when he
hears the news."

Mattie snapped her mouth shut, looking disappointed.
"Oh."

Preacher Owens drew in a relieved breath and beamed
at her. "Of course, of course! I knew what he meant. And
it's good that you're preparing what to say before you arrive.
George expected you to marry Jon Paul DeMent , didn't he?"

Savannah spoke hurriedly to cover the sound of Mac's
ominous growl. "Yes, he did, but he knows that I've
changed my mind, and he's always thought very highly of
Mac. Once he adjusts, I know he'll be pleased."

Preacher Owens nodded thoughtfully. "He'll want to
arrange a proper wedding, of course, in our church."

Oh . . . dear . . . God! Savannah's knees went weak. She
clutched Mac's strong arm for support, when what she really yearned to do was close her hands around his neck and
strangle him! "Yes . . . yes, of course." What more could
she say without arousing suspicion, thanks to Mac?

"What brings you to Paradise?"

It was Mac who asked the question, looking disgust-
ingly happy about the entire miserable charade. Savannah
shot him a murderous look that he ignored.

"We were on our way home from Richmond when Ju-
dith developed one of her sick headaches," Preacher
Owens explained. "We disembarked from the train . . . the
noise, the smoke." He clucked his tongue in sympathy.
"This episode is particularly bad. We've been in Paradise
for two days now, but we hope to leave in the morning.

Mattie and I were going downstairs for a bite to eat. Would you care to—"

"What in the hell is keeping you two so long?" a familiar voice bellowed from the stairwell. Footsteps pounded along the hall as Roy came trotting toward them, his coat flapping against his legs. He had a firm hand planted on top of his hat to keep it from sailing backward.

Savannah froze, wishing the floor would open up and swallow her. She had not thought the situation could get any worse!

"I'm starving, waiting on you two, and what are you doing?" Roy panted, reaching them. "Chatting it up with this old—"

Mac very casually reached out and clamped a hand over Roy's mouth. "*Preacher* Owens, Miss Owens, meet our new friend, Roy Hunter. He'll be going home with us, and you will most definitely see him in *church*."

Not even Roy, who was known to be a little slow taking hints, failed to understand Mac's threat. His eyes widened above Mac's hand. Mac slowly took his hand away.

"Um, sorry, Preacher. I didn't know you was a preacher." When Mac elbowed him, he hastily bowed to Mattie. "Sorry, ma'am."

Preacher Owens squeezed Roy's shoulder hard enough to make him wince. He smiled at the boy, his eyes glinting with amusement. "No harm done, son. I'll look forward to seeing you in church."

"Yes—yes, sir," Roy stammered, gulping hard.

They'd been on the train for two hours before Mac lost his patience with Savannah. She wouldn't speak to him, not one single word. In fact, she wouldn't look at him, either.

"Go get something to eat, Roy," Mac ordered the restless boy in a voice that brooked no argument.

But, of course, Roy argued anyway.

"But I'm not hungry!"

"Then go pester the engineer."

Roy perked up at this. "Really? He won't mind?"

Mac didn't care if he did. "Go."

When Roy had gone, Mac sat next to Savannah, who had shown him nothing but her profile since the train pulled out of Paradise. He eyed the angry thrust of her jaw and sighed. Of course she was furious, but dammit, what else could he have said to Preacher Owens?

He folded his arms and studied his boots. Finally he asked, "Would you have preferred that I let the preacher assume the worst about you?"

She didn't blink or move a muscle. She continued to sit with her hands clenched tightly in her lap, staring out the window as if the scenery was the most awe-inspiring sight she'd ever witnessed. It *was* beautiful country, full of rich green forestry and majestic hills. But they'd been seeing the same scenery for two hours, so Mac knew she wasn't *that* interested.

Mac tried again. "Your reputation would have been ruined. Your father would have been devastated. I had no choice." He felt a flash of hope when she stirred slightly; that hope turned to anger when he realized that she'd turned more fully away from him.

"Is it such a horrible thought being married to me, Sav?" he prompted softly, attempting to quell his rising anger. Stubborn minx!

Still, she didn't answer.

He reached out and cupped her chin, forcing her to look at him. His eyes blazed into hers as he ground out, all pretense of patience gone now, "Have you forgotten how good we are together? Because if you have, I can certainly remind you."

"I have no intention of marrying you just to protect my reputation . . . or because we please each other in bed," she stated bluntly.

So bluntly Mac winced. "And what of our friendship? You can't deny that friendship is an added boon to any relationship."

She gave him a pitying look. "Mac, none of those reasons are enough to convince me to marry you."

"What about love?" Mac declared recklessly. If he'd lost anyway, what harm would it do to confess his true feelings? At least Savannah would know how he felt.

A tender, rueful smile curved her mouth. "I wondered how long it would take you to get around to claiming you loved me." She shook her head, her eyes shimmering with tears. "Oh, Mac, you are the sweetest, most honorable man I know. That's exactly why I don't believe you. You'd say or do anything to convince me, just to protect me." She pulled from his grasp and presented him her profile again.

Frustration nearly choked Mac. She didn't believe him! He'd never considered that she might not believe him when he finally told her. For a few moments, Mac sat fuming in silence. He'd never met such a stubborn, willful, mistrustful woman in his life! Selfish motives aside, he had to make her understand the import of what they'd done—what *he'd* done—in telling Preacher Owens they were married.

Soon everyone in Angel Creek would know. Mattie Owens and the preacher would spread the news—not as malicious gossip, Mac knew—but in joyful celebration. George Carrington's battle to find a suitable husband for his wealthy daughter was no secret.

News traveled fast in a small community like Angel Creek, and with the use of telegraphy, Mac wouldn't be surprised if George didn't find out before they could tell him. And while the prospect of marrying Savannah at last made his heart beat faster, Mac didn't want an unwilling bride on his hands. An *angry* unwilling bride. He'd spoiled her plans for the future—

The reminder of her plans gave Mac an idea. He didn't like it but he loved Savannah enough to want her to be happy, with or without him.

"Savannah, what if we go ahead with the wedding? Then, after a while . . . a month or two, maybe, we could move to Jamestown. You could open your shop, and I could go about my own business. Take up bounty hunting again. You said yourself you weren't certain you ever wanted to marry, and I, well, I don't have any plans to marry, either." *If I can't have you,* he added silently. "We could be married but live apart." The words pained him to the depths of his soul, but he was desperate to make her see the potential disaster that could arise if she refused to marry him when they reached Angel Creek.

The preacher and his daughter had witnessed their exit from a hotel room. If they didn't marry, there would be whispers and speculation. Savannah's reputation would be quietly and thoroughly ripped to shreds.

Savannah spoke, so softly that Mac had to lean close to hear her.

"What do I care what the people of Angel Creek say about me if I'm not going to be living there?"

Mac felt like shaking her. "And your father? Do you not care that he'll be left behind to suffer the whispers and gossip? That every time you return to visit people will be talking about you, pointing at you, whispering behind your back?" Mac had never cared what people thought about him, but he knew women were different. Even Savannah, as strong-willed and brash as she was, would be affected.

"Will you at least think about my suggestion? I swear to

you that I won't stand in your way when you decide to leave Angel Creek. I'll leave at the same time, and no one will be the wiser." It would give him an opportunity to continue his pursuit of Barlow, he thought.

"In the meantime," she whispered, "we live as husband and wife?"

"I don't see any other way, do you?"

She turned to look at him, her eyes searching his face for something Mac couldn't fathom. "You would do this for me, Mac? Why?"

It was on the tip of Mac's tongue to repeat that he loved her, that living with her could never be a hardship, but her penetrating gaze lodged the declaration in his throat. She'd said she didn't believe him, and right now, in the emotional state she was in, he realized the futility of trying to convince her.

"Because you're my friend, Sav. I care a lot about you, and I don't want what's happened between us to ruin the rest of your life."

Her gaze softened as she reminded him, "No regrets, Mac. We agreed there would be no regrets."

"Then let's make certain, shall we?" he coaxed. "Let's get married." He held his breath as she continued to study him for a long, tense moment.

Finally she nodded.

Mac gripped the seat to keep from jumping to his feet and shouting for joy. No need to get ahead of himself, he cautioned. Savannah might marry him, but that didn't mean she would love him. Still, he would have more time, more opportunities to make an impact on her soul. Then, if she still insisted on leaving when the time came, perhaps she'd soon realize how much she missed him and come back to him.

It was his only hope.

Savannah grabbed his arm, startling him out of his thoughts and nearly out of his skin. Her voice was urgent as she pointed along the aisle. "Mac, look! Roy's in trouble."

Mac saw Roy standing near the entrance to the door leading to the observation desk. Towering over him was a huge bear of a man, red-faced and obviously angry. Even from this distance Mac could see the fear in Roy's expression.

Before Mac could reach them, the man grabbed Roy by the collar of his coat and lifted him high. He shook him as if he weighed nothing more than a pesky pup. "Teach you to try and pick my pockets!" the man roared. He turned with Roy dangling from his ham-sized fist and strode through the door to the open deck.

A red haze formed before Mac's eyes as he went after them. Sure, the kid irritated him sometimes, but he'd be damned if he'd let anyone mistreat him!

Mac's heart nearly stopped at the scene that met his eyes when he burst through the door. The man was dangling Roy over the side of the rail by the collar of his coat. Roy's face was bleached white, and his legs flayed helplessly in the air. Mac had never seen such terror in a kid's eyes before.

And he never wanted to again.

"Take it easy, mister," Mac warned the man in a low voice so as not to startle him. "You drop him, and he could die."

The man looked at Mac, then dismissed him with a snarl. The shoulder seams of his coat strained beneath the man's massive muscles. "He's a thief! He tried to pick my pockets, but I caught him red-handed!"

"The boy's with me. Put him down."

"Did you hear what I said? He tried to pick my—"

"If he needs to be punished, then *I'll* do the punishing."

"Looks like your brand of punishment doesn't work!" the man shouted, lowering Roy so that his heels bumped against the cross ties between the tracks.

"Do something, Mac!" Roy squeaked.

With a disgruntled sigh, Mac pulled out his gun and jammed it into the man's back. He'd tried to end this the nice way, but now it was time to get serious. "If you drop him, I'm going to shoot you. Is he worth dying over?"

The man's eyes widened. He looked at the gun, then back at Mac. He sneered, "I'm unarmed. You would shoot a man in the back? What kind of man are you?"

Mac's eyes narrowed at the brute's unspoken challenge. With a careless shrug, he threw the gun from the train. "How about we just settle this man to man? After you put the boy down, of course."

Roy shrieked, trying to twist around to see him. "Mac! I don't think throwing your gun away was a good idea! Did you get a good look at those—"

"Be quiet, Roy," Mac ordered. To the man he deliberately taunted, "Or are you afraid?"

For a moment, the man just stared at Mac, astounded. Then he threw back his head and laughed. When his laughter finally died away, he pulled Roy in and pitched him onto the deck. Roy scrambled to his feet and plastered himself against the coach wall, his terrified gaze darting between the two men.

The man was big. Mac came to his burly shoulders and was half as wide—and he was no small man. They eyed each other warily, waiting to see who would make the first move.

Mac remained relaxed, his arms hanging loosely at his side. He waited, his gaze intent on the man's face, on his eyes. They flickered once. Twice.

One beefy fist rose in the air, and Mac took a casual step forward, chopping the side of his hand into the man's windpipe.

The surprised brute clutched his throat and gagged, his face turning purple. While he was occupied with trying to breathe again, Mac sank his fist into the man's stomach, doubling him over. And while he was on his knees, Mac landed a hard blow to the back of his neck. He collapsed to the deck in a heap, unconscious.

Mac ran a hand through his hair, straightened his vest, and reached for Roy. He hauled him across the threshold and into the passenger coach, passed an open-mouthed Savannah—who'd been watching through the door—and to their seats.

Once there, he pushed Roy down and stood over him, tempering his silent fury. "You just cost me a good gun, brat."

Roy's mouth opened and closed. He regarded Mac with eyes brimming with admiration and awe. "You were wonderful, Mac! Where did you learn to—"

"Never mind where I learned to fight," Mac snapped, driving his fingers through his hair again. "You nearly got yourself killed! What if you had been alone?"

The boy's face fell into a scowl. "He accused me of trying to pick his pockets, Mac! I didn't, I swear!"

"Then what *were* you doing to make the man think it?"

Savannah came up silently behind Mac, then promptly sat down on the seat opposite Roy's. Mac spared her a quick glance, noting that she looked pale and stunned. She had probably thought the man would drop Roy, he mused, growing mad all over again.

"He had this—this pocket watch," Roy explained, thrusting his chin out in a defensive way Mac was beginning to recognize. "It was shaped like a wolf's head. I was *looking* at it, and he thought I was trying to steal it."

Green eyes clashed with brown. Mac stared at Roy long and hard, weighing the truth of his words with the honesty of his expression. Either he was a fool, or the boy was telling the truth, he decided. Expelling an exasperated sigh, Mac sat down beside Savannah. Delayed reaction set in, and he began to tremble. He couldn't seem to shake the image of Roy's terrified face from his mind. What if the bastard had accidentally dropped Roy? He closed his eyes, trying to blot out the horrible image of Roy tumbling head-over-heels along the tracks until he came to rest, broken, bleeding, perhaps dead.

"Mac, are you all right?"

It was Savannah's sweet voice that revived him and thankfully dispersed the horrid images. He opened his eyes to find her face close to his own, her eyes clouded with concern. He smiled faintly. "I'm fine. It's the brat you need to worry about. I'm surprised he's lived *this* long." He hesitated, captivated by her tender gaze. "Do you still think he's bounty-hunter material, darling?" The endearment had been intentional, and he was overjoyed to note that she didn't object.

"Hey, that's not fair—"

"I don't know, Mac," Savannah said softly, ignoring Roy's protest as she continued to gaze into Mac's eyes. "Maybe you were right. Maybe he's not cut out for the dangerous job of hunting down criminals."

"Now, wait just a damned—" Roy sputtered, only to be interrupted again by Mac.

"He *is* a little rash," Mac agreed.

"And hasty."

"Yes. Wouldn't hurt for him to mature, learn to stay out of trouble. Stop cursing."

"Hm," Savannah agreed. "Curb his curiosity before it gets us *all* killed."

"Fine," Roy snapped. He folded his arms and slumped against the seat, sulking. "Go ahead and talk about me like I'm not here. When you two finish rearranging my character, let me know. I just got one thing to say. I did *not* try to steal that bastard's watch!"

Mac and Savannah burst out laughing.

Chapter Twenty-five

Her eyes unfocused, Savannah watched the hypnotic sway of the telegraph lines rushing by outside her window.

In less than thirty minutes the train would pull into Angel Creek, and Savannah would disembark as Mac's wife. They had lied to the preacher and Mattie Owens, and Roy and everyone else along the way.

There was no way out.

She would become Mac's wife, and while the idea thrilled to the very heart of her, in an odd way it also repulsed her. She knew Mac was doing it just to save her reputation. She'd be married to a man she loved but who didn't love her. She'd have to live with a man who thought of her as a dear friend and nothing more.

Savannah shuddered, staring out the window to keep from looking at Mac again. Each time she looked at him, she got lost in the jade depths of his eyes. He was so tender, yet exciting. Considerate, yet demanding. He was everything she'd ever dreamed of finding in a man, and he'd been right beneath her nose most of her life!

How could she have been so blind?

He had brought her more pleasure than she could imagine, and yet he was nothing more than a friend to her. A lover and a friend. Her father had hired him to bring her back to Angel Creek, but instead Mac was forced to bring her back as his bride.

A chill swept over Savannah. It was all her fault, and eventually Mac would realize it. He'd start to resent her. The resentment would turn into hate.

She couldn't bear it to happen!

But there was no other way. She'd thought and pondered and plotted, but to no avail. They had lied to Preacher Owens, and he believed them to be wed, had seen them emerge as lovers from the hotel room. Yes, she could run again, before her father could arrange a proper wedding, but she wasn't a coward, and she couldn't do such a thing to her father again. He would be humiliated, and very probably Mac would become the hunted instead of the hunter. George Carrington had always been fiercely protective of her; it wasn't likely that he had changed since she'd been away.

Sending Mac after her . . . offering him a large sum of money was proof that her daddy hadn't changed. He wanted her safely married, she knew, and in his heart he meant well. Savannah sighed, conscious of Mac watching her profile. George Carrington would finally get his wish, but at what cost to Mac?

The only way she could redeem herself was to do everything in her power to make the situation as painless as possible for Mac. After the wedding—the *real* wedding—they would wait a few weeks, then announce their decision to move to Jamestown. She would then go her way, and Mac would be free of this impossible trap.

In the meantime she would try to make it up to Mac in the only way she knew how; by loving him.

• • •

In another ten minutes Mac would realize his dream; that of introducing Savannah as his wife. Only she wasn't, not yet. But she would be very, very soón, if Mac knew George Carrington. Carrington was a businessman through and through, and he would leave nothing to chance. Mac and Savannah would be married before the entire church congregation so there would be no question, for better or for worse, for richer or for poorer.

Lawfully and legally.

Mac took a deep breath as the full impact of what he'd inadvertently done sank in.

Savannah didn't look too happy about it, Mac reflected as he eyed her ramrod-straight back and the way her chin angled forward and out. In profile, her eyes held a bright gleam of something he couldn't identify.

He thought it might be fear.

Hoping to ease her tension, Mac leaned forward to whisper teasingly in her ear, "If you don't find a smile before we get off this train, your daddy's going to think I've been mistreating his little girl."

She turned abruptly, her eyes so full of misery that Mac felt his heart leap in sympathy. He recognized the gleam now—it was tears.

"Oh, Mac, I'm so sorry," she whispered. "This is all my fault!"

I'm so sorry. Mac struggled to hide the pain her words caused. He forced a tight smile as he drawled, "I believe there were two of us in that bed, making mad, passionate love."

She didn't look appeased, casting a quick glance at Roy before she whispered the delicious reminder, "But I came to bed *naked.*"

"So did I."

"It was my fault!"

"It wasn't anybody's fault," Mac argued patiently. If only she knew how her words wounded him. "We wanted each other, so we made love. You said yourself there should be no regrets. We never intentionally set out to hurt anyone—which is why we're going to get off this train as Mr. and Mrs. Mackenzy Cord." Taking her cold hands in his, he gave them a gentle squeeze, but his eyes glinted with mischief as he added in a low, seductive voice, "Just think of all the fun we're going to have playing house."

"You're wicked, Mac." But there was a ghost of a smile playing about her mouth and a heartening glint of anticipation in her eyes. "We don't have to tell anyone right away."

Mac lifted a chiding brow. "Would you rather George hear it from someone else?"

She didn't hesitate. "No, I wouldn't."

"Then we'll tell him together." Belatedly Mac remembered that George wouldn't be as shocked as Savannah expected him to be. But he couldn't explain—couldn't tell her. If she knew that he'd declared his love for her she'd feel more trapped than ever. Best he make this as painless as possible for her. It was the least he could do for putting her in this undesirable situation in the first place.

Which meant that he had to get to George Carrington first, beseech him to keep their earlier conversation to himself. Mac's speculative gaze landed on Roy, who had been dozing off and on for the last few hours. Maybe it was time to test the brat's loyalty.

He nudged Roy's foot with his boot, jarring him awake. Roy opened his sleepy eyes and focused on Mac, frowning.

"What? Did you kick me?"

"I want to talk to you about your manners—before we arrive," Mac said, nodding toward the door. "Outside."

Roy groaned, closed his eyes, and resumed his sleeping pose. "I don't need any lectures—"

"Outside," Mac repeated more forcefully. He rose, and Roy reluctantly followed him. Once outside, Mac inhaled the fresh, cool air rushing past them. It was noisy, but the observation deck was blessedly empty. In the distance he could see the rooftops of houses and businesses; a church steeple reached skyward.

Angel Creek, a prosperous, peaceful town where Mac had spent the majority of his life—when he wasn't hunting dangerous criminals for bounty.

"You don't have to worry," Roy grumbled as he came to stand beside Mac. "I'm not going to embarrass you or Mrs. Cord."

"I know. That was just an excuse to get you out here."

Roy did a double take. His eye's eyes widened. "Huh?"

"I've an assignment for you. Think you're up to it?"

The boy's chest expanded. He hooked his thumbs in his pants and rocked back on his heels. "Do bears shit in the woods?" he drawled with exaggerated arrogance.

Mac stifled a chuckle. "When we pull into the train station, I'm going to ask you to fetch a carriage for Savannah's trunks. I want you to refuse."

"You . . . you want me to *refuse?*" Roy squeaked.

"Yes. I need to talk to Savannah's father alone, so if you refuse to fetch the carriage, I'll have to."

After a baffled moment, Roy shrugged. "Sure thing, Mac." He looked suddenly anxious. "Everything okay between you and Mrs. Cord? I mean, you two seem like a happy couple . . . an' all."

"We're fine." Mac hesitated, not certain just how much

he should tell Roy. "Her father and I have a little business to discuss in private."

"Oh. And I guess this business is something you don't want Mrs. Cord knowing?"

"You're a shrewd boy, Roy."

"And you're a sly man, Mac."

"So it's a deal?"

"Sure thing." Roy rubbed his hands together with relish. "I guess bounty hunters have to be good at acting, don't they?"

"They do indeed," Mac murmured absently. He felt someone watching him . . . an itch right between the shoulder blades that always warned him in advance. It was this very instinct that had saved his life on more than one occasion.

Casually Mac turned around. He caught a flashing image of a man's face peering through the glass pane, but it was enough.

He recognized the deputy from Jamestown, the one Savannah said had followed him from the Empress Hotel in Paradise.

What did he hope to accomplish by following them clear to Angel Creek? Mac wondered. Did he believe they would still lead him to Barlow, or did the deputy have a more sinister motive for tailing them? Did he work for Sheriff Porter—or Ned Barlow?

The train began a series of long whistles announcing their final approach to Angel Creek. Mac considered going after the deputy and getting some answers, but he didn't have time to waste; he had to get to Carrington before Savannah did. His instincts told him the man wasn't a danger, just a nuisance.

Time enough to deal with him later, after he talked to

Carrington, and Savannah and Roy were settled in his house.

His house. Savannah would be going to *his* house as *his* wife—at least in everyone else's eyes. Mac's heart filled with a strange ache at the knowledge.

As the engineer engaged the brakes and the train began to lose speed, Mac returned to Savannah with Roy in tow. She had gathered her satchel full of drawings and her parasol, looking tense and unhappy.

Mac's heart continued to ache for her, knowing she was dreading the confrontation with her father.

When the train came to a full stop at the train station, they disembarked and moved to the baggage car to unload Savannah's trunks. Mac kept an eye on the few passengers who disembarked with them, but there was no sign of the deputy. If the man was good at his job, he would ride the train to the next town, hire a horse, and come back to Angel Creek in a less conspicuous way.

It was time to initiate the plan.

"Roy, go fetch a wagon for Savannah's trunks," Mac instructed, glancing at his pocket watch to see that it was an hour or so before dusk. He deposited the last hatbox on the pile of trunks and wiped his brow. It was unseasonably warm today, and when he cast a glance to the sky, he saw why; rain clouds had begun to gather.

To Mac's consternation, Roy groaned but flounced off in the direction of town. He stomped several yards away before he halted and spun on his heel. Mac recognized the mischievous twinkle in his eyes. *The brat!*

Thrusting out a belligerent chin, he shouted, "You know what? I think it's *your* turn to fetch the damned wagon! I'm not your slave." He stomped back and sat on one of Savannah's trunks, folded his arms, and clamped his mouth shut.

Mac bit back a smile at Savannah's astounded expression. Roy was a very convincing actor. "Roy," Mac said, injecting a weary note in his voice for Savannah's benefit, "just fetch the wagon. It's not only going to be dark, but also it looks like rain."

Roy gave a careless shrug and raised his pointed chin another notch. "Then I suggest you hurry. You wouldn't want your wife to get soaked."

"Roy!" Savannah protested, sounding injured. "This isn't the time or place to assert your manhood. Just do as Mac says."

"Nope. I'm staying right here. It's *his* turn."

With an aggrieved sigh, Mac muttered, "I'll go. There isn't time to argue with the brat."

"For once I agree with you—he *is* being a brat." Savannah found a trunk and flounced down, turning her back to Roy. "You go ahead, Mac." She sniffed loudly. "I'll be waiting right here with the brat—*in silence.*"

Her meaning was clear. Mac and Roy exchanged rueful, yet satisfied glances. Later Roy would have some making up to do, but Mac was confident the boy could weasel his way back into her good graces with the minimum of effort.

Chapter Twenty-six

George Carrington looked more haggard than ever, Mac noted as he thanked the butler and closed the study door behind him.

The older man rose slowly from his position behind the desk, removed his spectacles, and rubbed his eyes. His voice was thick with weariness as he indicated that Mac have a seat in the leather chair by the window. "Since Savannah isn't with you, I presume you failed to convince her to return."

"She's waiting at the train station now," Mac was pleased to inform him. "I'm supposed to be fetching a wagon for her trunks."

The man's face underwent a drastic change. His blue eyes flickered with a blatant mixture of hope and relief. "Thank God! I'll send Milton around to get her—"

"Not just yet, Mr. Carrington."

George frowned. "What's this about, Mac? Is she—does she not want to see me? Is that it?" He sat down heavily in his seat again.

"Nothing like that," Mac hastened to reassure him. "You see, I wanted to be the one to tell you the news."

"News? What news?" George stared at Mac for a full moment before realization dawned. A flush drifted into his cheeks, deepening his florid color. "By God, you succeeded, didn't you? You convinced Savannah to marry you!"

Mac hated to lie to the man, but he knew that he couldn't tell him the truth. In this instance, he believed a lie would be kinder. "Yes, I did. We were married in Jamestown." He hesitated, then plunged on. "I'd rather Savannah not know about our previous conversation that took place before I left, sir. She might not understand."

Bemused, George finally nodded. "Yes, yes. I can see why you're worried. Savannah has a suspicious mind." He rose and circled the desk, thrusting out his hand. "Well, congratulations, Mac. I'm mighty proud to have you for a son-in-law. I know that you'll take good care of my baby girl."

Mac swallowed a lump in his throat, accepting George's handshake. The disappointment Mac expected to find was lacking, and he was glad. "I *will* take good care of her, sir. You can count on it." *For as long as he had her, anyway.*

George dropped his hand, clearing his throat. "Yes, well, I'm anxious to see her. You bring her around to supper, you hear? Around seven?"

"Certainly." Mac rose, relieved the hard part was over. George Carrington would not betray him. "That will give us time to settle in. By the way, Savannah and I encountered a young friend along the way. He's determined to become a bounty hunter."

"Bring him along, too," George insisted with a careless wave of his hand. "The more the merrier."

"Thanks, Mr. Carrington."

"George. Call me George. You're family now."

Guilt swamped Mac as he left George and went to find a carriage.

Mac's childhood home was small, but Savannah found it utterly charming. There was a parlor, a kitchen, a living room, two bedrooms—and an attic room that Roy immediately declared for his own. The entire house was decorated tastefully but simply, a far cry from her own lavish home with its heavy, dark furniture and rich tapestry.

It was evident this house had once known the loving hands of a wife and mother—Mac's mother—and Savannah loved it. She could almost feel the other woman's loving presence.

As she moved from room to room, exclaiming over an exquisitely embroidered pillowcase on the bed, fingering the soft, worn red-and-white-checked curtains hanging in the kitchen window, she sensed Mac watching her anxiously. Roy was busy lugging furniture from one of the bedrooms up the narrow stairs leading into the attic, leaving them alone as they returned to the small parlor.

Savannah turned to Mac. "It's lovely," she said simply and sincerely. "I don't know how you stay away so long."

"If I had someone like you waiting for me, I wouldn't."

She shivered at his low, rumbling admission, despite the fact that she knew he didn't mean it. "Mac, you don't have to pretend. We're alone." Roy couldn't possibly hear them over the sound of his own cursing as he struggled with the furniture. She held her breath as Mac slowly approached her. His eyes deepened to jade.

"What would it take to convince you that I'm not pretending?" Mac queried softly.

He stroked the hair from her brow, then moved his hand to cup her neck, drawing her close. She inhaled the scent of wood smoke and soap, scents she had come to anticipate and love, as he drew her closer and closer to his mouth.

"I hunger for your kiss, Sav. It's been too long."

She forced a chuckle to hide the yearning his remark evoked. "What, a whole day and night?" she teased. His mouth brushed hers, then moved away. She whimpered and reached up, pulling him back. Perhaps it was wrong and selfish of her to want to make the most of her time with Mac, but she couldn't find the willpower necessary to resist him. Later, when it came time to leave him, she suspected she would pay the price for her weakness now.

"Would you care to test the bed?" Mac murmured seductively against her mouth. He slipped his hands around her waist and, with his mouth locked on hers, began to walk backward toward the door.

"What about Roy?" Savannah managed to gasp out before his mouth silenced her again. His big hands moved up, cupping the shameless thrust of her breasts. Savannah leaned into him with a moan. She could feel the hard length of him pressing against her.

In the end it was the enraged, muffled sound of Roy's screams that broke the sensuous spell.

"Daggumit! Somebody help! Get this thing off me!"

They found Roy on the stairs, buried beneath a thick, heavy goose-feather mattress. Laughing, they dragged the mattress from a red-faced Roy, who didn't think it was the slightest bit amusing.

"What are *you* laughing at?" he growled to Mac. "I could have used some help, you know."

"I was otherwise occupied, brat."

Roy looked from Savannah's flushed face to Mac's smug one. He shook his head and sighed. "I guess that means you want me to disappear?"

Savannah laughed at his resigned expression, feeling

her face heat even more. "No, Roy. Don't go. We're supposed to be at Daddy's house in half an hour. No time to . . . talk."

"Talk. Yeah, right. If you two were *talking,* then I'm picking cotton," he grumbled, kicking at the errant mattress. "Will someone *please* help me? I'd like to finish before midnight!"

Chuckling, Mac grabbed one end of the mattress and instructed Roy to grab the other. Savannah watched them for a moment as they struggled, tugged, and pulled on the bulky mattress, her heart swelling with tenderness. To anyone watching, they appeared to be a happy little family.

Her smile faded. *If only it were true.*

A half hour later in the Carringtons' formal drawing room, Mac stood by as George drew his daughter to him. He alternated between hugging and scolding her until Savannah laughingly protested.

"Daddy! I've only been gone a few weeks."

"It's felt like a lifetime, child," George said, his voice noticeably shaky.

And then came the moment Mac dreaded. George grasped Savannah's chin and forced her to look straight into his eyes as he asked, "Are you truly happy now, Savannah?"

Mac was impressed by the beautiful, spontaneous smile that spread across Savannah's face. If he didn't know better, *he* would be convinced by her sincerity.

"Yes, Daddy. I'm truly happy." She flashed Mac a loving smile that brought a peculiar weakness to his knees. "I only wish I had realized it sooner."

Roy cleared his throat, reminding them that he hadn't been introduced. In honor of the occasion, he'd left his treasured hat at home and wore his hair slicked back. His face was scrubbed clean, too, Mac noted, and he'd handed his long coat to the butler with a casualness that suggested it wasn't the first time the boy had faced a butler.

"George, this is our young friend, Roy Hunter." Mac nudged Roy forward. "He's determined to become a bounty hunter."

"A bounty hunter, eh?" George took the boy's hand and gave it a hearty squeeze, smiling benevolently. "That's a mighty brave yearning, son."

Roy nodded and stammered, "Y-yes, sir, Mr. Carrington."

The housekeeper, a reed-thin woman who'd been with the Carrington household for as long as Mac could remember, chose that moment to announce that dinner was ready.

"Thank you, Mrs. Hines. We'll be in shortly."

Dinner consisted of baked chicken, ham, quail, and a variety of vegetables served with hot, yeasty rolls and corn bread. Mac noticed that while Roy couldn't seem to get enough, he minded his manners. He and Savannah exchanged a mystified glance.

George pointed at Roy with his knife, apparently pleased with his appetite. "I like to see someone enjoying his food—other than myself, that is." He winked at Roy. Roy flushed and ducked his head. George then turned his attention to the apple of his eye just as Savannah popped a potato into her mouth. "So tell me all about your adventure, sweetheart. I want to hear every little detail."

Savannah choked on her food. She swallowed hard, looking like a rabbit caught in a snare. Mac used his napkin to hide a smile. He doubted Savannah's pride would allow her to tell George everything.

She proved him wrong.

Carefully she laid her fork onto her plate and placed her hands in her lap. "I'm not certain where to start, Daddy."

"How about at the beginning?" George prompted, blissfully unaware that his heart was about to receive a shock.

She began with meeting Ned Barlow and Raquel on the train. Mac watched the play of emotions on George's face as she spoke, wondering if he should interrupt. Savannah didn't know that her father wasn't in the best of health. Yet since their arrival, Mac had to admit that George didn't look ill at all now. Perhaps what he'd assumed was ill health had merely been grief and worry.

By the time she finished, George Carrington had gone white as a sheet. His eyes bulged with disbelief and horror. Finally he looked at Mac. His mouth moved, but it was a few taut seconds before sound emerged.

"Now you know why I was so eager to see her wed," he strangled out, then added with such heartfelt sincerity that Mac smiled, "Thank you, Mac!"

"My pleasure." Mac transferred his innocent smile to Savannah. She stared back at him, her beautiful blue eyes narrowed with suspicion. With an effort Mac maintained his bland expression until her suspicion began to waver.

"Well, now you can relax, Daddy. Mac takes *very* good care of me."

Roy picked up on her sarcastic inflection and snickered. Mac shot him a quelling glance. He sobered and reached for another roll to go with his third helping of baked ham.

"Now, hold on there, Savannah," George said, brandishing his knife again. "You didn't really think you were going to cheat me out of walking you down that aisle, did you? You're my only daughter—and I aim to see a wedding."

"It's really not necessary—"

"I'll give you two weeks. That should give you plenty

of time to prepare a wedding. I don't want folks around here to have any doubts that my little girl got hitched."

Savannah, apparently having realized it would be useless to argue, finally nodded. "Okay, Daddy."

Quick as lightning, George changed the subject, focusing on Roy. "Say, son, would you be interested in helping me at the bank tomorrow? You could stay right here with me tonight and give the newlyweds some privacy. What do you say?"

Mac silently urged Roy to accept George's offer. Getting Savannah alone sounded like the best idea he'd heard in a long time.

"I don't know, Mr. Carrington. Mac might need me."

"I think I can do without you for a few days," Mac said dryly. He caught the wicked gleam in Savannah's eyes, wondering if *she* was thinking what *he* was thinking. Just the possibility made him swell inside his trousers.

"Well, in that case, I'd sure like to. Will you show me the vault?"

George smiled at his boyish eagerness. "Of course."

Slowly Mac's gaze met Savannah's again. They exchanged a long, heated look that shimmered with promises and temptation.

The dinner couldn't end soon enough for Mac.

Chapter Twenty-seven

An hour later Mac and Savannah faced each other in the bedroom of Mac's house, the tension taut as a bowstring between them. Mac was glad he'd left a lamp burning; this time he wanted to *see* Savannah when he made love to her.

With their gazes locked, Savannah's hand reached for the top button of her blouse. "We probably shouldn't," she murmured even as she began to unfasten the buttons.

Mac quickly followed suit with his own shirt. "No, we probably shouldn't," he agreed, but didn't stop.

"It will make it harder for us when we go our separate ways."

"I don't think it could *get* any harder." The flaring of her eyes told Mac she hadn't missed his double meaning. Her gaze dipped briefly to the prominent bulge in his trousers, then returned to his face. Her eyes took on a sultry, half-hooded look that heated his blood. Mesmerized by her slow, deliberate actions, he watched her as she removed her blouse, revealing a thin white chemise that barely covered her rigid nipples and left her creamy breasts bare.

When she pulled the pins from her hair and let the heavy tresses flow around her shoulders, Mac caught his breath. Blood pumped heavily through his veins. Hawk's advice seemed like a distant dream. The wise Indian, Mac decided right then and there, had never been confronted with such an impossible temptation.

Her long skirt fell, pooling around her ankles. She drew one long, slim leg at a time. Mac's mouth watered at the bewitching sight. In two giant strides, he reached her, his trousers nearly bursting. He knelt before her as if to worship her, looking up into her angelic face without bothering to hide the love that welled within his heart. She had only to look to see it.

"You are without a doubt the most beautiful woman in the world," he said, and meant it. Her smile was soft and grateful.

"And you, Mac, are without a doubt the biggest liar I know," she countered softly. She rested a hand on his head, then let out a startled gasp as Mac grabbed her around the hips and lifted her high in the air.

He turned and carried her to the bed.

At the last moment Mac broke their fall by bracing his hands on either side of her. He eased gently onto her, fitting his body to hers from ankle to hip. Her hair formed a glorious golden fan around her face; her lips parted and gleamed in the lamplight. Time seemed suspended as they gazed into each other's eyes.

Words of love rose from Mac's heart and locked in his throat even as lust—primitive and relentless—threatened to obliterate his good intentions. Savannah reached for him, sliding her finger along his bottom lip, then tugging gently.

The provocative, spontaneous gesture melted Mac's bones.

He sucked her finger inside his mouth, watching as she closed her eyes and arched upward and into him. Suddenly her eyes flared open and burned into his with an erotic intensity that set flame to his groin.

"Don't shelter me, Mac," she scolded in a husky whisper, as if she sensed his inner struggle and disagreed with the victor. "Tonight I want you to forget I'm a lady."

Forget she was a lady? Mac groaned and shook his head. Just when he thought he'd mastered the beast, Savannah had to go and roust it again with her titillating request! Of course, with her limited experience, she had no idea—

"Shock me, Mac," she pleaded, proving Mac wrong. She raked her nails along his chest and whimpered, twisting beneath him. Her breasts quivered and heaved. Surging forward, she lapped at his throat with her hot little tongue.

A shudder nearly ripped him apart. She was pushing him beyond control with her husky pleas.

"Show me Mac the man."

This time she commanded him. Mac realized then how foolish he was to think he could deny Savannah anything. Not that he wanted to. To love Savannah without inhibitions was beyond his wildest dreams. With a deep growl of warning, Mac hooked his fingers in the neckline of her chemise and ripped the flimsy material from her squirming body.

Her eyes gazed at him, daring—challenging—him to continue.

Savannah wanted Mac the man . . .

Savannah would *get* Mac the man.

Rising onto his knees, Mac slowly pushed his trousers over his hips as Savannah watched him expectantly from beneath long, lustrous lashes. His manhood sprang free, erect and proud, eager to plunge into her fiery heat.

When she reached for him, Mac stilled her hands and shook his head, his expression full of lustful intent. His chest felt constricted, the air in his lungs hot and searing. Deliberately taking his time, he pushed her knees apart until she lay open before him. Slowly he stroked her silken thighs with hands that trembled, moving ever closer to the golden thatch of curls between her legs.

He watched her boldly watching him, her quick, excited breaths coming faster with each stroke that brought him closer to finding the treasure he knew lay nestled among the curls.

The moment his finger found her throbbing center, she gasped and surged into his hand. She cried out his name, and it was pure, sweet music to Mac's ears. He stroked her lightly, teasingly, driving her wild with need, ignoring his own need in his quest to show her Mac the man.

When he sensed an urgency to her movements, Mac halted his torture. She whimpered a protest, reaching for him as if to pull him into her embrace. Mac brushed her hands away once again. Gently coaxing, he urged Savannah onto her belly and lifted her hips until she was flush against his throbbing erection. He reached around her and found her moist center again, establishing a rhythm that soon had her thrashing against him.

Mac entered her with one swift plunge, rejoicing in her strangled cry of pleasure and surprise. She was hot and tight, her inner muscles closing around him as if to hold him inside her as he rocked against her. His free hand roamed over her bottom, trailed a teasing path along her spine and then back again, clutching her hip as his strokes grew deeper, harder, more urgent.

"Oh . . . God . . . Mac!"

At her hoarse cry, Mac turned her over with their bodies still merged as one. He wanted to see her face, to de-

vour her mouth as they reached their peak of pleasure together.

The lamp threw just enough light to reveal her flushed
cheeks, ripe lips, and glazed eyes. Gently now, Mac continued to meet her thrusts. He lowered himself onto her
and captured her parted lips, his kiss both rough and tender.

As the first wave of pleasure hit her, Mac commanded,
"Look at me!"

Her eyelashes swept upward, revealing the deep blue of
her smoldering eyes and the impending wonder of her release. Their gazes locked; they both tumbled over the edge
together, their cries mingling, their breathing harsh in the
aftermath of their joining.

To Mac it was not only a glorious joining of their bodies, but of their hearts as well. He'd never loved any
woman so deeply and thoroughly—and he knew that he
never would again.

Life without Mac would be colorless, dull, and un-
doubtably lonely. She would never feel whole again,
would always have an empty ache in her heart for this
wonderful, perfect man.

Savannah let out a ragged sigh and pressed her face
against Mac's damp chest, inhaling deeply, imprinting his
masculine scent onto her brain for future reference. His
deep, even breathing told her that he was asleep.

She couldn't begin to follow his path, not when each
moment in his arms could be the last. Tears dampened her
cheeks as she fought to control her sobs. She didn't want
Mac to wake up and find her crying, for he would surely
demand to know why.

And she couldn't tell him. Couldn't explain how she'd
fallen in love with her best friend, couldn't expose her

shame and fears to the one man she longed to tell. Mac would never let her go if he knew. He would feel duty-bound to stay with her, to pretend he loved her. Then, after their passion for each other waned—and without love Savannah suspected that it would, at least on Mac's part—he would be trapped in a loveless marriage. She couldn't bear the thought, not when it came to Mac's well-being, his future.

Convincing him that independence was the key to her happiness was all important. If Mac believed she wanted nothing more than to open her own business and live her own life—without him—then he could continue his own life with a clear conscience. Perhaps she'd at least have his continuing friendship to look forward to in the long lonely years ahead.

Savannah snuggled deeper against him, her mind refusing to give in to sleep. What if, in later years, Mac fell in love with someone? If that happened, then she would give him a divorce, she vowed. It was the least she could do to make up for the sacrifice he was making to marry her.

In the meantime . . . in the meantime she had two weeks to find joy where she could while convincing Mac she was looking forward to opening her own business in Jamestown. Two weeks to love Mac and stockpile memories for the lonely future ahead. After the wedding she would begin the weaning process—for Mac's sake as well as her own.

And if a child resulted from their passionate unions, she would treasure it. Having a part of Mac would surely ease the loneliness. Perhaps if there was a child, she would see more of Mac, for despite what she'd told him about declaring herself a widow to hush the gossip, she knew she could never deny Mac the pleasure of knowing his own child.

Sliding her hand between them, Savannah placed it on her belly and silently prayed. *Please God, give me this miracle, this precious extension of Mac so that I can always have a part of him with me.*

Chapter Twenty-eight

During the next three days Mac rarely saw Savannah. Her daylight hours were filled with fittings and flowers as she was literally hauled into the limelight by friends to plan her wedding. She seemed resigned now to the inevitable, which both gladdened and saddened Mac.

Roy, after Mac's repeated assurances that they wouldn't begin training until after the wedding, spent the majority of his time with George Carrington at the bank. George seemed equally taken with Roy, reminding Mac of his promise to Savannah that he would talk to her father about adopting Roy.

The nights were another matter entirely. Steamy, hot, and thoroughly satisfying as he and Savannah explored each other until there wasn't a patch of skin left on her luscious body that Mac hadn't tasted or touched. Savannah continued to surprise him with her sensual nature, eager and forever curious to learn everything there was to know about making love.

Sometimes she even shocked him.

Mac grinned in remembrance as he made his way to the jailhouse located next to Angel Creek's esteemed barbershop on the corner of Main and Calhoon Street. Across the street was Johnson's Mercantile, operated by Helen and Raedean Johnson and their bevy of children ranging from five to seventeen years old. Along the same boardwalk was a range of other businesses; a feed store, saddle shop, and a boot maker to name a few. Angel Creek also boasted a cotton gin and a lumber mill.

It was a small community, but its population continued to grow at a steady rate, increasing dramatically since the railroad put down tracks near the outskirts of town.

Sheriff Herbert Cannon was at his desk, his feet propped upon it, his chair tilted at a questionable angle. His eyes were closed, his hat pulled low over his tanned, weathered face.

Beyond the small office was a half dozen jail cells—all currently empty, Mac noted after a quick, amused glance.

"'Bout time you tore yourself away from that pretty wife of yours," Sheriff Cannon drawled lazily. He shoved his hat back and let the chair down with a snap, eyeing Mac with one bushy gray eyebrow lifted in challenge. "Kinda unexpected, wasn't it?"

Mac chuckled. Sheriff Cannon had never been known for his subtlety. "Just because I don't brag about my conquests doesn't mean they don't exist," Mac joked. Sheriff Cannon had never married, much to the disappointment of every widow within fifty miles of Angel Creek. Rugged, handsome, and still fit despite his fifty years, he wasn't averse, however, to easing their loneliness by warming their beds on occasion.

The sheriff's eyes twinkled. He scratched at the stubble on his chin, smiling. "Don't let them fool you—women love it when you talk about them. So, you sly son of a gun! You've got the bachelors frothing at the bit by snagging the richest, prettiest girl in town."

Mac didn't much feel like smiling as he said, "In the first place, I didn't snag her. Secondly, I didn't marry her for her money *or* her looks."

Sheriff Cannon's brow disappeared beneath a lock of iron gray hair as his amusement deepened. "You don't have to convince me, son. But you know other folks are gonna think differently."

"Let them think whatever they want—as long as *I* know the truth, it doesn't matter." Mac expelled an exasperated breath, furious with himself for letting the sheriff's comments get to him. Sheriff Cannon was a good friend and had merely been baiting him as usual. He settled his butt on the edge of the desk and summoned a rueful smile. "You were so busy trying to piss me off you forgot to congratulate me."

"Congratulations," Sheriff Cannon said amicably. "I guess this means you want me to retire earlier than we discussed?"

Mac shook his head. "No. I've got one last job to do before I settle down."

This piqued the sheriff's interest. "Anybody I know?"

Quickly giving him the details of Savannah's run-in with Barlow and their subsequent pursuit, Mac ended with, "I came by to look through your most recent Wanted posters and to ask you if you'd noticed any strangers around town lately. I figure the deputy from Jamestown will make an appearance, if he hasn't already."

"And you got no clue why he might be following you?"

With a shrug, Mac said, "I figure it's one of three things; he could be acting on Sheriff Porter's orders, he could want the bounty for himself, or he's in cahoots with Barlow." He waited patiently while Sheriff Cannon mulled this information over. It didn't take long.

"Seems mighty strange for a sheriff to send one of his

own men out of his jurisdiction on a wild-goose chase," he mused. "Unless he's got more than just a couple of suspicions." He hesitated. "You certain Savannah told you everything?"

"I'm certain." Mac hadn't told the sheriff about his own shameful suspicions, and didn't intend to.

"I don't know. . . ." Sheriff Cannon rubbed his bristling jaw again, shaking his head as if bewildered. "Barlow leaving Savannah's locket to taunt you just don't sound right. A wanted man usually goes out of his way *not* to draw attention. You ever considered that it was a signal?"

"A signal?"

Again the sheriff hesitated—with good reason—before he said, "For Savannah."

Mac's eyes narrowed. He fought to remember this man was a good friend as he explained tightly, "I told you, Savannah was innocently duped by this bastard. She would never willingly help someone rob a bank. Besides, he took her money as well, remember?"

"Don't go gettin' your dander up, son. I'm just trying to put the facts together and make some sense out of it."

"Well, don't blame Savannah," Mac growled. "She wants to catch Barlow as badly as I do."

"She know you're planning on going after him again?"

"No. I don't plan to tell her until after the wedding."

"Wedding? Thought you two had already gotten hitched!"

"We did, but George won't be satisfied until he walks his little girl down the aisle."

"Sounds like George, all right. He handle the news okay?"

Mac shrugged. "I'm sure he would rather she have married DeMent, but it's over and done with now."

The sheriff sat forward suddenly. "Speaking of DeMent, I don't know what Savannah ever saw in him. That boy's about as deep as that creek out behind my house."

"Sheriff, that creek dried up years ago," Mac reminded him.

"Just my point, just my point." He opened a deep drawer to his right and pulled out a stack of posters. "Now, let's see if we can find your man."

They didn't find Barlow—or at least they didn't find anyone with Barlow's name—but searching through the pile of crudely drawn sketches and faded pictures gave Mac an idea. Savannah had shown remarkable talent with her hat sketches. Perhaps she could draw a likeness of Barlow, something Mac could carry with him when he went after the outlaw.

Without a likeness, Mac could pass Barlow on the street without realizing it. The possibility made Mac want to howl with frustration.

Later that evening Mac walked into a scene that he knew he'd never forget.

Savannah and Roy were in the kitchen, cooking—or attempting to, Mac amended with a grin—fried chicken. Both were covered in flour. More of the powdered grain covered the floor, the chairs, and the wood-burning stove. Savannah wore an apron, but the material only covered the front part of her. Somehow, she'd managed to get flour on the back of her dress, right over the curve of her bottom.

Mac's first instinct was to cross the room and brush it away, mold his hands over her bottom, and caress her until she moaned and leaned into him. He forced himself to remain where he was, watching the domestic scene with a fierce ache in his heart.

"Something smells good," he said, his voice noticeably husky.

They both jumped. Savannah whirled around, looking

flustered and adorably mussed. "Mac! We wanted to surprise you. . . ."

"I'm surprised." He gave in to the urge to get close to her. After all, Roy believed they were married. In his heart, Mac believed it, too. Drawing her against his hardening body, he nuzzled her floured nose with his own, then placed a tender, lingering kiss on her surprised mouth.

Roy groaned in disgust. "If you two are going to start that again, I'm leaving."

Mac laughed and reluctantly stepped away from Savannah. He peered into the iron skillet on the stove, lifting a mocking brow at Roy. "I take it the menu choice was *your* idea, brat?"

"Don't you like fried chicken? I thought everybody liked fried chicken." Roy scratched his head as if he couldn't comprehend any other possibility, unending a tuft of hair so that it stood out at a comical angle from his head.

"I love fried chicken," Mac agreed. If they had been frying coon—which he detested—he would have lied and said he loved it. The idea of just the three of them sitting down at the table for a meal appealed to him more than either of them would ever know.

Working as a team, they set the table with china that had belonged to Savannah's mother. George had given it to them as a wedding present, along with a beautiful, cherrywood desk so that Savannah would have a place to work on her sketches.

It was during the delicious dinner of fried chicken, tender corn on the cob dripping with fresh melted butter, corn bread, and fresh green beans that Roy made his startling announcement.

"Mr. Carrington has asked me to come live with him after the wedding."

Mac and Savannah exchanged a satisfied glance. Curbing his amusement at Roy's anxious expression, Mac said, "I thought you wanted to be a bounty hunter."

Roy looked decidedly torn. "I do, Mac, but Mr. Carrington thinks I'd make a good banker." He leaned in close to whisper, his dark eyes round with excitement, "He even trusted me with the combination to the vault."

Savannah pretended to pout. "He never trusted *me* with the combination," she said, sniffing her outrage. "And he's known me all my life!"

Missing the twinkle in her eye, Roy tried to soothe her ruffled feathers, but only succeeded in stepping in deeper manure. "I'm a man, Mrs. Cord—no offense. Everyone knows that women can't keep a—"

"Roy," Mac interrupted quickly, hoping to save the boy. "I think you've said enough."

Bewildered, Roy glanced from Mac's stern expression to Savannah's suddenly glittering eyes. "Oh. Sorry, Mrs. Cord. I didn't mean to—"

"Roy," Mac said, louder this time.

"Okay, okay," Roy grumbled, grabbing another piece of chicken. "So what do you two think? Would it be okay with you, Mac?"

Mac shrugged. "If you're sure, it's fine with me." After a deliberate pause, he added, "What will your folks think?"

Roy's eyes clouded at the question, as if he were remembering something unpleasant. "I don't have any folks."

"Everyone has a mother and a father," Savannah said gently.

"Well, *I* don't, at least not any worth mentioning."

With his sullen gaze fixed on his plate, he resumed eating, leaving Mac and Savannah the impression that further attempts to find out about his past would prove useless.

It was obviously a painful subject for the kid, Mac

thought compassionately. Although he was extremely curious, he respected Roy's reluctance to talk about it.

He changed the subject, eliciting a relieved sigh from Roy. "Sav, I talked to Sheriff Cannon this morning about Barlow and went through his most recent Wanted posters."

"Did you find him?"

Mac shook his head. "No, I didn't, unless he has an alias. Do you think you could use your impressive artistic talents and draw a likeness of him from memory?"

She blushed at his compliment. "I can try, Mac. Truthfully, I've never attempted to draw a person's face before."

"I have complete confidence in your ability," Mac told her softly, eyeing her rosy blush and aching to pull her onto his lap. She lifted her gaze, catching the slumbering desire he didn't bother to hide. Her breath caught; her eyes darkened.

Roy heaved an exasperated sigh and pushed himself away from the table. He looked from one to the other, snorting. "You two act like lovesick calves! Don't you ever get tired of each other?"

Mac shook his head, and Savannah did the same, their gazes never wavering from each other.

"Well, hell!" Roy exclaimed loudly. "I guess I'll take Mr. Carrington up on his offer to exercise his horses." He took two clomping steps away from the table, then paused. "I'm going now." It was clearly a threat.

"Bye, Roy," Mac said, reaching across and capturing Savannah's hand. He threaded his fingers through hers, rubbing his thumb against her palm. Unseen beneath the table, Savannah's bare foot began a slow, tantalizing journey along his calf and onto his thigh.

"I probably won't be back until late," Roy added ominously.

"Okay."

"Might even be midnight."

"All right."

"Or maybe I'll just get drunk and stay out *all* night."

Savannah's lips twitched. With a spontaneous laugh, she broke away from Mac's heated gaze and focused on Roy, who obviously need *someone's* attention. Mac didn't dare follow suit; her foot had found him, hard and straining against his trousers. Slowly she used her toes to outline his length. Up. Down.

"Be home by dark, or I'll worry," Savannah told Roy sternly.

Roy grinned and saluted her. "Yes, ma'am!"

The moment they heard the door slam, Mac rose from his chair. He tenderly gathered Savannah into his arms and headed for their bedroom.

Chapter Twenty-nine

Just after dawn four days before the wedding, Mac was roused from sleep by someone pounding fiercely on the door. Thinking it was Roy, Mac stumbled through the house pulling on his trousers, cursing and mumbling to himself. He jerked open the door to find George Carrington on his threshold.

His future father-in-law looked pale, and Roy, standing beside him, sported an ugly, multicolored bruise on his right cheek.

Mac's eyes narrowed. Father-in-law or not, if George Carrington was abusing Roy, there would be hell to pay. "What happened?" He moved aside to let George by, but grabbed Roy before he could dart past him. He tilted the boy's face to get a better look at the bruise. "What happened?" he repeated.

Hot color flooded Roy's cheeks, further darkening the bruise. "I—I fell off my horse," he stammered, jerking free of Mac's hold. "Jeepers , Mac! You act like you've never seen a bruise before! I'm not a sissy girl, you know."

"I told him not to ride Aspen," George said impatiently.

He'd found the whiskey decanter and was now pouring himself a generous shot into a glass.

Watching George drain the liquid caused Mac's gut to clench in protest. It was hardly six o'clock in the morning; clearly something was upsetting the banker.

George waved the empty glass through the air, his wild gaze clashing with Mac's questioning one. "We didn't come to show you Roy's bruise—the bank's been robbed! Someone cleared the vault out last night."

Mac swallowed a startled gasp. "How did they get in? Someone would have heard the blast—"

"The vault wasn't blasted," George snarled. "And it appears they came in through an *open* window."

Savannah joined them, tying the belt of her robe as she entered the room. "I heard shouting . . . My Lord, Roy! What happened to your face?"

"He fell off his horse," Mac explained, looking at Roy once again. "But that's not the reason they're here. Someone robbed the bank."

"Someone who knew the combination!" George bellowed, drowning out the sound of Savannah's dismayed cry. Frustration was evident in his jerky movements as he began to pace. "The only people who know it are myself, Telly, and Roy here, and I trust them explicitly."

A unpleasant spiraling sensation traveled along Mac's spine as he stared hard at Roy. Roy stared innocently back at him. Although the boy had wormed his way into their hearts, Mac had to remind himself that they knew almost nothing about him. What they *did* know was that Roy knew the combination to the vault, and this morning he sported an ugly bruise. Coincidence? Mac intended to find out.

The spiraling sensation hit his stomach, making him

feel almost physically ill. He began to fasten his shirt, his voice gruff. "We'll rouse the sheriff on the way."

"I'll stay—" Roy began.

Mac cut him off with a quick, hard glance. "You're coming with us." He forced himself to add in a neutral voice, "We'll need all the eyes we can get to look for clues."

"I'll make coffee and start breakfast," Savannah stated. She seemed to glide across the room as she went to her father and hugged him. "Don't worry. Mac'll catch them and get your money back."

George blinked back unmanly tears as he enfolded Savannah in his bearlike embrace. His voice wobbled. "It's not my money, Sav, it's the town's money. Even Mac's savings, the money he's been hoarding so that he can give you everything—"

"Let's get going," Mac interrupted hastily. He placed a brief, hard kiss on Savannah's mouth before heading for the door.

Outside, the town was slowly coming to life. Mac's house was situated on Winchester Street—a few blocks from Main Street—so it didn't take them long to walk the short distance to the sheriff's office. Mac knew that Sheriff Cannon often slept in one of the jail cells instead of going home at night, and that's exactly where he found him.

Fifteen minutes later Mac, the sleepy-eyed sheriff, George, and Roy entered the quiet bank building. No sign of forced entry, Mac noted quickly, and none of the employees he knew would be careless enough to leave one of the high windows open, so that meant someone had *deliberately* left it open so the outlaws could get inside.

Once again his suspicious gaze returned to Roy, who was now looking as outraged as George sounded.

"I can't believe this," George said, cursing loudly and explicitly as he led the way across the gleaming mahogany floor into his office where the vault was located. The heavy iron door of the vault stood wide open, revealing the empty shelves within. "Them son-of-a-bitches didn't even have to *work* for it! Just walked right in and took it!"

"It was a clean sweep, all right," Sheriff Cannon confirmed, his bushy eyebrows drawn together in a perplexed frown. "They knew the combination to the vault."

George snorted. "Herb, any fool can see that!"

"No need to bite my head off, George," Sheriff Cannon rebuked mildly. "I ain't the one that took your money. Let's take a look outside, see how many there were."

They all followed Sheriff Cannon outside and around to the side of the bank building. The lawman hunkered down beneath the open window, studying the footprints while Mac combed the area where their horses had trampled the dirt.

"Looks like there might have been two or more," Sheriff Cannon said.

Mac grunted. "I agree. Three horses and a mule. They're probably using the mule to pack the money."

"How can you tell?" George asked, peering over Mac's shoulder.

"See those tracks there, leading away from the building? They're deeper. That means the mule was carrying a heavier load when they left." Mac frowned, kneeling down to get a closer look at the tracks. Slowly he said, "They've either got a spare horse or a light rider." He motioned the sheriff over, pointing at the faint imprint of the fourth horse. "What do you think?"

Sheriff Cannon nodded. "You're right, Mac. Looks like they've got an extra mount."

"We should get back to the house," Roy announced suddenly. "Savannah's cooking breakfast. She'll—she'll be mad if we let it get cold."

Three pairs of eyes looked at Roy as if he'd lost his mind. Mac rose, that ugly feeling in his gut returning like a toothache. How could the boy think of his stomach at a time like this? Usually, an event of this magnitude would excite the boy; why wasn't he excited now?

Softly Mac asked, "Is there any particular reason—other than food—that we should hurry back to the house, Roy?"

Roy swallowed so hard the sound was audible. His voice was nothing but a hoarse, agonized croak. "Please, Mac. Let's just *go!*"

Before Mac could think, he grabbed the boy's shoulders and jerked him close. He glared into Roy's round-eyed gaze. "So help me God!" he snarled.

Cowering before Mac's obvious fury, Roy nevertheless managed to stammer, "M-mac, we need to hurry."

Mac needed no further urging. His heart began to pound with fear as he loped in the direction of Winchester. Vaguely he was aware of Roy close behind him, and George and Sheriff Cannon panting to keep up.

When he reached the house where he and Savannah had spent two glorious weeks loving each other, he burst through the front door, shouting, "Savannah? Savannah, answer me!"

But of course she didn't because she wasn't there.

George and Sheriff Cannon raced into the parlor just as Mac emerged from the empty kitchen. Roy had checked the bedrooms and was coming down the narrow stairs from the attic room. The bruise on his cheek stood out in vivid detail against the paleness of his face. Guilt and ter-ror mingled in his eyes.

The banker's face was beet red from his exertion, and

he was breathing hard. Bracing his hands on his knees, he gasped out, "Mac, what the hell is this all about?"

Mac's burning gaze locked on Roy's frightened face. With deceptive calm, Mac said, "I think Roy can answer that, can't you, Roy?"

They gathered at the table where Savannah had begun laying out the materials for making biscuits; a mixing bowl, a wooden spoon, flour, lard, and an empty can for cutting the biscuits.

In the middle of the table lay her gold locket.

Mac fixed his gaze on it, his fists clenched, his jaw equally clenched as he tried to control his wild rage at Barlow's latest taunt. The bastard would pay with his life, he vowed.

His clenched fist hit the table with a thundering whack, startling the others—particularly Roy—who jumped as if Mac had struck him. "Start talking," he ordered.

Roy swallowed several times, his huge eyes focused on the locket. "He—he promised to leave Mrs. Cord alone if I told him the combination. He *promised,*" he added in an anguished whisper.

"And the window?" Mac hardened his heart against the anguish twisting the boy's face.

Instead of answering, Roy simply nodded and hung his head.

But Mac wasn't satisfied by any means. "Why did he hit you?"

Startled, Roy's gaze flew to Mac's. "I—I told you, I fell—"

"You didn't fall." Mac was certain of this, but why would Roy lie? What reason could he possibly have for lying about something that would *help* them to understand why he'd betrayed them?

"Look," George said, "if he said he fell, then maybe he did, Mac. As far as giving him the combination, the boy obviously had no choice in the matter. He knows how much my daughter means to me."

Mac ignored George, shooting questions at Roy and demanding answers. "Why did he hit you?"

Apparently Roy realized Mac wasn't going to give up. "He—he hit me because at first I refused to give him the combination to the vault."

"How did he know who you were?" Mac knew that Roy had seen the likeness of Barlow that Savannah had sketched, which would explain how Roy knew *him*. But it didn't explain how Barlow recognized Roy.

"I don't know. I was out riding Aspen, and they jumped me."

"How many?"

"Just—just Barlow and that woman, Raquel."

"You're lying."

"For God's sake, Mac—" George began.

Mac held up his hand to silence the banker without taking his eyes from Roy. The sheriff remained silent and watchful. "He's not lying about how many, he's lying about Barlow not knowing him," he explained. "Am I right, Roy?"

Roy's shoulders slumped. His gaze fell from Mac's as he whispered miserably, "Yeah, he knows me."

"Was the third horse for you, Roy?"

The silence seemed to stretch as Roy took his time answering. Finally he mumbled, "Yeah, it was for me, but I didn't want to go with them." His lifted his pleading gaze to George. "I wanted to stay with you, learn how to be a banker."

"And you never wanted to become a bounty hunter?" Mac guessed shrewdly.

"No. I heard you two talking outside the hotel that first night in Jamestown. That was the only excuse I could think of, so's you'd let me go with you and Mrs. Cord. I—I was supposed to stick with her like a burr on a dog."

Not Roy's own words, Mac sensed as the disturbing pieces of the puzzle began to fall into place. Just as Savannah had been taken in by Barlow, they had *all* been fooled by Roy. It stung his pride to realize he'd been so gullible, but the pain of betrayal hurt far worse than his pride. Now he knew how Savannah felt!

"You've got to believe me, Mac!" Roy suddenly cried, jumping to his feet. He was visibly trembling, his eyes pleading with Mac to understand. "At first I went along with his plans, but then I—I started to like you and Mrs. Cord. I wanted to tell you, but I couldn't. I just couldn't. You all treat me like a real *person*."

Mac pointed at the chair, and Roy sat abruptly. "How long have you known Barlow was going to rob the bank?"

"I *didn't* know!"

"But you knew that he planned to carry out his original plan to kidnap Savannah."

Roy's mouth worked uselessly. Finally he strangled out in a shameful voice, "Yeah, I knew. But I thought I could change his mind. I—I thought if I told him the combination to the vault, he would take the money and leave us alone."

"Why didn't you just come to me? Or tell George?"

"Because I was ashamed. . . ." Roy's skinny chest hitched as he fought an unmanly sob. "I didn't want you all to know the *real* me."

George cursed softly. "What do they expect me to use for ransom? *My* money was in that vault, too."

They all looked to Roy for an answer; he clearly didn't like this type of attention and didn't know what to say.

It was Mac who finally shocked them all by saying, "I don't think Barlow kidnapped Savannah for money."

"I think you might be right," Sheriff Cannon said, speaking for the first time since the entire conversation began. "This sounds more like an act of revenge. Mac, are you certain you didn't recognize Barlow from Savannah's sketch?"

Mac shook his head. "I'm certain."

"He didn't kidnap her out of revenge *or* for money," Roy blurted out. When everyone looked at him again, his face reddened. "He's just mad because she got away from him the first time." His hand touched his bruised cheek, and he winced. "He doesn't like to be crossed."

"How long have you known him?" Mac asked, wishing he had his hands around Barlow's throat. Despite the fact that Roy had started out deceiving them, Mac didn't find it difficult to believe he'd had a change of heart. Otherwise Roy would have left with Barlow, he reasoned. Or perhaps this was just what he *wanted* to believe.

"I've known him a long time," Roy admitted reluctantly, as if he were ashamed of the fact.

Sheriff Cannon leaned forward, placing his elbows on the table. His piercing blue eyes bore into Roy's. "He any kin of yours?"

Roy took forever to answer, and when he did, George, Mac, and Sheriff Cannon had to strain to hear his whispered words.

"Yeah. He's my pa."

Chapter Thirty

Mac fancied he could smell the lingering scent of jasmine in the air.

A kettle of water boiled on the stove. He knew he should tend to it, at least remove it from the heat, but somehow the sight of the steaming kettle was soothing, reminding him that not so long ago Savannah was in this room, preparing breakfast. A knife-like pain hit his chest at the thought of Savannah in the cruel hands of Ned Barlow.

He and Roy were alone in the small kitchen. Sheriff Cannon had left to find Mac a fast horse, and George had gone to the bank to inform his employees of the robbery.

Silence stretched between them; the air was heavy with conflicting emotions—disappointment, shame, and a black fury such as Mac had never known before.

Roy's betrayal stunned him, but Savannah's absence left a gaping hole in his heart. Fear twisted his gut into a painful knot. What if Barlow planned to kill Savannah? Why else would he take her, if not for money?

He glanced at Roy. He wanted to believe that Roy didn't know Barlow would take Savannah, but after all the lies and deception . . .

"Hawk and Patricia know you," Mac said abruptly, ending the tense silence. "That's why you didn't follow Savannah to Sunset Ranch, and that's how you knew how to get there."

"Yes," Roy whispered. He stared at his hands, which were locked together on the table in front of him.

They were trembling.

Mac eyed the telltale motion with grim satisfaction. Until Savannah was safe in his arms again, he didn't think he could forgive the kid. "You also warned Barlow in Paradise, didn't you?" Another shame-filled nod. Mac fought down his rage, reminding himself that Roy was just a kid. "Where will he take her?"

"Hawk was right. Ned bought some land outside of Paradise." Roy pressed his thumbs into his hands until his knuckles turned white. "I reckon he'll take her there."

"And wait for me to come after her?"

Roy shook his head. His bottom lip trembled, but he stopped the gesture with his teeth. "I didn't want to say nothing in front of the sheriff, but Ned's plannin' on making a deal with you. He don't want to be hunted the rest of his life."

Ned. Not Pa, but Ned. Mac stored the information away for future contemplation. "I thought you said you didn't know he was going to take Savannah."

"I—I thought I had talked him out of it—after he told me what he was plannin' to do!" Roy struck the table with his fists as Mac had done earlier, in frustration and anger. "He lied to me! He ain't done nothing but lie to me since Ma died!"

At another time Mac would have prompted the boy to continue, to let it all out and lance the boil that had obviously been festering since his mother's death, but right now with Roy's betrayal fresh in his mind, Mac could think of nothing but Savannah. "What's the deal? My silence for Savannah's life?" he asked, not bothering to hide his contempt.

"Yeah, only . . ." Roy darted a fearful glance at Mac before he continued in a low voice. "Only he wants you to tell everybody you killed him."

Mac uttered a soft, four-letter curse. Was Barlow that confident Mac couldn't rescue Savannah? Was he that arrogant? Mac clenched his jaw as rage swelled, lethal and ugly. His voice shook as he asked, "Do *you* think he will kill her if I don't agree with his deal?"

Roy frowned as if contemplating the question. Finally he said, "I don't know, Mac. Ned's pretty mean. He might."

"If he does," Mac growled with complete conviction, "there won't be a hole left for him to hide in."

"What are you going to do?"

"I'm going after Savannah. When I find her and get her to safety, I'm going to bring Barlow and his lady love in. Dead or alive. Makes no difference to me." In fact, he preferred Barlow dead.

"I want to go."

"No." Mac said it sharper than he intended. It was obvious the boy was suffering massive guilt and regretted his part in Barlow's dirty schemes, but he would have to work it out on his own for now.

He rose and, without a backward glance at the miserable boy, left to start his journey. He figured Barlow had ridden to the next town to catch the morning train.

Mac wasn't about to wait until the next train out— which wouldn't be until tomorrow morning—before he began the hunt. He would ride like the wind, changing horses along the way. Thanks to telegraphy and Sheriff Cannon's many contacts, there would be fresh horses waiting for him in many of the small towns that crossed his path.

When he reached Edmondsville, North Carolina, he would catch the train to Paradise. With any luck, he would arrive only hours behind Barlow.

Ned Barlow and Raquel looked like any wealthy couple traveling first class. Ned wore a striped woolen suit and a solid black vest, and carried an ivory cane that with a flick of a switch revealed a rapier-sharp knife at the tip; he'd wasted no time showing it to Savannah, warning her that he wouldn't hesitate to use it if she cried for help.

Raquel wore her dark hair piled on top of her head with artfully curled ringlets cascading over her shoulders. She was dressed in a burgundy traveling suit that looked uncomfortably tight.

Savannah bit her lip and turned her face to the window again. After a grueling horseback ride, they had caught the morning train from Calliecut, a small town not more than five miles from Angel Creek.

Did Mac and her father know she was gone yet? she wondered. For all she knew they were still at the bank, looking for clues, discussing the robbery while Barlow took her farther and farther away. She hadn't even resisted, not after Barlow informed her that he had Roy and would kill him if she didn't come peacefully.

He'd lied, of course. Once they were on the train heading north, Raquel couldn't wait to tell her—laughing gleefully—the startling news about *Roy*. Savannah drew in a long, shuddering breath. How could that sweet, clumsy boy be Barlow's son? How could she and Mac have overlooked something so important? They had blindly trusted the boy, believing his sad story when he told them he didn't have any folks.

No—he'd said he didn't have folks worth *mentioning,* which certainly made sense now that she knew the truth. And if he truly *was* part of Barlow's devious plans, then why didn't he come with them? Had Barlow left him behind to continue spying on Mac? The possibility made Savannah clench her fists until her nails bit deeply into her palms. She didn't know what Barlow planned for her, but she knew Mac would come after her. He wouldn't give a thought to his own safety.

Was this Barlow's plan? Why did he hate Mac so?

Her heart skipped a painful beat. In the last two weeks she had fallen even more in love with Mac, so much that she had considered begging him to give them a chance to be more than friends . . . and lovers. Considered blurting out that she was in love with him.

Now she might not have the chance.

Savannah slowly unclenched her fists, ignoring the painful grooves left by her nails. She lifted her chin and squared her shoulders. Somehow, she vowed, she would find a way to escape Barlow and his cold-hearted lady friend before Mac had a chance to get himself killed trying to rescue her.

Mac pushed his horse hard as he rode north hell-for-leather. He knew Roy followed, had known from the start, but he studiously ignored the boy in the hopes that he would give up and turn back.

He couldn't trust him, didn't know if he was friend or foe, and didn't have time to belabor the issue.

In Albert City, a thriving cow town hugging the border of North Carolina, Mac thundered up to the marshal's office to change horses and fill his canteen. Sheriff Cannon had wired ahead, and Marshal Crow was waiting for him on the boardwalk outside the jail.

The big-boned, heavily jowled marshal tipped his hat at
Mac as he slid from the heaving horse. The lawman held
out a saddlebag, a fresh canteen, and a big hand to shake.
Mac took all three with a grim thank-you before he
mounted the fresh horse and kicked it into a gallop.

Roy would never keep up without a fresh horse, Mac reflected as he slowed down long enough to take a deep pull
from the canteen. The sun was sinking, but Mac continued
to ride hard until full dark was upon him. He finally
slowed the gallant gelding to a walk, knowing a lame horse
wouldn't do him any good.

Sometime during the early-morning hours, Mac dozed
in the saddle. Each time the horse stumbled, he jerked
awake. An hour before sunset he stopped long enough to
water his horse and eat a chunk of corn bread the marshal
had given him.

The air was cool and sweet, but Mac knew it would heat
up when the sun came out. Fall was slow in arriving this
year, and winter was still some weeks away.

He spent another hard day in the saddle, cutting across
rugged terrain avoided by most travelers, and splashing
through creeks and streams—some deep enough to soak
his boots—and crashing through dense forests. He rode
into the town of Sweet Water just as the sun was once
again sinking in the sky. With the minimum of conversation, he changed horses, refilled his canteen, and gratefully
accepted another offering of food from the sheriff before
riding out again.

He was exhausted, but he knew that even if he stopped,
he wouldn't be able to sleep. Each time he closed his eyes
a mental image of Barlow filled his mind, and the fury returned. When his eyes were open, he thought of Savannah,
his sweet, passionate, loving Savannah. He remembered
her delightful laugh, her husky voice urging him to touch

her, love her, when they were making love. He recalled the numerous times he nearly told her that he had loved her for a long time. Without any effort he brought to mind a vivid image of her flushed, excited face when she spoke to him about plans for the future.

Now Mac wished he *had* told her, because he couldn't bear the thought of either of them dying without her knowing how much he loved her—how much he looked forward to marrying her, and how much he'd like to live with her as husband and wife until the end of their days.

Mac stumbled into Edmondsville two hours before the evening train was due. Edmondsville was one of the few towns that boasted both a morning and evening north-bound train. Mac estimated that would put him about twelve hours behind Barlow.

He left his horse at the jail and bought a ticket to Paradise, then settled on the empty train platform to eat a cold supper of biscuits and bacon, compliments of the sheriff's wife.

The shrill whistle of the approaching train startled Mac out a light doze. Tired, dirty, with his face stinging from the numerous scratches he'd received crashing through the forest, he boarded the train that would take him closer to Savannah. The moment he lowered his aching body onto the padded seat, his eyes began to close. *Hold on, Savannah, I'm coming,* he thought as he drifted off.

What seemed like moments later, someone shook him awake. Mac rubbed his heavy, swollen eyes and blinked at the man who had rudely interrupted his sleep. He gathered by his sharply creased suit that he was the conductor. Fumbling inside his coat, Mac found his ticket and held it out to him.

The conductor took the ticket, but instead of moving on, he asked, "Are you Mac Cord?"

Mac came fully alert. The way the man was frowning reminded him of another time. But, no, it couldn't possibly be—

"We have a young man who claims that you know him." The conductor's thin lips nearly disappeared in a disapproving frown. "He stowed away on the baggage car."

For a wild moment Mac considered shrugging and telling the conductor that the stowaway must be confused, that he knew nothing about a young boy brash enough to stow away on a train. But his conscience wouldn't let him—and he knew Savannah would tear him limb from limb.

The thought of her spirited reaction nearly made him smile. He let out a long, put-upon sigh and said, "Yeah, I know him. Might as well take me to him."

Roy looked worse than Mac. The deep scratches on his face clearly mapped his path through the same uncharted forest Mac had struggled through. His boots were wet and muddy, his clothes torn and dirty, and his entire frame shook from exhaustion.

For the first time since he discovered Roy's duplicity, Mac felt a stirring in his heart, a remembered fondness for this brash, loudmouthed boy. On the heels of this surprising emotion, Mac experienced a wild moment of paternal pride that Roy had managed to keep up with him on the grueling journey.

"Do you have a bed available on this train?" Mac asked the conductor. When the conductor remained silent, Mac fished a persuasive amount of money from his coat pocket and offered it to him.

The reaction was instantaneous.

"Why, yes, Mr. Cord. Happy to oblige, Mr. Cord." He glanced from one scratched, dirty face to another before he added, "I'll get him some fresh water, too."

"Thanks," Mac said dryly. "And food? Did I give you

enough money to cover that, too?" When the conductor hesitated, Mac sighed and fished out another incentive.

The conductor whisked the coin from his hand and made it disappear. "Yes, sir. I'll see what we've got in the way of food."

When they were alone in the private bunker, Mac folded his arms and tried to look forbidding as he glared at the shamefaced boy. It was difficult to be angry with a kid who looked as if he'd stumbled into a catfight, and who could barely hold himself upright. Deliberately Mac reminded himself that Roy was Barlow's son. He'd been trained to deceive.

"Why did you follow me?" Mac demanded.

Roy struggled to keep his eyes open. His belly gave an ominous rumble as he said sluggishly, "I wanted . . . to prove to you . . . that I'm not like you . . . think I am. I wanna . . . help get Sav . . . Mrs. Cord back."

As Mac watched, Roy's eyes drifted down again. He crumpled slowly onto the bunk, his legs still hanging over the side. Within seconds he'd begun to snore.

Shaking his head, Mac removed Roy's muddy boots and settled him more comfortably onto the mattress. He drew a blanket over his thin shoulders. Roy stirred and mumbled something in his sleep. Mac bent close so that he could hear.

"I . . . lost my damned . . . hat," Roy whispered in a weary, little-boy voice. "Gotta find . . . it."

"We'll find it," Mac promised, swallowing a lump in his throat and cursing his foolish heart. Common sense told him Roy couldn't be trusted, yet here he was, tending the boy like a soft-hearted woman.

If only Savannah could see him now.

Chapter Thirty-one

"You can sleep over there, by the fireplace. I'm sure it's not up to your standards, Princess, but it's the best I can do."

"Over there" was a blanket on the hard floor, but Savannah was too exhausted to care. She mustered a haughty look for Ned's benefit as she stumbled to the blanket. If he expected her to complain, plead, or become hysterical, he was in for a disappointment.

She stretched out on the blanket and cradled her head on her arms, struggling to keep her eyes open. She should stay awake, plot how she was going to escape from these cruel people.

Sometime later Savannah awoke to the sound of low voices—Ned's and Raquel's voices. She lay very still, keeping her eyes closed as she listened.

"What if he brings a posse with him?" Raquel asked.

"He wouldn't dare," Ned sneered. "Roy says he's besotted with her. He won't risk her life."

"I hope you're right."

"I am."

Savannah was amazed at the man's arrogance. Ned was

right about one thing; Mac wouldn't bring a posse. But he *would* come for her.

"What if he won't agree to your deal?"

Ned made a vicious sound in his throat. "Either he agrees to tell everyone that I'm dead, or *she* dies."

Cold chills swept over Savannah at his words. Mac was an honorable man. Could he—or would he—agree to such a deal? To lie to everyone, claim that Ned Barlow was dead, just to save her life?

Savannah bit her lip, knowing the answer. Mac would agree, but in agreeing, he would be compromising his integrity. He would lose a piece of himself.

She couldn't let that happen! Mac had already done so much for her in the name of gallantry. Gathering her courage, Savannah pushed herself to a sitting position.

Conversation immediately ceased. The couple turned to look at her. Ned's lip curled. Raquel smiled, a tiny, superior smile that made Savannah shiver.

"Well, well, well," Ned drawled. "If it isn't Sleeping Beauty, awake and refreshed after her nap."

Her voice thick with contempt, Savannah said, "There's something you should know about Mac and me."

"Oh? And what, pray tell, would that be?"

"Mac doesn't love me. In fact, we're not really married. We're just friends."

"And you expect me to believe that?"

"It's true. He pretended to be my husband to get me out of jail, then Preacher Owens saw us coming out of my hotel room, so Mac lied about our relationship again to save my reputation." Savannah shoved her tangled hair from her eyes, willing Ned to believe her. "So you see, Mac will never agree to let you go free. Unlike you, he's a man of honor."

Ned's black eyes glowed with a feral light. "Unfortunate for you, my dear, if what you say is true."

Savannah tried another tactic. "I met your sister. She's a wonderful, sweet person. Too bad she doesn't know what a monster you are."

When Ned made a threatening move toward Savannah, Raquel grabbed his arm. She laughed derisively. "Ned! Shame on you. Can't you see she's trying to bait you? She's lying, of course."

"I'm not lying," Savannah stated with dignity. "So you might as well kill me now, because Mac will never agree to your sordid plans."

The maniacal light in Ned's eyes brightened. He removed a small derringer from his jacket pocket. Slowly he pointed it at her, his unholy smile full of devilry.

Savannah closed her eyes and braced herself for the pain.

The conductor had brought them a loaf of bread and a comb of raw honey. When Roy awoke he sat on the side of the bunk and ate the loaf of bread and the entire comb of honey as Mac looked on, amused by the boy's voracious appetite.

Roy licked his fingers clean, flashing Mac a sheepish smile when he realized Mac was watching. "Mr. Carrington gave me some money, but I didn't have time to buy food."

Mac's brow rose. "That's how you were able to trade horses?"

Roy nodded. "It took me a little longer to make the exchange at the stables, but I managed."

"I take it you also didn't have time to buy a train ticket?"

"Nope. Got here just as the train was pulling out."

"You're lucky they didn't throw your carcass from the train," Mac scolded.

"I don't think I would have cared if you had said you didn't know me," Roy retorted, his vulnerable expression tugging at Mac's heartstrings.

They stared at each other for a long moment. Finally Mac sighed. "What makes you think you can help me?"

The vulnerability vanished so quickly Mac was suspicious that it was ever there. The boy definitely had a talent for acting.

Roy's face became animated as he talked. "I *can* help, Mac! I can convince Ned that I've changed my mind, that I want to live with them." He made a face. "It's the *last* thing I want, but I could convince them. I know I could."

"And how would that help?"

Briefly Roy outlined his plan. When he finished, Mac said, "Why should I trust you? How do I know you won't warn Ned of our plans? Your pa would be mighty proud of you."

Mac's quick reflex saved him from a fat lip. He caught Roy's wrist, holding him at bay as the furious boy struggled uselessly. His face was red, and the way his skinny chest heaved told Mac he was near tears. Roy's reaction both surprised and reassured him.

Breathing hard, Roy snarled, "I hate him! He's not my pa—not the one who raised me! He's nothing but dog meat!"

"Then why did you go along with his plans in the first place?" Mac taunted softly.

"Because—because he said I wasn't nothing but a skinny little kid, a sissy. He said—he said that if I let Mrs. Cord out of my sight, he'd—he'd send me to an orphanage."

Mac felt the fight go out of Roy. Slowly he let go of his

wrist. The boy sat hard on the bunk, his breathing quick and shallow.

"I know now that I'd *rather* go to an orphanage than to live with him and that mean—mean harlot." His chest hitched in a sob; his big eyes swam with tears. "After Ma died, I didn't know what to do. Just before . . . before she died, she told me who my real pa was. She didn't want to leave me alone."

"How did your folks die?"

"My pa—my step-pa—was coming out of the feed store and walked into a gunfight. He'd been blasting tree stumps and couldn't hear very good because he'd gotten too close to the dynamite." Roy's gaze fell to his feet, his face a mask of sorrow. "Leastways, that's what me and Ma figured happened."

"And your ma?" Mac prompted softly.

"I reckon she died of a broken heart. After Pa died, she started gettin' sick and laying in bed all the time. Old Doc Fender said he couldn't find nothing wrong with her."

A man would have to be made of stone not to react to Roy's sad story—and Mac was no exception. But Mac was also a cautious man, and he'd seen firsthand Roy's talent for convincing people. "How do I know that you're telling the truth now?"

"I don't reckon I blame you if you don't believe me," Roy whispered tearfully. He wiped his runny nose with his dirty sleeve and drew a shuddering breath. He looked Mac dead in the eye as he added, "But for Mrs. Cord's sake, can you try? I can help get her back—I *know* I can. Maybe then—maybe then you'll forgive me."

"It would be dangerous."

"I don't care!" Roy cried passionately. "If it means we can get Mrs. Cord back, and Ned will go to jail, then I don't care how dangerous it is."

Mac fell silent, amazed that he would even consider trusting Roy. Stunned that he would consider sending a boy into a potentially explosive situation. Savannah's life was at stake. Did he dare take such a chance with her life hanging in the balance?

"Get washed up and join me in the passenger car," he instructed Roy. He had to do some thinking and he couldn't do it while Roy was staring at him with those big, wounded eyes.

"Does this mean you'll think about it?" Roy asked hopefully.

"I'll think about it but I ain't making any promises."

"I swear to you, Mac, that if you'll give me a chance, I'll make it up to you and Mrs. Cord. She—she reminds me of my ma, and I don't want anything to happen to her."

"Neither do I, brat. Neither do I."

The possibility was unthinkable.

Chapter Thirty-two

When Mac and Roy stepped from the train the next morning in Paradise, a pleasant surprise awaited them.

Mac stared at the tall, dignified Indian, then trailed his astounded gaze over the horses at Hawk's side. He shook his bewildered head as he approached his friend. "I guess it would be useless for me to ask how you knew."

Hawk grinned. "How can I say what I cannot explain? I come to repay the favor you did for me in Cornwall."

"Are you talking about West?"

"Yes. He has decided not to kill me, thanks to my good friend Mackenzy Cord. I can now go into town without fearing for my life."

Mac wasn't fooled. "You don't fear anyone, Hawk, but they'd be wise to fear you."

"Tell that to my Patricia," Hawk said, still grinning. He focused his penetrating gaze on Roy, who stood beside Mac, gaping at him. "So we meet again, Bristling Feather."

"Bristling Feather?" Mac cocked a brow at Roy, who flushed and scowled at Hawk.

"That's just some ole dumb name Sparrow gave me. It don't mean nothing."

Hawk chuckled as he handed Mac the reins to a beautiful bay gelding. He indicated to Roy that he should take the other mount, a spotted pinto pony. "You can tell me your plans on the way to Barlow's land."

"You mean you don't know?" Mac joked, stifling a groan as he mounted the gelding. Roy didn't bother hiding *his* agony; he groaned and cursed, fidgeting in the saddle as if his butt was full of prickly burrs.

"Don't worry, Bristling Feather. Soon you will grow numb and feel no pain."

Roy snorted at Hawk's comment. "Well, isn't that reassuring, Eye of the Hawk. And my name is Roy . . . *Hunter,* not Bristling Feather. I don't have a drop of Indian blood in me."

"You do not have to have the blood of an Indian to possess the heart of a warrior, Roy Hunter."

Hawk's compliment, delivered so casually, took a moment to sink in. Amused, Mac watched as Roy flushed with pleasure.

"Well, in that case, my *Indian* name is Bristling Feather."

As they rode through town, Mac could feel curious eyes on them. Hawk didn't seem to notice or care, which sparked Mac's admiration.

Roy broke the silence the moment they left the town behind them. "Aren't you going to give Mac a name, Hawk?"

When Hawk hesitated, Mac's curiosity was aroused. "Well?" Mac prompted.

"It is difficult to give a name to a man with so many admirable qualities," Hawk hedged.

Mac felt childishly disappointed. "So Whistle Britches here gets a name and I don't."

"I think you've hurt Mac's feelings, Hawk."

"Shut up, brat, Bristling Feather, Roy Hunter—whatever the hell your name is."

"Hey, don't get mad at *me!* I'm not the one who—"

"Heart of the Mountain Lion," Hawk interjected.

They fell silent. Mac turned the name over in his mind, deciding he liked it. He gave in to the temptation and shot Roy a smug look. But Roy wasn't paying attention; he was squinting over his shoulder.

"I think someone's following us."

"He, too, hunts for Barlow," Hawk informed them.

"He might interfere with our plans." Mac frowned, looking back at the speck of dust in the distance. He couldn't make out who it was, but he figured it was the deputy from Jamestown.

"Do not worry," Hawk said. "He rides a soft horse."

Mac was amused. "I take it it's not one of your horses?"

Hawk's faint smile was his answer.

Another companionable silence followed before Roy asked, "Does Aunt Patricia know what you're doing?"

"Patricia knows that I am helping a friend."

"Ah, so she *doesn't* know that you're aiding in the capture of her outlaw brother."

"I am helping a friend," Hawk insisted, but a guilty flush darkened his leathered cheeks.

Mac slanted Roy a quelling look and kicked his horse into a canter, forcing Hawk and Roy to follow suit.

The building was just as Roy had described; nothing more than a squatter's shack. With a sagging front porch, one window, and a storm-damaged roof, it was hard to imagine anyone wintering here—and staying warm. He hated the thought of Savannah trapped inside those wobbly walls with Barlow, perhaps hungry and cold, possibly hurt. Did she know that he would come for her?

He and Hawk had crawled along the ground until they could peer over the hill to the shack below. Roy was preparing to launch their plan as Mac and Hawk took stock of their enemies.

"He must have picked up the henchmen in town," Mac whispered to Hawk, nodding toward the dilapidated porch where two men with rifles stood guard. Mac could see the shadow of another armed man guarding the back entrance to the shack. He frowned. "I don't like the thought of Roy barging in. They might shoot first and ask questions later."

"Remember, Barlow wants amnesty," Hawk whispered back. "If he kills you, he knows there are others who will hunt him."

Despite Hawk's reassuring logic, Mac continued to worry about Roy. If something happened to the kid . . . "So you think they have orders not to shoot?"

Hawk nodded. "Yes, that is what I think."

"I hope you're right."

"So do I, Heart of the Lion, so do I."

Mac fell silent, tension humming along his veins. It was almost time for Roy to make an appearance. How the henchmen reacted to Roy would give them an idea of how well-trained they were.

He heard the sound of pounding hooves long before Roy came into sight, knew the exact moment the henchmen heard it, too.

They raised their rifles and pointed them at Roy. One of the henchmen shouted the alarm, presumably to alert Barlow.

Fearlessly Roy hauled on the reins and ground to a halt before the armed men. Catching sight of the rifles, the frightened horse danced and rolled his eyes. Roy's boyish voice carried clearly to the hill where Mac and Hawk held their breaths.

"I'm here to see my pa."

• • •

Of the three of them, Savannah couldn't say who was the most stunned to hear Roy's voice through the open window. Ned leaped to his feet, his face registering shock. Raquel's eyes flared wide, then narrowed with displeasure.

She was clearly lacking in motherly instincts, Savannah noted. She arched her back, attempting to relieve the pressure on her spine from hours of holding herself stiffly upright without support. Roy was here. Did this mean that Mac wasn't far behind? Or was Roy merely finishing the job and here to report to Ned? Despite what she'd learned about Roy's parentage, she refused to believe that Roy was following in his father's footsteps.

Ned's explosive reaction strengthened her belief.

"What the blue blazes is *he* doing here?"

Raquel moved to the shack's only window and peered out. "Maybe Cord sent him to make the deal," she offered, but didn't sound convinced.

"Bring him to me!" Ned bellowed to his henchmen.

After a short silence Roy stumbled into the room, helped along by a rough shove from one of the armed men. Savannah's heart leaped at the sight of Roy's dear, familiar face. She silently compelled him to look her way, to give her some reassurance that everything would be okay.

But Roy seemed to deliberately avoid looking in her direction. He stood tall and faced his angry father, his chin lifted so bravely that tears stung Savannah's eyes. The bruise on his cheek had faded to a sickly yellow, but he now sported a multitude of scratches on his face.

Only Savannah seemed to noticed his trembling hands. The sight of that betraying movement gave her hope.

"I came to warn you that Mac, the sheriff, and a couple of deputies are on their way here. Mac said he wasn't agreeing to no deal with you."

Ned's hand was just a blur as he smacked Roy in the

face. Roy reeled from the blow but didn't flinch. He kept his hands to his sides and resumed his brave posture. If anything, his chin went up another notch.

Savannah gasped. She struggled to her feet, weak and dizzy from lack of food. "Don't you *dare* lay another hand on him!" she ordered, her voice trembling with fury.

Raquel casually pointed the derringer at her, effectively halting her movements in Roy's direction. "Stay right where you are, Princess."

Ned ignored the women, his eyes blazing into Roy's defiant face. "What are *you* doing here?"

"I came to help," Roy said, his voice low and earnest. "I rode here as fast as I could, staying ahead of Mac." He traced a particularly vicious scratch on his chin. "That's how I got all these scratches."

"So you changed your mind, did you?"

Roy nodded, then hung his head as if ashamed. "When Mac and Mr. Carrington found out who I was, they were gonna turn me over to the sheriff."

"Now why would they do a thing like that?" Ned asked, his voice deceptively soft.

When Roy lifted his head again, his eyes blazed with hatred. "They think they're too good for me now. I don't know why I was ever fooled by them in the first place. I belong here, with you and Raquel."

Savannah shook her head, refusing to believe what she was hearing. "Roy, you can't mean what you're—"

"Shut up, lady!" Roy snarled at her. His eyes were narrowed to hateful slits. "I never liked you to begin with, you with your haughty, I'm-better-than-everyone-else ways! You make me sick."

With her hand to her throat, Savannah backed away from his murderous gaze. Her back touched the wall. She slumped against it, shocked to the core by Roy's vengeful tirade. How could Roy be loyal to a man like Ned?

"You should set up an ambush, finish them off before they get here," Roy urged Ned. "If you don't, we'll be trapped."

"Then I'll kill his lovely wife," Ned informed him in a vicious whisper. "Just like I shot that sissy stepfather of yours."

Roy jerked as if Ned had delivered another blow. His voice started out faint, but quickly gathered strength as if he were pushing something ugly behind him. "That's not his wife . . . Pa. They were supposed to get married tomorrow. Mac said he just went along with it because her rich daddy offered to pay him five thousand dollars if he married her." Roy shot Savannah a glance so filled with contempt, she flinched beneath the force of it. "But Mac's changed his mind. In fact, he's hoping you *will* kill her so that he don't have to marry her." His hateful laughter seared her to the bone. "I don't blame him. She does nothing but whine and complain."

Savannah couldn't muster a protest.

Her heart was breaking.

Chapter Thirty-three

Mac watched two of the henchmen mount up and ride away from the shack in the direction of town. He could hardly believe his eyes. "It worked!" he whispered to Hawk. "But we've got one left—the one around back."

With a sly gleam in his eyes, Hawk unsheathed a wicked-looking knife from his boot. "He's mine. When I give the signal, you go in the front way and take care of Barlow and Raquel."

Hawk had slipped away before Mac realized he didn't know what the signal would be. A few moments later Mac heard the call of a coyote, a long, mournful sound that seemed to go on forever. It sounded very close, and could be none other than Hawk, Mac decided, scrambling to his feet and running toward the shack.

He reached the building and plastered his body to the side, edging around the corner to the porch. Finding it empty, he stepped onto the rotting boards, gingerly picking his way to the door. He burst through with his gun cocked and ready, catching Barlow by surprise.

"Don't even try it," Mac warned as Barlow reached for his gun. From the corner of his eye, he saw Raquel slide her hand into the folds of her dress. Thanks to Savannah, Mac was able to say, "Ma'am, I wouldn't do that if I were you. It pains me to shoot a woman, but I'll do it if I have to. Here, Roy. Hold this gun on her." He pitched Roy a gun and prayed the boy wouldn't shoot himself accidentally.

With supreme satisfaction, Mac watched Barlow's face as Roy aimed the pistol at Raquel. Surprise, then fury contorted the outlaw's features. Mac didn't dare look at Savannah; he couldn't afford the distraction yet.

"Why, you little bastard!" he snarled, glaring at Roy. "How can you do this to your own pa?"

"You ain't never been my pa," Roy quavered, suddenly aiming the gun at Barlow with deadly intent. "And thanks to you, the man who *was* my pa is dead now. You killed him."

"Roy . . ." Mac warned, recognizing the very adult rage in the boy's eyes.

"And now I'm gonna kill you," Roy continued as if Mac hadn't spoken. "If you're dead, you can't hurt anybody anymore."

"Roy," Mac tried again. "He's going to prison for a long time. He can't hurt anyone there."

A lone tear streaked down Roy's face. He rubbed at it with his sleeve. "He deserves to die, Mac! He said he killed my pa. The man who raised me! And if he killed my pa, then he also killed my ma."

Mac's deep-rooted sense of justice wavered. He, above anyone, understood Roy's anguish and rage. Hadn't he wanted Barlow dead himself? As he hesitated, he heard the rustling of skirts.

Savannah touched his arm, but her compassionate gaze was focused on the trembling boy. Her soft voice flowed over Mac like warm honey, reminding him how much he'd missed her.

"If you kill him . . . then you become him."

Roy glared at her, a glimmer of hysteria in his eyes. "That ain't true! I could never be like him!"

"That's right, Roy," she continued to croon. "You could never be like Ned, so give me the gun. Let Mac handle this."

The tears flowed freely now, peppering Roy's tattered shirt. He couldn't wipe them away fast enough. Mac tensed as Savannah approached Roy and took the gun from his unresisting fingers. The boy went to his knees, giving in to the wrenching sobs. Savannah pressed his head against her skirts, stroking his hair with her fingers. She used her free hand to train the gun on Raquel.

Mac removed Ned's weapon, then held out his hand for Raquel's gun. He stepped back again, glancing down at Roy. The boy's sobs had eased somewhat.

"Roy, can you tie them up?" He was hoping to help the boy take his mind off his grief.

Roy nodded and got to his feet. His eyes were red-rimmed and swollen from crying. He retrieved the rope from Mac's saddle and tied Ned's and Raquel's hands securely. Together they marched them onto the porch.

Hawk stood in the yard. On the ground at his feet were the three guards, trussed and gagged. Apparently Hawk had gone after them, knowing they would return when they realized Roy had lied.

Mac flashed his friend a grateful smile. "Can you help Roy get them on their horses while I look for the money?" Hawk nodded, and Mac turned to go back into the shack.

"I know where they put it," Savannah said, following him.

The moment they were inside, Mac grabbed her and pressed her tightly to his chest. He was shaking. "I was so afraid," he whispered, inhaling her scent as if it were the very air he had to breathe. "When I realized you were gone, I thought I would go insane."

To Mac's surprise, Savannah remained stiff in his arms. He frowned, tilting her chin to look into her eyes. She stared back at him without expression. Where was the warmth, the desire? he wondered, alarm skirting along his spine.

"Shouldn't we get going?" she inquired coolly, stepping free of his embrace. "I, for one, can't wait to get a bath and some food—in that order."

Still flabbergasted, he followed her to a small, sparsely furnished bedroom. Taking a good portion of the floor space was a mound of cloth sacks filled with money Barlow had stolen from the banks.

"I'm sure Daddy will be relieved that you've recovered his money," Savannah commented with that same, cool reserve he'd never heard before. "I'm certain you're glad as well."

At her puzzling comment, Mac glanced sharply at her. She gazed back at him in silent condemnation. "Is there something I missed here?" he asked softly.

"No. There was something *I* missed, Mac."

Before he could demand an explanation, she turned her back on him and walked stiffly from the room.

In Paradise, Savannah and Roy went on to the hotel while Mac and Hawk stopped at the jail to drop off the prisoners. The sheriff would appoint a deputy to take Barlow—and the money—to Jamestown to stand trial. Barlow would then be brought to Angel Creek to sit before a judge and jury for the robbery of the Angel Creek Bank.

Mac, Savannah, and Roy would safely return the rest of the money to George Carrington.

After the arrangements were made and Mac and Hawk

suffered through numerous back-pounding congratulations, Mac said his goodbyes to Hawk outside the hotel.

"Come for a visit soon," Hawk urged. "Bring Savannah
and Bristling Feather with you."

"Thanks. I will." Mac hesitated, then plunged ahead.
"What will you tell Patricia? We should know in case . . ."

"I have decided to tell her the truth. There should be no
lies between a husband and his wife."

Although Mac agreed with Hawk, he didn't envy his
friend. He watched Hawk walk away, his gaze sliding beyond Hawk's shoulder to the horse and rider limping along
Main Street. Mac's gaze narrowed in recognition.

It was the Jamestown deputy, and he looked about as
happy as a fly on a porcupine.

Mac sauntered into the road, blocking the deputy's path.
The weary horse stumbled to a halt. "Looks like you had a
stroke of bad luck," Mac drawled.

The deputy glared at Mac. "She knew where Barlow
was all along, didn't she? Sheriff Porter was right."

"Nope." Mac squinted into the sun, then turned to look
at the jailhouse behind him. He could have explained, but
he had more important things to do. Leaving the fuming
deputy in the road, Mac continued to the hotel. The sheriff
would tell the deputy what he wanted to know.

Since Mac didn't know which room Savannah was in,
he stopped at the desk to inquire.

"I don't have a Mrs. Cord registered, I'm afraid."

Mac stared at the clerk, convinced he'd made a mistake.
"Of course you do. Mrs. Savannah Cord. I'm her husband."

The clerk was shaking his head before Mac could finish. "I'm sorry, sir. I have a Savannah Carrington in room
fourteen—"

Mac took the stairs at a fast trot. It was time to find out
why Savannah was treating him as if—as if they were

mere acquaintances! After what they'd been through, after what they'd shared, Mac was hurt by her behavior. Besides, he'd vowed to tell her that he loved her—and make her believe it—at the first opportunity, and there was no time like the present.

He skidded to a halt in front of room fourteen and pounded on the door. The door to room fifteen opened abruptly. Roy stuck his head out, but after one glance at Mac's set, angry face, he quickly closed it again.

She wasn't answering. Mac pounded on the door again, not giving a damn who heard him. "Savannah? I need to talk to you." After another endless moment of silence, Mac raised his voice to a shout. "I will not leave until you open this door!"

All along the carpeted hall, doors began to open. Faces peered around corners; an elderly couple stepped into the hall to openly stare at him. Even Roy risked another glance through the crack in his door.

Mac ignored them all. He meant what he said—he was not leaving until Savannah talked to him. "There's something I've been wanting to tell you!" Mac shouted. "I love you, and I want us to be married. I mean, I want us to be *truly* married, not just living together and pretending to be."

The couple in the hall gasped simultaneously.

"I want us to have babies together, grow old together." Mac leaned against the door, his palms flattened against the wood. His voice thickened with emotion. "Savannah . . . will you marry me? Do you think you can eventually learn to love me—not just as a friend but as a man?"

Vaguely Mac was aware that more people had stepped into the hall to watch the scene unfold. He simply didn't care.

"Savannah, I don't think I can live without you."

"Mac," Roy whispered loudly, opening the door wide

enough to stick his entire head out. He glanced up and down the now crowded hall. His eyes bulged. "You're making a spectacle of yourself!"

"I don't care!" Mac growled, sweeping his audience a disgusted glance. "This is a private conversation."

"But you're *shouting*," Roy pointed out.

"Because she won't talk to me!"

"Maybe she's mad at you."

"Which is exactly what I'm trying to find out!" Mac thundered, ready to throttle the boy. Roy suddenly looked fearful, arousing Mac's suspicions. When he tried to close the door, Mac quickly thrust his boot into the opening. "Roy? Would you happen to know why Savannah refuses to talk to me?"

"Um, maybe it was on account of what I told her," Roy mumbled.

"And what would that be?"

"Um, I just told her the truth, that Mr. Carrington paid you five thousand dollars to marry her." He shrugged uneasily. "I thought she already knew."

Mac was struck speechless for so long that his audience began to grow restless. A low murmur swept through the crowd as they waited to see what Mac would do. When he finally found his voice, he was amazed at the levelness of it. "What gave you the idea that Carrington *paid* me to marry Savannah?"

Nervously Roy licked his lips. He looked left, then right as if seeking reinforcement. "Well, I heard Mr. Carrington telling Telly to put the money into your savings account. He said that he promised it to you and that you earned it."

"And by that . . . you gathered that he meant I earned it by marrying his daughter?" Mac asked so softly the crowd dared to strain forward.

Roy nodded, obviously aware by this time that he was

in deep horse manure, but uncertain how he'd gotten there. "Um, isn't that what he meant, Mac?"

"No, Roy, that isn't what he meant," Mac explained through clenched teeth. "Mr. Carrington hired me to find Savannah and bring her back to Angel Creek. He didn't know that I was already in love with her, you see"—he paused as a wave of silly sighs came from the crowd—"so I made a deal with him. If I could convince Savannah to marry me, then he would give us his blessing and he could keep his five thousand dollars. I don't need his money— I've been putting my earnings away for several years so that I could buy us a bigger house and give Savannah the things she's used to having."

The door to room fourteen opened abruptly. Savannah stood in the doorway, her eyes red-rimmed and swollen. It was suddenly so quiet Mac fancied he could hear his heart pounding.

"I like your house," Savannah told him. Her tremulous smile turned his knees to jelly. "And I don't need fancy dresses or anything else . . . as long as I have you. I've loved *you* since you kissed me in that jail cell."

This revelation caused more than a few startled gasps from the fainthearted.

Mac swallowed hard. He found that his hands were trembling as he reached out and pulled her into his arms. "Does this mean you *will* marry me?"

Savannah wound her arms around his neck. "Yes, I will marry you."

Cheers erupted around them as the crowd surged forward to congratulate them. Mac had to shout to be heard. "What about your hat shop?"

"I can open one in Angel Creek!" Savannah shouted back, laughing. "Hold on a minute. There's someone I want you to meet." She pulled free and stepped back into the room.

Curious, grinning like a fool, Mac waited patiently for her to emerge.

She came forward again, tugging a red-haired girl into the hall. "You were never properly introduced before," Savannah said. "This is Alissa. She's going to work for me in my hat shop."

Mac felt certain his face turned red as he remembered that *this* was the Alissa who had tutored Savannah on how to please him. Without a doubt he owed her a debt of gratitude! "Welcome to the family, Alissa," he said, and meant it.

Savannah walked back into his arms and pulled his head down for a lusty, satisfying kiss. Mac cupped her bottom, pressing her intimately against him.

Roy's door was the first to slam shut. One by one the other guests silently returned to their rooms until Mac and Savannah were left alone in the hall.

"Do I have a room?" Mac mumbled against her mouth.

"Mm. At the end of the hall."

He chuckled as he lifted her into his arms. He stared into her impish, smiling face, so happy he could burst. "I've got a feeling I won't miss the excitement of bounty hunting with you around."

Savannah spread her hand across his chest in a possessive way that thrilled Mac to the bone. "You can count on it, darling. There's still a few tricks I haven't shown you. . . ."

Mac wisely headed in the direction of his room.